The Clef Hanger

By Troy Burkman

Contents

CHAPTER ONE: "Thunderstruck"

Mikey Gross had a funny name. It didn't help that he wasn't a handsome boy either. He was short for his age and had bad eyesight; therefore, he had to wear large, oversized, circular glasses. His father, Bob Gross, was the new high school band director at Kinish Technical High School, and they both looked alike. They had the same round glasses and shared a recessive gene that caused hair loss. Mikey had quite thin hair for his age, although he kept his hair messy to hide his loss. His dad sometimes called him "mophead," but Mikey didn't mind; it was endearing to him. Despite the bully comments from other kids, he remained a jovial child. His 'pop,' as Mikey called him, tried to ignore his hair loss by growing a moustache and a slight beard. It seemed to Mikey that many men did this. He once told his dad, trying to convince him with his wisdom, "When men lose hair on top, they try to make up for it with beards, goatees, and moustaches."

Bob wanted to just do the mustache thing, which he felt made him look more distinguished and also covered for hair loss. With time, he grew a beard, which he trimmed, but eventually, he wanted to shave it off.

"One day, I'll just do the mustache, son. I prefer it, I promise," said Bob to Mikey when he asked, "What's up with all of the facial hair, Bruh?"

They also both had small beer guts, which they referred to as their 'dinky-do's.' They joked it was because their bellies stuck out more than their 'dinky-do.' They would both grab their bellies and laugh. They were very close as father and son, except when they were at school, where they had to distance themselves on purpose.

Mikey was in the school band, which was difficult for two reasons. First, his dad was the band instructor, and the other kids felt there was huge favoritism because of it. Second, Mikey was a horrible player. He played the oboe, which didn't sound right unless it was played correctly.

Mikey didn't play it correctly.

When Mikey practiced, even the pests ran and hid. That's how bad his playing was, yet he kept trying and practiced quite frequently. It worked really well to keep bugs away from the house. There were even rumors that their neighbor, "Old Lady Pettibon," actually passed away upon hearing his playing. The paramedics would neither confirm nor deny this wild rumor.

Mikey was a creative kid, and he often tried to tell imaginative stories to anyone who would listen. However, they didn't because of how he looked, so he told those stories to his oboe. Mikey felt it was a good listener and his only friend. He frequently took it everywhere with him in his backpack, unassembled in three parts.

One day, he jumped on the city bus with his backpack, and his friend, the oboe, to go to the Salzman Music store, where he could buy new oboe reeds. Something happened that day that changed everything in his life.

Mikey was talking to his oboe while sitting on the bus.

"The night was one of those cold nights where your breath just pumped out of your mouth as you breathed like an industrial smokestack. Something was going to happen that changed everything from good to something questionable. I know it changed my safe and secure life to one of chaos and confusion, but let me try and tell you the story. I don't know all of the details, so

I will fill in what I am not sure about with my imagination. You can thank me later because my imagination can be pretty crazy."

Mikey then made shooter fingers with each hand and put them together like *Steven Spielberg,* the movie director, would do, where he 'framed the shot,' creating a rectangle with his fingers. With one eye closed, he used the other to peer through his fingers, making his handmade imaginary film frame.

Mikey then said quietly to the oboe, "So, back to cold breath entering the camera view, leaving a hanging mist of carbon dioxide pumping into the air like smoke...This story gets pretty, um, interesting. Let's leave it at that because I don't want to spoil it for you."

#

A sinister figure pulled a cold, white iron mask down over his face, his eyes disappearing into the darkness like a superhero who was hiding his identity.

The figure was dressed all in black, wearing black armor that peeked out from under a long, black trench coat that almost reached the ground. It was very 'Matrix-like' if you ever saw the movie. Only his mask was white, which contrasted with the rest of his armor. It was very futuristic armor, like something anime characters would wear in a video game, with LED lights blinking on parts of it, as if they were wired to weapons and other gadgets.

From opened pelican cases, a cacophony of futuristic weaponry, sleek and alien, were being distributed. They appeared to be otherworldly-looking rifles that took rectangular cartridges with soft, ambiently lit edges that clicked into place. One soldier, his face obscured by a helmet, made the pretense of aiming his new rectangular weapon at something unseen, his gaze fixed on the sight of the weapon. Surrounding them were crates overflowing with military ordnance, a veritable arsenal of advanced weaponry. They had everything they needed for a battle.

Of these twenty soldiers, there were four figures, all of whose names were unknown, and they were only called 'the warriors.' They moved around with quiet efficiency, distinct from the rest. Of them, one of the warriors, with a sleek, ninja-like mask with a reflective eye channel, jerkily sprang up following a series of high-pitched musical notes. The tune was unfamiliar yet haunting, and he froze, head cocked to one side as he listened intently. Apparently, the others didn't hear it, for they didn't falter in what they were doing.

They were all in a dark, icy cavern, and it was very cold, with ice stalactites hanging from many items. Even new items brought into this place had already started to freeze over and begun to get small icicles magically formed on their edges. The warrior who heard the musical tones seemed to be the 'leader' who motioned to a dark entrance at the back of the cavern and performed a sweeping arm gesture pointing there, followed by a quick nod at the other three warriors. The four of them slowly walked towards the back with footsteps crunching snow beneath their waffle-soled military boots. The other sixteen soldiers fell in behind and followed, the other two flanking them but spaced out slightly like a chevron formation. They marched directly to the opening, pacing evenly and slightly crouched. They had definitely done this before.

#

A large, black, orb-shaped metal generator with blinking lights and cables protruding from it, sat quietly humming at the back of the large cave where the four were heading. The cables protruding from one side of the giant metal ball were gathered and tethered, then tied like hair braids twisted sloppily by little girls on the playground. The braided wires led across the floor for about 50 feet and then seemed to connect to a robed man's back, who was kneeling on the floor in prayer with his head bowed inside an oversized black hoodie. His face was not revealed, and was in a dark shadow.

The man's hands had long, thin fingers, which were now purposefully configured in a strange manner, like a gang symbol, yet they were trembling slightly. His knuckles were ragged and bony and looked like they were full of arthritic pain, which was probably why they were shaking. His body jerked back slightly, as if he got 'hit' by an unseen force and was trying to resist a pull from that 'something' that was somewhere.

A large set of stairs were leading down, hewn from stones and covered in snow and ice, towards a giant round seal with ancient carvings and letters on it. It was surrounded by high-tech machinery on both sides, like a *Stargate* movie setup. The machines also had LED lights in shapes that matched the odd symbols on the archway seal, yet none were currently lit.

From behind the kneeling man, the four warriors entered with their robes flowing. The black robes all looked the same, with large sleeves featuring red circles at the wrist and a red orb symbol on their chest with a digital quarter note in the center and a musical fermata symbol above, as if to say the digital note was to play forever. The other soldiers caught up but were still approximately 10 feet behind the four warriors.

The four continued marching to the icy stairs and stopped in unison. The leader raised his gauntlet and, with the other hand, swiped at it like a smartphone - a matrix of numbers appeared and lit up on its 'face.' He tapped a series of numbers and hit an enter symbol. Immediately, the orb generator behind them all activated loudly with a low blast of bass sound. This jolted the kneeling, hooded man who was connected to it. He threw his head back with a grunt of pain; the act revealed his face. He had long, white hair and eyebrows, which were extremely long. They covered his eyes and flowed down the sides of his face to his neck. He also had a rather large protruding chin, larger than normal, and an unusually long, pointy nose.

A burst of energy and light came from the orb, that connected to the cables and into his back, pumping this energy into him. He began glowing while swirling lights flew around his form in a circular pattern.

He rocked back and forth, dealing with the pain but not breaking his hand symbols... in fact, he raised them toward the seal, and the room erupted with more energy and began to shake. The bass 'noise' grew louder. He held as still as he could, with hands still trembling, and the symbols on the seal started to glow one at a time in sequence. As they glowed, the machinery with matching symbols and lights also glowed, and each light 'locked' onto their respective symbols with a blue glow, which was very similar to what was seen in the movie *Stargate*.

The warriors all braced themselves and planted their feet firmly in the snow, and one even had to divert his eyes away from the seal and the bright lights, yet they all held firm with robes billowing in this magical windy energy. The soldiers behind them all fell to their knees and dipped their heads down to avoid the blast of icy wind. Eventually, all symbols lit up blue, the seal flashed, then a large whoosh of water and lights swirled into the room from the center, then retracted into the new 'gate' that was made. They had opened something...something ancient. *Was the Stargate just like the movie, a real thing?*

A series of musical notes played in the warrior leader's earpiece again, and he started to walk down the icy stairs towards the magical gate, with the other three following cautiously. Machines were humming, lights flashing, and snow started coming through the portal, not water, as they approached. The kneeling soldiers got up, and some orders were barked and they started to march slowly in unison towards the warriors and the gate.

An eerie mist of low-lying fog billowed from the orb generator and fell upon the steps as if magically leading them to the portal. The four cautiously entered the gateway one at a time and dissolved into light as they were zipped into it, followed by the marching soldiers who also popped through the gate with whooshing sounds as they dissolved. The gate 'sealed' back up as everything powered down into darkness and complete quiet. The only thing left moving was the dark mass, which was the wizard, who was breathing hard and panting for air.

In the darkness, he looked up slowly from his tired stare from the floor to the gate. A trickle of blood slowly crept from his nose down his chin and dripped to the ground, now covered in crunched snow. It slowly got absorbed in the white snow and creepily spread outward like tentacles reaching for something.

"They know not what they are doing. The fools will meet their folly."

#

A High School marching band was trying to practice in a Six Flags amusement park parking lot.

The band director yelled on a bullhorn, "I know we can't just move the cars, so just march around them, please- we need the practice if we want a first division."

A parent handed Bob, the band director, his kid to hold while the man got an ice chest from the back of his mini-van.

The kid dangled in the air while Bob handled him like a 'thing.' The kid grinned.

"Thanks, Bub," the dad said, and took the kid back.

"It's Bob, actually. And you're welcome." Bob chuckled and replied.

Bob got back on the bullhorn, "Let's take it from the top, um, the Kinish Tech fight song please...a one, and a two, and a three and four."

Bob gave a downbeat, and the kids started playing and moving through the parking lot, avoiding cars the best they could.

Mikey yelled, "Get your toes up, and roll with the foot...c'mon guys, march like you mean it!"

"Man, that Wonder Woman coaster better be worth this band trip to San Antonio!" one of the kids said to another.

"Dude, it's the only reason I joined the band this year. It will be epic, I promise. Let's get through this..." the other replied.

Inside a glass orb held upside down by claws like eagle's talons, a dark figure looked inside it, hunched over it and intent on what was going on inside it.

The voice said, "Let's see how you deal with a little whimsy and a touch of anthropomorphism, Mr. Gross..."

The dark figure glided from the Palantir to a large bookcase. A woman's hand with long nails reached out from the shadows for an old dusty book in the bookcase, then used her long fingernail to retrieve it from the top, angled it towards her, then snatched it with the same hand and slid it out slowly. The spine of the book said, "Aesop's fables and other stories." The book opened on an old wooden hewn desk, and the shadowy figure loomed behind it, looking down upon the open gilded pages.

"Oh, I do hope a valuable lesson is learned from this. For all involved..." The figure made a pulling gesture upwards from the book's pages and slight snow flurries actually sprung from the pages into the room.

The shadowy figure laughed and laughed even harder, which became a swirling wind of snow, focused directly over the open book on the table.

#

Eighty high school band students were now tracking through what looked like the Himalayas in Tibet. The very band that was just at Six Flags…

Mikey made a fist and held it to his mouth like a microphone, then said in his best imitation broadcaster voice, "Facing the many dangers upon setting out...the cold, snowy conditions, the treacherous, rocky landscape, and the low oxygen levels at such a high altitude…how did they get here?" Then, in Mikey's normal voice, he said, "And where the hell is… pop? Whaa happened?"

Mikey watched his dad, who was observing the mountain peaks around them as he walked, lowering his bullhorn to his side.

Bob stopped and took a 360 degree look around the snowy nightmare, then shrugged his shoulders and nodded unknowingly to his son Mikey.

"Bruh. I don't really know," Bob said. "I think everything will be alright."

A frost began to crawl upon the band instruments as they tried to play; some kids dropped their instruments in disbelief. Four clarinets landed in the snow with frost on them, almost perfectly lined up...

The entire marching band was astonished and started bundling up and trying to stay in lines the best they could. The parking lot had completely disappeared, and everyone was wondering just how they were earlier at Six Flags and now here...with Bob Gross and his son Mikey at the front.

Mikey and Bob pulled some hoodies from Mikey's backpack and got all bundled up so only their glasses were visible, and they both somehow already had cups of hot cocoa in their hands. A girl pointed at them and asked, "Hey, where did you get those?!"

"It's a secret." Mikey smiled.

The band kids all scrambled to zip up their coats and freaked out because of where they were. They just realized their perilous situation. They all started taking shelter along the canyon walls and huddled together. Band practice was over.

Bob grabbed the bullhorn again and said, while completely ignoring where they were, "C'mon kids, isn't this the best band trip ever? Um, can we please try to stay in the chevron formation, hmm? Please?"

Bob got hit with several snowballs that he tried to dodge.

To get even warmer, Bob pulled from the backpack again and threw on a Kinish-Tech letterman's jacket, which had a pipe symbol under his embroidered name, "B. Gross." Mikey kept that backpack close to his side and by his feet. It's an odd backpack that is old and leathery with a large single compartment and a large flap that buckled at the bottom. It almost looked like the grimacing face of an angry person.

Some kids said in unison, "What happened? Where are we? Boo! You suck! What the hell, man? I can't breathe! I'm freeeezing!"

#

A fully armed and stern-looking man in military boots and pants was standing in the snow.

The man ordered, "Ok, this is it, men. Lock and load, it won't come out again if we screw this up. He said we only have one chance."

Two huge lights turned on, aimed at a cave entrance in the snow.

Instantly, a low roar was heard echoing throughout the mountain peaks.

The band kids stopped in their tracks, listening to the roar.

Many kids looked worried, clenching their frozen instruments closer to them.

"This isn't Six Flags, man! Where are we? I didn't sign up for this, Bruh, band isn't supposed to get you killed," said one boy holding a french horn.

Men started screaming in the distance, and sounds of rapid gunfire and roaring continued violently.

A feeling of terror started to spread like a disease.

"Say, pop, doesn't that sound like a low C?" Mikey's voice trembled.

He held out his hand like an opera singer, and sang the note, "Bruhhhhh."

"You got it, Mikey, but you need to go pianissimo because the roar is so far away.

Mikey imitated the sound again but was really quiet this time..."Bruhhhhhh," and he held his hand lower."That's it!" Gross said.

Screams of men, gunfire, and roars got louder.

Explosions were also heard.

"It sounds more Mezzo forte now, son," Bob said.

"Sweet." Said Mikey.

To the bewilderment of all, a portal opened from the mountain side, and the warriors passed through with long trench coats flowing in the wind and their weapons raised. The band kids pointed and yelled, "Check that out!"

The warriors headed toward the gunfire, with more screams and blasts heard as the kids watched, shivering and confused. The warriors turned the corner and immediately scattered in different directions, with one of the 'warriors' climbing the mountain quickly and stealthily like a ninja.

Several white-skinned, very muscular but thin humanoid-like men, with white hair and short, unkept beards wearing nothing but tan leathery shoes and a furry skirt of long hair were seemingly everywhere...there may have only been about 10 of them, but they ran, and moved so quickly it seemed like an army of 40.

Methodically, they moved in teams to attack a soldier one at a time, or several soldiers at once, completely dodging and evading gunfire while dismantling them. Helmuts got pulled off and thrown aside, and the wild men leaped onto shoulders and flipped men down to the ground, completely disarming them. Men were getting punched in their throats, and their legs were being swept. Judo throws, and uniforms were grabbed, and men were thrown into each other, with men shooting at each other and tracking after one wild man at a time while firing, yet shooting another soldier who was in the way.

The soldiers were completely getting pulverized and outfought easily.

The trench-coat warriors then decided to join in the fray using their high-tech weapons and tools of death. The ninja-type warrior leaped up into a tree and started throwing glowing ninja-type stars, which struck two of the wild men - one in the leg and one in his back. The stars seemed to slow them down a little but, really, only made them angrier as they pulled them out and cast them to the ground. One of the warriors got a panicked laser shot out of his weapon, which caught one of the wild men leaping at him. The wild man tried to twist and avoid it but got his side blasted, which made him scream out a loud, horrible cry of pain.

The other wild men heard this cry, paused, and looked- then got angry. They all howled with their heads turned upwards. This startled the remaining soldiers...are they animals? The laser gun only made a gash, which remained open as he continued fighting. Oddly, no blood spilled, but rather, something that looked like water leaked from his wound.

A loud rumbling shook the ground, and from a nearby mountaintop, a silhouette appeared, but only one eye glowed where the head was in the darkness. Twisted horns could be made out upon its head of billowing white hair. It seemed to be wearing a robe that also blew in the wind like an anime character brought to life from the comic books. This one was bigger and very different from the others. The shadowed outline seemed like this one was as big as a bison.

The sky darkened, and a single lightning bolt cracked in the distance.

The shadowy figure charged down the mountainside, going left and right to avoid gunfire that was now aimed at it.

Mikey said, "Hey pop, that reminds me of American Ninja Warrior and the beginning of the standard course with those platforms one must jump on- one foot at a time without falling into the water!"

Bob simply stared at the beast moving towards them and said, "Indeed."

Mikey reached into the "mouth" of the backpack and found an old yellow Sony Walkman cassette player and headphones. He quickly put it on and pushed 'PLAY.'

The dark clouds seemed to follow above this bounding figure, which was growing even more menacing and dark. Lightning began to roll through the dark cloud formations above it, while thunder began to grumble louder and more frequently.

The figure plowed straight at a group of six men shooting towards it, but before it reached them, a lightning bolt cascaded from the dark clouds above, and a crash of thunder was heard at the same time, which shook everyone back a bit, which was nearby. Some soldiers fell to the ground. The bolt from the blue then destroyed the soldiers easily in a burst of energy and light. They disintegrated into dust, which blew away in the snowy wind.

Mikey watched with his mouth agape, and when the thunder and lightning struck another group of soldiers, he turned to his dad and said, "Pop, they've been thunderstruck! You know, just like the song."

Mikey pointed to his headphones happily, "I'm listening to it right now!" The figure then turned direction and headed directly towards Bob and Mikey, with thunder rumbling and brewing…and the music in Mikey's ears grew louder and louder. They started to run from the beast but halted at a mountain with nowhere to go. It was a dead end.

CHAPTER TWO: The Door

The beast kept charging towards Mikey and Bob. The ground shook, and thunder rumbled above as the thing got closer and closer to Mikey and Bob.

Bob quickly reached into the grizzled backpack at his feet and frantically searched for something. Mikey was panicking, "Pop, what are we gonna do? What are you looking for?"

Bob pulled out a yellow hardcover book, small in size, and smiled because he was so proud of himself.

"This should do it!"

"What? How? What is this?" Mikey was confused.

The yellow cover was a bit worn and old looking, with silver letters outlined in black: "The Boy's Book of Survival: How to survive anything, anywhere." It had a picture of a 1940s Normal Rockwell child trying to start a fire and smiling goofily in the center.

Bob quickly swished through the pages and stopped, yelling "AHA!" and pointed to a section in the book and then read intently.

The beast was 10 feet from them when Mikey stopped his Sony Walkman and yanked off his headphones before dropping to his knees, covering his face and whining.

"This is the end, Bruh. I know it. I should have been a better person. Why didn't I do better in school? I should have helped out more around the house..." He wailed, and wrapped himself in a fetal position as he continued to mumble. "I never even kissed a girl or learned to drive...man, this sucks!"

Bob quickly reached into the backpack and magically pulled out a silver tray that couldn't have possibly been in there nor fit inside. He placed it on top of Mikey, then drew from the backpack a small silver kettle with steam coming from it and placed it on the silver tray. He told Mikey, "Don't move, son, it's hot. Stay still."

Next, he pulled out two China tea cups and placed them on the tray next to the kettle.

The beast was about 5 feet from them now and luckily stopped to look around and behind him, then roared quite loudly. This gave Bob a little more time. Bob also looked around and noticed that all of the soldiers were dead except for the ninja warrior who somehow disappeared in a flash of smoke before the AC/DC lightning could strike him. Bob thought ninjas tend to do that quite well!

Bob poured the tea into the cups and grabbed one, which he held out towards the fuming beast. The background was littered with small fires and smoke plumed with carnage from a small war everywhere.

"Tea?" He said, trying to smile exceptionally big to the monster's massive face.

The beast was within Bob's reach, and its demeanor changed. It was surprised and not quite sure what to do but stopped and stared at Bob, breathing heavily. Mikey was still on the ground with the entire tea set on top of him as a human, trembling table. Bob's glasses fogged up completely with each 'hit' of the beast's heavy breath pushing at Bob like a billowing smokestack. Bob noticed the beast only had one good eye that glowed brightly with a yellow tint.

Bob wondered if that was a childhood accident or did something happen to him that made him lose his other eye.

The beast nodded as everything else seemed frozen in time, unmoving. All except for the slight-trembling coming from Mikey below imitating a table. One of the Wildman Yetis reached out, took the hot tea cup, and held it in front of the beast. The beast took it from the other Yeti very gingerly and, with its massive hand, gulped it down its throat in one arm swoop. He placed the cup back on the outstretched hand of the helper Yeti.

"Mmmm, rhododendron tea. How very kind of you," bellowed the beast in a true bass voice that could put James Earl Jones' voice to shame. "I am Polybius, the third leader of Shen -Yun, a magical village here in the Himalayas. My people have named me the snow king. Who are you?" The beast seemed to grow larger as he asked that last question as if to threaten Bob if he didn't like the answer expected.

Bob stood up straight and extended his hand, then said, "I am Bob Gross, and this is my son, Mikey Gross. It is a pleasure to meet you."

Polybius shook his hand with a cloven hoof that Bob didn't expect. It seemed the beast had one good hand and one hoof for hands.

A part man, part beast thing going on here, Bob thought.

The beast sighed heavily and said, "Gross one, why do these men keep coming here and attacking my peaceful village? We are monks and scholars and although we are a peaceful race, we have been having to train in the art of war more frequently than ever before."

"Excuse me, sir," said Bob as he cleared the tray off of Mikey and helped him up off of the ground. Mikey was still shaking and looking up at Polybius with eyes very wide and uttering nonsense words and noises. "Abaa abba, babba baa. Pop…poppa, wha…how…bruh?"

Bob handed Mikey the yellow book and then pushed it into Mikey's chest as if to say, this is mandatory. Bob said, "Don't ever leave home without it! Look at page 64."

Mikey stopped shaking and didn't say a word. There was nothing to say, so he opened the book and looked down into it, adjusting his crooked glasses so he could read better.

The book page opened with the heading "How to survive a visit from an abominable snowman."

"Wow, Pop. That is very unexpected."

Bob put his arm around Mikey's shoulder, "You have a lot to learn, young padawan." A reference to *Star Wars* he knew Mikey would understand.

Polybius then asked, "Would you care for some snow cookies?"

Bob said, "Only if you have a smoke with me, Polybius."

"A smoke, you say? Indeed. We have the best Southern Star pipeweed that you'll probably never find anywhere else other than in the shire. I do like their Longbottom leaf almost as equally, but I find their Old Toby weed too sweet for my liking."

Bob said, "I would be honored to share your Southern star with you and have some of your snow cookies." Bob's heart fluttered a little, and a sense of relief washed over him.

"Thank you, Polybius." Bob then reached into his coat pocket and pulled out an old black calabash pipe and smacked it a few times on his knee to clear out any remaining ashes inside of it.

Polybius smiled, the best way a one-eyed Yeti could smile, and pulled out a long briar pipe, ornately decorated yet very curvy, like a child's silly straw from his shawl. He then bellowed in a low tone with the pitch intentionally rising, "Edwaaaard" he called, and a small black and white snub-nosed monkey came jumping from a temple door carrying a small bag tied with a drawstring and leaped onto another Yeti's open hand near Polybius. The Yeti held the monkey up to Polybius' pipe, and the monkey packed it full of pipeweed.

He does this quite well. He must do this all of the time. Bob thought.

The monkey being held did the same weed packing ceremony for Bob's pipe too.

Polybius snapped his fingers with his human hand- precisely centered above his pipe, and said, "Bim Sala-Bim!" Poof! Fire ignited in a small flash in the pipe, catching the weed on fire so he could smoke it. He then put his hand over Bob's pipe and was about to do the same thing when Bob leaned in a bit too close, "Bim Sala Bim!" Poof! Bob's pipe was lit with a small blast of fire, which also singed Bob's face and blew his hair back.

"Sorry, gross one."

Mikey said to his dad, "Pop, I thought you gave up smoking?"

Bob said, "It's a pipe. It doesn't count."

#

A woman's voice said, "How is it that this imbecile eschews my traps?!"

The shadowed figure then turned hurriedly away from the glass Palantir she was looking into. She bit on her lower lip and clenched her fists in anger. Her internal rage was building to a boiling point. "He won't learn any consequential lessons if he continues to use temerity towards my lessons!" She turned to the bookshelf rapidly and began to inspect all of the book binds and their titles very closely.

"Very well. He foiled my first trap; therefore, I will have to expend my energies better and revise a more transcendent challenge for him and his son. This is an arduous task, but I predict that this next disparate adventure will end your teaching tenure, Mr. Gross. Let's see how you emerge after experiencing a new soul-rewarding toil."

She then grinned widely, clasped her gnarled hands in front of her, and started to laugh. She then started softly singing to herself while smiling. She also started wildly spinning and dancing around the floor, arms raised and flailing around like a dervish. Her long, black cape and flowing gown began to flail wildly about, unfurling completely, often raising and dropping repeatedly. She sang louder and louder, almost screaming it to the nothingness in the castle chamber, with the last word echoing down the hall.

"Double, double, toil and trouble"

"Fire burn, and cauldron bubble"

"Double, double, toil and trouble."

"Something wicked this way COMES!"

#

Polybius made sure all of the children were safely found and accounted for and escorted into a grand, ominous cave opening where a large door filled the space from ground to ceiling. It was an odd door, dark but also light in color because it looked like it was made of pixels and light that kept glitching out of synch often.

"Cool door," Mikey said. "Looks like a videogame screen."

Polybius quickly looked down at him with a scowl on his face but didn't say anything.

As they all got close to the electronic-looking door, Mikey had a sense of dread wash over him. For some reason, this part of this adventure seemed like they were being herded like cattle towards their doom.

Mikey thought about a piece of music the band was playing at the music festival they were missing. It was a piece called, *Symphony No.2 by John Barnes Chance*. Rumor had it that it was the last piece of music the composer ever wrote. It was late at night, and as soon as the composer finished it, he had gone to investigate "strange demon sounds" coming from his backyard. He was found dead, lying in the yard the next morning by his neighbors. The paramedics claimed that he was electrocuted, but nobody could tell how. That second symphony was a creepy one, and it always made the hair stand up on the back of Mikey's neck and gave him goosebumps. That music seemed to play in his head as they marched through this creepy valley towards that bizarre electronic door.

When they arrived in front of the massive doorway, Polybius placed his human hand on a plate next to the door, which glowed brightly and diminished abruptly.

The light beam energy that was the door, began to rise slowly to the top of the door frame, and once it got to the top, it went dark. Totally off. A counter above started counting down, with little line marks of light in a circular clock pattern, every time a few seconds went by.

Mikey said, "Does that mean we only have that long before the doorway shuts again?"

Polybius said, "Indeed, little Gross one. The doorway is in tune with my body only, and any part of my being can open or close this gateway. It is mostly for protection from outsiders."

The Yeti monks hurried the school kids in through the doorway as Mikey climbed and stood on a stone beside the door encouraging the kids to hurry as he watched the ticking countdown.

"Come one, come all. Come to the light, young ones," he said, imitating the lady from the first Poltergeist movie.

A random band kid yelled, "Put a sock in it, loser!"

Mikey was just trying to liven up the menacing atmosphere and thought he had favor with Polybius, which was more than the attention he got when in class. So, he was now eating up the attention that he wasn't used to. He felt like a celebrity.

He felt special for once.

As the last student made it in, the timer actually had just expired, and the door of energy ignited brightly and started to slowly crawl down the opening, zotting, spurting, and buzzing until it closed fully.

Mikey thought to himself that this still seemed scary, and also why could only Polybius open or close this thing? Where were they now, and when could they eat something? He was starving. His stomach growled loudly at him.

Mikey thought, "A-minor. Definitely a stomach growl in the key of A-minor."

CHAPTER THREE: Something wicked this way comes

The accommodations for the children were actually pretty nice, thought Bob. Each room had a single twin bed, a nightstand, a lamp, and a desk with a rolling chair. There was an attached little bathroom for each room with a sink, a commode and a walk-in shower. The rooms all had a small window, and they all smelled musty, like a damp rag. The windows were inset into the wall about two feet, which was odd, but the view was pretty spectacular. They seemed higher than when they went in, and the windows seemingly glowed just a little around the edges, which was a bit strange, but nobody cared.

They were out of the cold, they were warm and they had a decent place to stay even if it wasn't home.

Mikey counted the band kids, and the total was forty-two, including himself.

Kinish-Tech was not a big school, but their school motto ironically was "Tiny, but Mighty." So, they had some semblance of school pride even for a smaller technical arts high school. Bob felt lucky to have gotten to teach band there since his predecessor was a legendary Band director, John Faraone. That man led their band to State honors and even received a few invitations for the school band to perform in the Rose Bowl parade and halftime football show, which they never went to.

"Just too expensive and not in the budget," said their high school principal, Bob Kirtley.

Mikey then thought of something.

There were forty-two members in the band. FORTY-TWO!

Proud of himself, he muttered, "That's the secret to life, the universe, and everything." It came from one of his favorite book series, *The Hitch-Hiker's Guide to the Galaxy,* by Douglas Adams, one of his favorite science-fiction writers. He had the book with him in his backpack, too. So, as he thought about it, he fondly reached over his shoulder, smiled quirkily, and softly patted the backpack he was wearing on his back.

The snow king asked that everyone gather in the main throne room so he could say a few things and administer the 'rules' of this castle in Shen Yun.

The throne room was in the center of the complex castle, made up of a myriad of rooms, odd tubes, hanging cables, and hallways, which didn't seem to make much sense to Mikey as he looked around as they all were herded towards the center.

"As castle layouts go," said Mikey to his Pop, "This one doesn't seem to make logical sense. There are small ante-chambers next to larger rooms and odd-shaped hallways. And what's with the random pillars, cabling and line markings in the walls? This place almost looks as if we're standing on a giant circuit board inside a computer!"

Bob said, "Interesting. That's your area, kid. I don't know much about computers. But I think your imagination is getting overworked."

"Maybe, but I am still not sure why we're here and if this is a safe place, Pop," Mikey said.

Bob answered quietly, "They did save us from those hooligan military guys, right? But I can't answer your question about safety here. I am just wondering if we're going to be disqualified for not showing up to play at Six Flags!"

Mikey wasn't concerned with that because he was actually pretty nervous to perform at that show. He had not practiced as much as he should have, and he had a solo to play on English horn, which was not his oboe. Yes, it was a double reed instrument too, but way bigger and louder. If he messed up, everyone would surely hear it. It was the solo at the beginning of the fourth- movement of *Ottorino Respighi's Pines of Rome*. A difficult-tone poem musical piece in four movements, which was all about Rome, the fountains of Rome, and its Roman Festivals. The piece depicted different scenes of the pine trees in Rome, some in the present and some in the past, reflecting the composer's tribute to his country's capital and its history. It was pretty well known, so Mikey didn't want to suck.

Every once in a while, an electrical buzzing could be heard and sometimes the lines in the walls seemed to carry a current that surged from the castle walls to a direction directly towards the throne room.

Mikey told his dad upon seeing a surge go down the walls, "Gee, that's shocking to look at, eh, Pop? Get it?" He smiled big and looked for a reaction from his dad, who bleakly smiled and said, 'That's so punny, I forgot to laugh." And then chuckled as they continued the hallway walk.

The kids all squeezed into the throne room, facing a large throne that was oddly connected to a myriad of cables attached to the floor on all sides, and the walls looked like circuit board patterns. The snow king was already sitting, but then he stood and addressed the crowd of children, "Welcome to Shen Yun! I hope you enjoy your stay. There are only a few rules to abide by…um, for your safety."

"First, the east wing is off-limits. There are some dangerous things there because we are doing some renovation work, and we wouldn't want any of you getting injured. The second thing is that after dinner, we must insist that you go back to your rooms so we can lock down the castle from intruders. Yes, your energy door will be activated then, so it's best if you just go to sleep because it won't be open until the next day. I have given you all music headsets that you may use to keep you entertained, which are attached above your bed. You're welcome. Now, enjoy dinner."

Mikey had a question, so he raised his arm, and to make it higher, he used his other hand to prop it higher, "Um, sir, snow king, how long are we going to stay here, and when are we going to be able to get home?"

Polybius paused and said, "This thing, all things devour. Birds, beasts, trees, flowers. Gnaws iron, bites steel. Grinds hard stones to meal. Slays king, ruins town, and beats high mountains down."

Mikey was puzzled at that answer but with a thinking expression, yelled, "TIME! That's from the *Lord of the Rings* books, right? So, you are saying that it will take some time?"

"Yes, gross one. Now, leave me be. Maybe you are already home?"

That didn't give Mikey too much satisfaction, but he remained quiet.

Outside the castle, a snowstorm was building. It was dark and the storm clouds lit up with temporal flashes of lighting which rolled along the clouds' undersides almost in a pulsing manner. The wind had picked up, which made the snow swirl in different directions. It was violent. The great door they went into could be revealed more with the lightning flashes lighting up the sky. Creatures were flying in the storm towards the doorway. They flew very erratically but at the same time in a murmuration and whirled in ever-changing patterns. To anyone who could see this, it was probably mesmerizing, like an aerial ballet.

The children inside had some stew and bread, which was more than adequate since they were all famished.

Some children decided they were bored and wanted to try the music headsets, so they retired to their rooms. Mikey had other plans.

"Hey, Pop, can I go look around a little before bedtime?"

"Sure. Just be careful, and remember to stay away from the east wing, OK?" Said Bob.

"Bruh, I'm not an imbecilic nerd." Mikey stated firmly. "Well, maybe not imbecilic." And he grinned really big.

"Don't be too late, and besides, you need to practice your solo. We'll be out of here soon and we may just make our performance time window."

"Ugh, don't remind me…" Mikey said under his breath.

Bob said, "What was that?"

Mikey said, "You're right, Pop. Thanks for reminding me." Mikey really wished his fellow oboe player, Kristin Hickman, was doing that solo instead. Her mom worked at the school like his dad did, but as a guidance counselor, so if she screwed the solo up, it would blow over more quickly. She didn't seem to like Mikey because she thought he was getting preferential treatment, so whenever she saw Mikey approach her, she pretended she was talking on her phone and walked away.

Mikey always thought, "Wow, that girl is always on the phone. I bet she's going to have some serious head radiation one day. Probably going to make her hair all fall out, and she'll be bald. That's what 5G will do to you. Yeppers."

Mikey then began thinking about the solo and started to sweat profusely. "Gotta split. Laterz, Dad." He threw a sideways 'peace' sign like a gang member would throw a gang symbol. He started walking off all cool and walk-squatting like he had a new swagger or something in his pants bothering him. It wasn't convincing.

Bob just shook his head. "Youth today, sheesh."

#

Mikey walked cautiously through the winding hallways, poking his head into rooms when he could, and looking into windows and doorways, without being seen. That was a game he used to play with his dad, pretending they were both ninjas. "Try not to be seen," it was called, and the only drawback to the game was that they were often seen. Especially when they played it at the mall and in department stores, the game didn't go over too well in those places, and often security or store managers would find them in some clothing rack or display window and would ask them to leave before they had them arrested.

"I insist, sir, that my son and I are just doing some father-son bonding and don't mean to cause you or anyone any harm. It's just a game we play," said Bob.

Who knew that those Master ninja practice sessions would come in so handy now?

Mikey hummed a mission impossible type theme to himself as he skirted along the rock walls and crawled on the floor. "Duh da tahhh, duh da tahhh, duddut," he sang softly. "I know something is going on heeere and we're not being told everythiiiiing. I can feel it in my boooones. Duh da tahhh, duh da tuhhh, duddut."

Mikey turned a corner and saw a menacing sign that read "East Wing and service entrance. Selected personnel only." There were two Yeti guards standing on each side of an elevator whose doors were emblazoned with a scary skull logo that split the doors equally. The two Yetis there were beefier than the normal ones he had seen before. These guys wore hairy outfits and were very thick. They meant business and were probably there as a very strong deterrent to anyone not authorized to go in that elevator.

"That's interesting. I wonder where that thing goes, and why is it guarded so well? I have to go tell Pop." With that, Mikey dashed back the way he came but quickly stopped running when he got near the throne room again. He then abruptly started to walk leisurely and whistled with his hands in his pockets- trying to walk cool.

"What's up, my guy?" Mikey said as he pointed to a Yeti guard in the throne room who just grimaced at him. Mikey headed back towards the hallway with the dorm rooms to find his dad's room.

It was going to be a bit scary being locked in a room for the night but Mikey thought it might be a good time to practice a bit on his oboe. He thought to himself, "I should really work on that English horn solo for Pines, but my oboe needs some Mikey attention!"

He ran into his Pop, walking down the hall. He was asking the band kids to call it a night and get to their rooms. Sort of shooing them into their rooms like herding cats. "We should all be so thankful for these sweet rooms and accommodations. See you all bright and early!"

As each child went into their rooms, a Yeti guard came by and pushed some buttons, which created a door of energy and light, thus sealing them in their rooms. As more rooms were sealed, the hallway outside became very magical, with the reflections of energy and lights dancing all over, creating a myriad of shadows and activity. It was very beautiful to see, like a light ballet.

In each room, the kids all did something different. Some drew, some of the boys exercised, and some got in the shower, but all eventually ended up in their beds with the headphones on. They all listened to the music that played. All of them. Then they fell asleep.

Oh, the dreams they had. Was it their subconscious, or did the music have something to do with it? Some of the boys dreamt they were on the football team and scoring the winning points. The girls also dreamt about various happy things and situations, and all seemed to be good dreams. All dreams were about them personally winning at something or about something they deeply cared about, their pets, or the fantastic food they were eating. All of them had their parents in their dreams, cheering them on or congratulating them and hugging them. Lots of love and good feelings.

Mikey was now in his room and getting ready for bed. He didn't practice. He reached inside the backpack fumbled around in it, biting his tongue to find just what he wanted from in there…and he pulled out a pair of pajamas, complete with Darth Vader faces and poses with a lightsaber stamped all over them. He put them on proudly, sat on the bed, and then turned off the lights. He then lay down and put the music headset on. The door for the room was glowing, so there was no need for the typical tie-fighter nightlight that he used at home. "It helps me find the way to the bathroom, Pop," was his reply to his dad when Bob asked why he still needed it.

His headset was playing *Maurice Ravel's Bolero*, which he felt was a pretty cool music piece to fall asleep to. Mikey knew that Ravel was truly the greatest French composer ever, and Mikey really liked the impressionistic style of his music- even though Ravel himself rejected that term. He remembered that the rhythms of *Bolero* were inspired by the machines at his father's factory, and that made Mikey ponder why this piece was chosen by the Snow King. As he drifted off, his dream wasn't anything he could have ever imagined.

#

In the heart of the ancient town of Shen Yun, ominously embedded in the jagged mountains, stood the foreboding silhouette of the castle. Its towering spires pierced the night sky, and atop its highest rooftop, a spectacle of the supernatural unfolded each night.

As the sun dipped below the horizon, the castle's rooftop came alive with a flurry of activity. Giant bats, their wingspans as wide as a grown man, emerged from the caves nearby and the castle's hidden crevices. Their eyes glowed with an eerie luminescence, casting an otherworldly glow on the weathered stone of the castle. Giant bats swirled and circled until some wires at the top of the castle started to glow. The cables seemed intertwined and came from salient parts of the castle rooftop. Although the cables came from different locations in the stone roof, they all ended up leading to a castle tower, where they entered the base. The cables pulsed as they seemed to drink energy, while the turret seemed to swallow the energy down.

The bats swooped and dived, their wings cutting through the air with a chilling screech. They were drawn to the thick cables that snaked across the rooftop, pulsating with raw energy drawn from the castle's ancient power source. The bats attacked the cables feverishly, their sharp fangs sinking into the rubbery insulation. A strange hum filled the air as they fed, drawing the energy into their bodies. They needed to quench their thirst as well. The locals called them parasitic draw bats because they fed off of energy, any kind of energy.

The townsfolk lived in constant fear, their homes cast in the long shadow of the castle. Whispers of the bats' nightly feast spread through the town, fueling their terror. The bats were growing larger and more powerful with each passing night. The townsfolk feared that once the cables could no longer satiate the bats' hunger, they would turn to a new source of energy - the townsfolk themselves. Each night, as the castle rooftop buzzed with the sound of the feeding bats, the townsfolk huddled in their homes, praying for dawn. The castle, once a symbol of their town's proud history, had become a haunting reminder of their living nightmare. The eerie glow from the rooftop served as a chilling beacon, a stark reminder of the fear that gripped their town under the cover of darkness. As the bats drank, their bodies glowed different colors; some were red, some blue, some green and some yellow. Once full, they darted back up into the sky. Their murmuration always seemed to form the scary face of a skull, but seemingly just for an instant.

#

The dorm room energy doors flickered in the night, and so did the headsets the kids were currently wearing as they slept.

Their dreams changed into nightmares, which caused them to twist, kick, and cry in their beds - truly in emotional and physical pain.

"Hey kid, wake up! This is your stop, right?" Said the burly bus driver to Mikey as he gently nudged Mikey's shoulder.

"Gee, thanks, mister. Sorry about that." Mikey stated sleepily as he grabbed his headphones off his head and put the Walkman back in his backpack. There were some drawings done in Crayola colors on the seat next to him. Mikey grabbed them up, "Oops, almost lost Aunt Irma's drawings!" He glanced quickly at the top one, which seemed familiar. "That's interesting," he said. It actually looked like a bunch of bats flying in a funnel shape with swirling lines all over the page and lightning bolts throughout. He stuffed the drawings in the backpack, swung it over his shoulders, and hurried off the bus.

He was standing in front of the "Bunker Hill Memory Care and Assisted living facility." A short, flowered median and walkway led to some gates, for which Mikey had a key fob. The place was all red, white, and blue, with decorations everywhere. It really played up on its patriotic name and even flew the American flag proudly out front. He pulled the fob from out of his pocket, placed it up to his chin, and clicked. He felt it always worked better when touching his chin. He always told people driving in who couldn't open the gate easily to try his 'chin trick,' which they never did, and would rather keep clicking and clicking, raising their arms higher and to different sides, hoping one of those directions may work.

Mikey would tell them again that he learned it online, yet they would ignore him.

"Just trying to be helpful. Here, I will open it." He put his fob to his chin, the door buzzed, and the gate slowly swung open.

"Remember, drive only 10 miles an hour in here, OK? Be safe, and have a wonderful day."

It was dark and cloudy outside, and Mikey hurried to the front door and typed his code on the keypad to get into the lobby before the rain started. He signed in at the desk and wrote in the "Who are you here to see?" category, "Irma Ruby Gross. Then, he said, "Ah dang, I forgot again…" and crossed out "Gross" and re-wrote the last name 'White" instead. She had been married to Bill White for many years until he passed away from a heart attack when helping to move 'the purple beast' which was the band's practice tower that the drum majors and director would get up into to watch over the formations when they practiced their drill for their show. It was actually painted purple by the senior class band members' of 1984 when they raised the money to purchase it for the band's use. Irma never forgave the band for that accident, and she blamed them directly for not helping him more as a volunteer. Upon becoming a widow, she retired early from teaching at the school- she was the senior class advanced placement or AP English teacher at Kinish Tech. It was just too hard to continue working at the school where her husband had passed away.

Irma was so happy to get rid of her last name as well when she married Bill. Her initials on her office door at school had been "I. R. Gross," and that was something the kids always made fun of.

"Dude, are you gross?"

"Yeah, man, I *are* gross. Hahaha!"

When he heard stuff like that, Mikey tried to get them to stop saying mean things about her name but ended up getting bullied for it and often pushed into a locker or thrown into the school dumpster. One day, they locked him in the atriums that were in between the buildings. That's where the 'bad kids' hung out, sneaking away to smoke cigarettes or make out with girls. The windows all looked into the atrium, so the other kids could see Mikey's terror as he ran from window to window, pleading to be let back into the school. He hated missing anything academic and, worse, to be trapped in that place.

Irma White was one of the toughest English teachers to have. The kind of teacher who assigned homework over the holidays and papers assigned on Friday- due Monday. She meant business, much to the dismay of her classes. On the other hand, because she worked them so hard, many were more prepared for college-level English courses and became quite adept at writing and researching for later needs in life.

Irma sat in her room, often medicated pretty heavily by the staff in order to "ease her anxiety," they said. This made conversations with her pretty one-sided and similar if you had just spoken to the wall, or to the curtains in the room, or just to yourself. Mikey felt sad about that, so he took it upon himself to go and see her as often as he could after school. Sometimes, he found her in the computer lab, but today, she was in her room. Family was important to him, and he felt she needed some family around her. Maybe his visits would cheer her up?

Mikey came into her room, "Whazzzup, Bruh? How are you today, Aunt White?"

She was sitting at the table coloring with the Crayola crayons given to her. She looked up at him, then just kept drawing and coloring. Pretty much trying to ignore him. The wall behind her was plastered with her previous drawings. Many looked very disturbing, but others had suns and flowers depicting a man and a woman running happily, holding hands, and smiling. The happy ones were pinned up heavily on the right side of the wall, with the darker ones on the left. Words were written on many of them, such as "Foible, Circumspect, Nebulous, Mischievous, Tomorrow." As she finished her drawings, she would slide them to Mikey to look at and take. He could tell she meant for him to take them, so he didn't want to hurt her feelings. He would take them and look at them later. He took the previous ones from his backpack and said, "Well, Auntie White, these should go up on your Art wall. Shall I put them up in order of dark colors to light?"

She didn't say anything but just stared out the window.

"Boom, this one will go here, and this one will move this one over here, and I'll put this one on top over here…" He did his best to fit them in and color-match them to the similar colored sibling pictures. He stood back after completing this job and got a strange feeling.

"Some of these look-like things that are familiar to me. Here's one with a big door in a mountainside, and this one here looks like some soldiers fighting snowmen, but my dream was about soldiers fighting Yetis. Hmm, that's very interesting. Great minds must think alike I suppose! Was that a dream? It felt so real."

Mikey looked briefly at the new drawings given to him. "Wow, look at that- another snowman drawing. He looks angry, and he's fighting those other snowmen. Cool! You have a great imagination, Auntie White. Oh, look, a little puppy, how cute! I have always wanted a little dog like that. Too bad they only allow cats in this place Auntie. I bet a little dog would cheer you right up! I know it would make me happier for sure. I don't have any friends, really."

Irma then pointed to another one of the drawings she gave him with her crooked, arthritic pointer finger. It was of some kids laying in beds, just stick drawings, but they had squiggly lines coming from them, their eyes just black discs, and their mouths were open. They looked like they were in pain. She said, "Feel."

Mikey was all like, "Whoa, she said something! That's great Auntie. You said 'feel.' You're talking to me today. That's great!"

Mikey felt the crayon drawing. "Doesn't feel like anything but waxy Crayola to me, but um, ok."

Mikey now had some colors on his hands. "What's with the little squiggly lines here? Do they smell bad? It looks like they have a tummy ache, and they might be tooting. Maybe too much Mexican food, Haha!"

Irma didn't like the comment and whipped her hand away quickly as if it were burned.

Mikey said, "Thanks for the drawings. I will check 'em out on the flip side, Auntie White. I gotta split. It's getting late. Oh, and thanks for the laugh too, Haha." He kissed her forehead, grabbed his stuff, and swung the backpack back over his shoulder. On the way out, he said to himself, "Mexican food. Now I am going to have *La Suerte de Los Tantos* by Stan Kenton from the album Cuban Fire stuck in my head tonight." He then whistled some of the tune as he left and thought about the fact that the song was written for the actress Grace Kelly and the Prince of Monaco.

Mikey intensely felt a sharp pain in his stomach and bent over a little, "Ouch! What caused that? Feels like I ate some bad Mexican food, Yo!" He then had intense pain all over his body and dropped to his knees. "Argh! What the heck, man? What's happening?!" He grabbed his head with both hands and covered his ears, which were also in pain.

Mikey collapsed outside in the median of flowers face down. Totally out. A small trickle of blood seeped from one ear and ran down his cheek. Rain started trickling, then pouring down on him. Dark, ominous clouds blocked the remaining light of day. The red, white, and blue banners from the patriotic complex whipped in the rising wind, and the American flag whipped in a fury while its chain clattered on the pole, echoing in the silence.

CHAPTER FIVE: A puppy named Presley

Bob sat at the wooden desk provided for him in the dorm room made of stones that were also provided to him and all of his band students. This was a refuge from whatever nefarious beings were outside, like those soldiers and the ninja who attacked them upon mysteriously arriving here. This was Shen Yun, somewhere in Tibet, he thought. The name seemed really familiar to him but he couldn't place it. He didn't remember a Shen Yun anywhere on the map in this part of the world, but then again, he was no *Jeopardy* game champion in geography either.

The kids had constantly asked him how long they had stayed there and when they were going home. Being the person in charge of them, Bob decided to try to find something out. He couldn't just sit all day and write in his journal. He did enjoy the meal that night, but this thunder and storm outside had him worried. The other children had gone to sleep, but he was still stirring a bit and wished he had gone to sleep before this electrical storm hit. It was very creepy.

"Oh well, let's try and find out something before I go off to bed," Bob said and then headed towards the door of energy flickering quite a bit as the storm's intensity grew stronger and more violent. Bob approached very cautiously and reached out slowly with one finger in order to just barely touch the door.

ZAP! He whipped his finger back and noticed that the tip of his finger was charred black and smoking a little. "Buh, that smarts! There's got to be a way to open this thing manually from in here."

He started looking everywhere, on the sides of the doorway and at the bottom. He even took the chair and stood on it to see the top. He couldn't see anything that would open the door. So, he thought, "Maybe the window?" He went over to the odd window recessed into the wall quite a bit and then had to lean into it to get a good view.

"That's odd. The storm seems worse outside than what I am seeing here." Then it happened. As another lighting strike hit and made all of the lights flicker in the room, including the energy door, he saw the window actually flicker as well!

"What gives man? How can a window flicker unless it's not a window at all?"

Bob was confused and felt betrayed. He had trusted the snow king to be upfront with him, and they even shared pipe weed! The nerve. "I have to get to the bottom of this…this betrayal!"

He then went as close as he could to the door and yelled, "Guard! Guard, yo, who be boo! I need some help here. C'mon man, I know someone is out there." He had his hand on the cold stone near the door, leaning on it and propping himself away from getting charred himself, and he could just see between the flickering that a Yeti was approaching.

"Ah yes, my good man. Thank you, thank you for coming to my aid." Bob said as the Yeti came to the door and punched a code into the keypad on the outside, and the door turned off. The Yeti stood in the doorway and stared at Bob, who was now grinning stupidly, and asked him, "Can I possibly speak with Polybius and make some plans for my departure from this wonderful facility? Some storm huh? Is it always like this?" Bob noticed a pin on his weapon strap now that wasn't there previously, just the initials HWLA.

The Yeti guard turned and marched Bob down the hallway toward the throne room, but before they got there, Polybius emerged quickly from the room, and the door closed abruptly behind him. To Bob, he looked bigger now and seemed to have a slight glow about him.

"Wow, hey, Mister Snow King. You, ah, look healthier now. Have you got a workout room or something in there?" Bob said jokingly.

"What do you need, gross one?" Polybius bellowed in a deep bass voice, almost shaking Bob, who was standing there. "I am very busy, and it is late. Why are you not sleeping?"

"I want to know when we are going to get out of here. Are we going to be able to leave soon?"

"There is someone I want you to meet, so if you go now, you'll never get that opportunity, so I think you should all hang around here for a good while until he arrives. Trust me, you'll be dying to meet him," said the snow king with a chuckle.

"Golly," said Bob. "Who is it?"

"Oh, he is a big fan of yours and loves your kids. You'll see just how much very soon. Now, please go back to bed. Morning shall come soon, and this storm will be ending quickly."

"Ok, but can I say goodnight to my kiddo? I didn't see him at all after dinner. I just want to check on him."

"Guard, take this gross one to his gross son and then see to it that they both get to bed, HWLA." The Yeti hit his own chest with a thud and repeated, "HWLA, your Highness."

Bob looked confused, "HWLA? What is that?"

"It is of no concern to your kind, but we are very religious, and you can take it to mean he will live again." Said the snow king, trying to make a praying sign with one hand and one hoof while bowing his beastly horned head.

"Well, HWLA to you too, then," said Bob. "Shall we go?" He said to the Yeti guard, putting his arm out as if he wanted him to take him by his arm like a date would do. The guard looked at his arm, sneered, and marched away in disgust.

Bob said, "Touchy, touchy, aren't we?" and followed the guard down the hall as Polybius watched them disappear round the corner.

#

Mikey lay sprawled across his bed, drenched in sweat. One leg dangled off the edge while the other was tucked beneath him. His face was buried in the pillow, his headset still on. He moaned and groaned, occasionally jerking dramatically with a loud 'Buuuuuhhh" rattling from him.

The energy door raised, and Bob was standing there in silhouette. Flashes from the other doors in the hall cast him in a flickering shadow. He saw Mikey and ran to the bed. He shook him and said, "What's wrong, son? Mikey, wake up kid!"

He flipped Mikey up and held him in his arms, "C'mon, kiddo, wake up. You are having a bad nightmare. Pop is here." But Mikey just said with a drooped head, "Buuuuhhh."

Bob yanked the headset off of him, and Mikey jolted and went stiff. Then relaxed. Bob tried to stir him gently, saying, "I don't know what that was all about, but c'mon kid, wakey, wakey." Mikey slowly stirred and saw his dad.

"Hey, Pop. You won't believe the nightmare I was having…"
He then wiped tears from his eyes and coughed a bit. Eventually,
he sat up on the side of the bed next to his dad.

Bob was relieved and hugged his boy, with Mikey letting out
an, "Ow! Too tight, Bruh."

Bob leaned in and said quietly, "Son, I don't know what's
going on, but this is not what it seems, and we need to amscray
ASAP." Bob winked at him and pretended to yawn while
stretching his arms high up and then pointed at the backpack upon
bringing them down. Then he said loudly- so the Yeti guard could
hear him, "Man, look at the time, son! Time to get some shut-eye.
I am glad you are safe and sound. I'm off to my wonderful room
to get some sleep, too. See you in the morning."

Mikey nodded in acceptance, still groggy from the effects of
whatever had happened to him. His thoughts were nebulous at best,
but he felt like he understood that this wasn't a place to stay any
longer. He would think of something. He would be sure it involved
their magical backpack.

Bob stood in the doorway so that the guard couldn't shut it,
then he pulled his pipe out and said, "Can I have a late-night smoke
on the way? Do you mind?" He purposefully put his fingers in the
opening and got lots of ashes and soot on his hand, then purposely
dropped the pipe a little distance away from the guard. "Oopsie
Daisy! Would you mind getting that for me, good man?" The Yeti
grunted at him and turned to get the pipe from the floor. Bob
shooshed and pointed his hand behind his back at Mikey to get the
backpack and do something quick.

Mikey was alone and miserable. All he wanted was a friend.
He needed something to lift his spirits, someone who would never

let him down, someone who was real and not just a figment of his imagination. He craved unconditional love and a way out of their current predicament. With a gulp and a flicker of hope, he squeezed his eyes shut and said, "Please, please, please…I need a friend."

A little puffy white curly-haired puppy emerged from the pack after knocking it over, trying to get out. It didn't bark at all, and it was wearing a miniature service dog vest because it was a small breed of dog, like a tiny poodle, but way, way cuter. It was a little white puffball of love, all perky and happy to be out of the backpack. Mikey looked astonished, with a welt of tears pooling up in his eyes. "I am going to name you Presley! Yep, you are a puppy named Presley, and we are going to be the best of friends!" Presley jumped up into his lap, very happy to see him.

The Yeti guard hadn't seen what happened nor heard anything but Mikey talking to himself because this puppy was a Bichon Frise breed, and they hardly bark. Their manner is to be extremely cute. At least, that is what most people would think if they saw him. Presley popped up on the bed next to Mikey and gave him kisses, but Mikey calmed him and said, "You are my best friend now, and I need you to help me." Presley inquisitively tilted his head to one side as he listened like a dog would. "Run out of here and down the halls, and don't get caught. Avoid everyone but me and my Dad there." He pointed to his father. "Think of it as a game of 'don't get caught,' ok?" Then he put Presley down and said, "Go!" Presley skirted through the doorway under the legs of both Bob and the Yeti guard.

Bob got his pipe back and said, "Thank you, thank you, my good man! How can I ever repay you?" While he grabbed the Yeti's hand, he shook it rapidly and wiped soot and ashes all over his fingers using his own dirty hand. The Yeti guard saw the puppy dash away and wanted to give chase, but he had to shut the door to run. He bumped Bob aside and attacked the keypad with his dirty fingers. Beep, beep, beep, beep. The door of energy came down and closed. He then looked at Bob and turned to give chase towards the puppy who was already rounding the corner.

Bob looked at the keypad, and only 4 numbers were covered in soot: 5, 6, 7, and 8. Bob started punching different combinations of those four numbers, but nothing worked. Mikey then said, "Pop, what are the numbers?"

Bob said, "5,6,7, and 8. But nothing is working. I tried them like that, and backward, then started with 6, then 7, nothing is opening."

Mikey thought a second and said, "How about 8,6,7, 5?" Bob tried it, and the energy field rose up and disappeared. Mikey smiled. "Good ole Tommy Tutone."

Bob said, "How did you know?"

Mikey said, "It's the first part of Jenny's phone number from the 1982 hit song by Tommy Tutone. It's one of my faves. 867-5309." He sang the numbers, so Bob would have a reference. The number combination worked.

Bob said, "Interesting. Good job. Now, let's get outta here and save the other kids. Something is not right here, and if the others are suffering what you went through, we have to be quick about it."

Mikey said, "Pop, did you see him? Isn't he wonderful? I always wanted a friend, and now I have one pop. He's so cute…but I don't feel so good." Mikey collapsed in Bob's arms. Probably still suffering from whatever was happening to him from wearing those headphones.

An alarm claxon went off inside the castle hallways, and Bob could hear many footsteps running in the halls, but he just held Mikey and said, "What have they done to you, son? Don't worry, I will get you home…somehow. I'll get your little friend too and treat him like family. I promise because I am a Gross!" The footsteps got closer.

Bob ran down the hall carrying his son and wearing the backpack. He had to duck into corners, hide behind pillars, and dart into alcoves while Yeti guards ran through the hallways, apparently looking for them. He had to find a safe place to go and be able to lay Mikey down so he could get some rest. The effects of the headphones were still apparent, and his kid needed some real rest.

Suddenly, Presley came trotting around the corner and came right up to them both. They were hiding behind a pillar, and Presley was going to give them away!

"Shhh! Presley, that's a nice doggie. Will you get back in the backpack, please, little guy?" Bob pleaded. He put the backpack down, and Pressley looked at him again with a tilted head. If he were a person, he would be saying with his body language, "What's the deal, bro? I just got out of there. You actually want me to go back in?" But then, when Bob opened the flap, Presley jumped right in but kept his head out. He wasn't going to go in all of the way this time.

"Oh my, that is such a good puppy! Wait until Mikey hears how good you are! Thank you, little guy."

Some Yeti guards just ran by, and Bob saw an energy door across the hall where one of the band kids was. He ran across the hall with Mikey and Presley in tow and punched in the numbers on the keypad, 8,6,7,5, and whoosh, the energy door turned off. There was a girl in this room, and she was obviously suffering like Mikey, so Bob quickly removed the headphones from her as well. She also looked weak but stirred and slowly woke up. She saw

Bob by the bed looking over at her, and he said, "How are you feeling? You, OK?"

She sat up, looked at him in bewilderment, then leaned over the bed and barfed all over his shoes.

"Great. That's really great. I guess I should have expected that," Bob said, keeping the backpack away from the vomit and scootching to the side to get to the little bathroom on the other side of the room. He cleaned up his shoes while Mikey lay on the bed next to the girl and started to wake up again. Mikey opened his eyes and said, "Kristin? What are you doing in my bed?"

Kristin said angrily, "Mikey Gross, this is my bed, and you're the interloper here, not me! Tell me what the heck is going on…I don't feel too well."

Bob came back in and said, "Both of you need to keep it down. Kristin, I brought him here because there is something going on that's not right here, and I have to get you all out of here before it's too late."

"Why in here?" Kristin asked.

"Because we are trying to get away from those Yeti soldiers who are looking for us."

"I thought they were helping us," she said.

"I thought so, too, until I saw what they were doing to you all. It's why you feel sick."

"I feel really weak too," Kristin said with bags under her eyes that were not there previously. She then got up and went to look in the mirror in the bathroom. "Eek! What happened to my eyes? They're so tired-looking and all sunken in. What gives?!"

Bob said, "I think it has something to do with those headphones. What's playing on them anyway?" He then placed them on his head. It was overpowering to him, and he instantly fell on the bed after letting out a 'Buuuuhhh.' It was nearing the end of *Ravel's Bolero,* and the trombone glissandos were playing loudly with the drum beats ever so louder.

Mikey, as tired as he was, leaped to his dad and said, "Nooo!" But it was too late, Bob was out cold on the bed. No stirring him nor shaking was waking Bob up, even after Mikey removed the headphones. The song ended in a climax of brass and triple forte, and when it ended, Bob also seemed to stop. Except he was pianissimo now.

Mikey tried and tried to wake him to no avail. He knew he wasn't dead, but he just wasn't waking. Mikey said, "There's some evil magic going on here. I guess I am going to have to do this on my own." But then Presley popped out of the bag and jumped up on the bed by Bob and Mikey sitting there. Kristin said, "OMG, what a cute puppy! Where the heck did he come from?"

Mikey proudly said, "This is my puppy, Presley. He's my best friend in the whole world." He then gave Presley a little hug and squeeze. Presley was happy and did a circle walk in place and started panting happily while wagging his tail.

"He looks thirsty. Can I give him some water?" Kristin asked.

"Oh wow, I hadn't thought of that. He's been cooped up in that backpack for quite a while, I suppose. He's probably hungry too! We need to get him some food."

"Kristin, will you watch over him and watch my dad? I need to go get some food and find us a way out of this place."

"Well, I guess. This is all very weird, Mikey. I don't like this one bit, but I will help. Presley is too cute, and I still feel like caca, so I will stay here and watch them both. Hurry back!"

Mikey put the backpack on without Presley in it this time and started heading to the open door. Claxons were still going off, but there wasn't much activity out there at the time. They must be somewhere else in the castle, he told himself. "Kristin, I have to keep you all safe, so I am going to shut the door. I can open it when I get back, so don't freak out, ok?"

She nodded yes. Presley then jumped off the bed and started towards Mikey. Mikey stopped him and said, "Presley, you have to stay here with Kristin. She will be nice to you, and I will get back to you shortly. Be a good puppy, ok? Watch after them, please. good dog!" He then patted him on the head, picked him up with both hands placed on Presley's sides, and turned him around like a toy car he just picked up and made go in the other direction while it was running. "Direction change," Mikey said. Presley did his tilted head thing again but stayed put.

Beep, beep, beep, beep. The door whooshed full of energy again as Mikey input the code. "Ok, where is the kitchen, and what am I going to do to get us out of here? What am I thinking? I am nobody. Man, this is crazy. I guess I will try and follow my nose." He started trying to smell the air like a dog would. "Maybe the backpack can help me?" Mikey spoke to the backpack. "Yo, magic backpack, can you get me something that can help me find some food and find a way out of here?" Mikey reached in and fumbled around inside the pack, where he brought out a thermometer. "What gives man?" He dove back in and searched around. Nothing new and just the regular things that he always kept in there- his oboe case, a bag of Sour Patch Kids candy, a folder of Clarke studies practice sheet music exercises, his band music folder, his Aunt White's drawings, his Walkman and cassette mix tapes he made, and his dad's little yellow book of survival. He pulled out the book and started looking at the table of contents to find anything about how they could get out of there. "Great, if I need to know how to survive falling off a horse, survive a zombie invasion, or survive a duel, they're in here. Nothing about how to escape a dungeon or use a stupid thermometer to find food. Thanks a lot, backpack! You always come through for us. Is something not working right?" Mikey looked at the straps of the backpack, which resembled that leathery angry face. "Sheesh, OK, I will trust you. Don't get all mad about it. Touchy, touchy." He then slung the backpack back on.

Mikey turned the thermometer over and looked at the back. There were some words written on it: "Don't be cold. Be cool. You'll find a friend, you fool."

"Funny. OK, I guess I will look for somewhere cold?" He then held the thermometer out in front of him like he was holding a divining rod, and he started to walk and watch the temperature gauge on the thermometer. He based his direction on whether it got colder or not. He meandered through many hallways and odd rooms that were open and avoided all Yeti guards. He seemed to be going further into the castle's bowels, knowing that he may have a hard time finding his way back. But that didn't deter him because he knew everything rested on him if they were going to survive.

Mikey turned a corner, and the temperature drastically dropped. He could feel it get colder as if a door from the snowy outside world was opened. He looked ahead and thought he saw some light on the left side of the hallway and some snow flurries.

He got some shivers and tried to bundle up into his coat a little more. He was still wearing his Darth Vader pajamas and only had time to throw his coat and backpack on when he ventured out. At least he still had his Vans high-tops on because going barefoot wasn't an option. He approached the opening slowly and listened as he did for anything strange. He heard swooshing sounds, then clicks. More clicking, and then an electrical arc noise like an electronic buzzing.

Mikey realized the wall on the left side, where all of this was coming from, was laden with white, almost chalky-looking bars. They were jail cell bars yet white in color, and whatever was inside was making these sounds. He got to the edge of the cell, then slowly peered his head around the wall to look in the opening of the first bars. The thermometer Mikey held was maxed out blue, and the indicator light was glowing as he had succeeded. He put it in his pocket slowly as he looked in. His eyes got large and he gasped because he wasn't sure he was seeing something that was real.

#

The snow king barked orders at the Yeti who were conferring around him and pointing in different directions to send them off to different areas of the castle to search for the dog and find where Bob was hidden. As they dispersed in different directions, the snow king headed towards the back area of the throne room, towards the hall, and to that elevator Mikey had seen before. The two guards saw him approach, and both turned with their backs against the wall of either side as he passed them. He entered the passcode, and the skull-laden doors slid open for him. He got in and pressed a button that had a sinister-looking skull on it. It took him down and opened into a large open cavern area, which was pitch dark except for some glowing lines of blue, red, and green lights in the distance. They seemed to be spaced perfectly apart, and colors were bundled in a way that all blues were together all reds together, and the same for greens. As he started walking forward down the path, motion sensor lights in the stone path near him lit up that area of the path in dramatic fashion. He finally approached the ordered lights, and as that area was lit up it revealed that they were cannisters filled with energy that emitted their colored glow. Each cannister's energy swirled and moved like a ghostly apparition trapped inside. Polybius passed them and came to a fork in the path. One direction led to a large sliding door and labeled across it, was 'MCP,' and the other had a sinister skull that matched what was on the elevator button. Sort of a geometric and angled skull, almost laughing in evil. Polybius turned to the MCP door from the fork and walked to it. The door swished open, and as he stepped inside, a loud whirring and spinning sound could be heard. Polybius stood still in front of a large cylindrical tower that looked like it was made of glass. Inside the tower of glass was a red and orange vortex spinning and whirring but now slowing. The colors lit the room in the same fashion. It finally came to a stop to reveal a sizeable geometric face that stretched from the top of the cylinder to the bottom. It looked computer-generated and geometric. A booming voice then broke the silence when the face spoke.

"Greetings conscript. Report your status. I grow weary of your failures."

CHAPTER SEVEN: Meet the Glitch

Mikey pulled away from the jail bars and flattened himself against the stone wall with a gasp and a look of worry. What did his eyes see? The sloshing noises continued, as did the clicking noises. He decided to take a really good look this time to see if what he saw was real or just his wild imagination. He looked again and saw something that looked like a snowman, but not completely. It had only two ball-type sections, a head and a body, yet it was mostly made up of interlocking and overlapping gears covered with some snow. Mikey thought it was like a steampunk snowman. A creature made from snow and code? The floor of its cage was wet because there was wet melting snow on top of the stone floor. The creature travelled smoothly around the small space, spinning and whirling around over the melting snow spots, often frantically, and this caused the sloshing noise. It had a face of melting snow and gears as well. It did have a carrot nose though, and a worn-out top hat with a black scarf around its neck. Its eyes were completely digital and were glowing red. It didn't have any arms at all, and its buttons, which would traditionally be made of coal, were replaced with three shiny gears that glowed the same color as its eyes. The hat had something stuck in its hat band. A piece of paper that was torn a bit, but the word on it said 'Glitching.' The 'ing' was just hanging on by a shard of paper, though and waved around frantically as the snowman spun around and clicked.

Mikey stood there, ready to run away from the bars if anything happened, but the thermometer sent him here, so he was going to take a chance.

Mikey said nervously and with pretend confidence, "Um, hey there. My name is Mikey. What's yours?"

The creature stopped, then turned to Mikey and rushed to the bars at him, clicking rapidly at him. As it reached the bars, it seemed to cry out in pain with an electrical noise as it pinned itself against the bars, trying to get out. It quickly recoiled and darted for the back corner, hurt and as if in trouble. Snow from its body fell off its wireframe and onto the floor, creating more wet snow to slosh upon. The bars seemed to be smoking now after the attack on them, and Mikey thought, what are those things made of?

Mikey said, "Hey, I am sorry if I said something to anger you, bro. I just wanted to see if you were ok. Are you doing alright?"

The creature gradually stopped cowering and slowly turned to look at Mikey again, its eyes and buttons turning blue.

Mikey asked, "Can you talk or just click?"

The snowman shook its head no and just clicked at him sadly.

Mikey said, "Are you in trouble for something? Why did they lock you in here, and what the heck are these bars made of?" He got closer to a smoking bar and decided to touch it. He quickly pulled his finger away but realized it did nothing to him. So, he got really close to it and smelled it. "Nothing," he said. "But it looks familiar."

Mikey then got a look on his face of joy. He had figured out what this was.

"It's salt!" "Just regular ole salt but made into bars. I can see where this would hurt a snowman, but it couldn't hurt anyone else." He thought about it and said, "Well, maybe a snail too, but that's all I got. Salt melts ice, and you, sir, are made mostly of snow."

Mikey then said, "I don't think you meant to hurt me, right?"

The snowman shook its head again, a clicking sound accompanying its gesture. The snowman approached the bars slowly, its calmness masking the sadness that weighed heavily on its heart. Mikey said, "I am sorry for being so circumspect, but I have never seen anyone like you before. Were you just trying to get out?"

The snowman nodded yes and clicked more.

Mikey said, "I think I can get you out of here, but you'll have to stand back."

The creature sloshed to the corner again.

Mikey then said, "Lucky for you, I practice Gross-fu! Actually, I made that up because I'm not really good at martial arts, but I pretend that I am. Pretending confidently usually keeps kids away from bullying me sometimes. I guess they think I'm either really crazy or that I really do know martial arts, so they leave me alone. Ok, here goes something…"

Mikey crouched into a fighting stance, his right-hand whirling in circles, two fingers extended and joined. His left hand formed a fist, tucked close to his side with his elbow bent. He yelled, "Kum-bye-yah!" He then kicked the salt bars, which shattered and broke into pieces on the floor. This caused more melting snow to vaporize into water. Mikey extrapolated that this was why he was sloshing around so much. Poor guy, he must have been trying to escape often. Whoever did this to him was going to pay.

The snowman was so happy that there was a hole to escape from that it sped out to Mikey, almost jumping out of the opening while clicking madly the entire time. His eyes and buttons then all lit up with a bright yellow glow.

Like a cat, he bent forward to rub his head on Mikey several times to thank him.

Mikey smiled and said, "No problem, buddy. What do I call you anyway?"

Then Mikey saw the paper in his hat. "Glitching, huh?" Then he said, "May I?" He then reached up to the paper and held his hand there inquisitively, seeing if there was a reaction from the snowman.

The snowman nodded yes.

Mikey tore off the 'ing' from the paper, and the word now said simply "Glitch."

"Well, that settles it then; Glitch is your name! Nice to meet you, Glitch. May I now ask you some questions?"

Glitch clicked and buzzed as they continued walking down the hallway away from that cell. He was happy and enjoyed being free so much that he often just slid around in circles quickly around Mikey. A magical snow flurry appeared above Glitch and showered Mikey and Glitch with small snowflakes everywhere. Mikey stuck out his tongue and let some land on it. "Wow", he said. "That's a cool trick, Glitch. Can you create snow at will?"

Glitch clicked happily, blue lights flashing. He circled Mikey again, and more snow fell around them.

"Well, that answers that. Ok, my laconic friend. Let's go find me some real food, or I am going to have to munch my Sour Patch kid's candy, and that will wig me out!"

Mikey had made a new friend of this gentle, magical snowman named Glitch. Mikey thought fondly, "Just wait until Pop sees him!"

#

Kristin applied a warm washcloth to Bob's forehead as he lay passed out on the bed in her room. She thought about this man who was her new band director and how he had faith in her to have the primary solos in the musical pieces they were performing. He could have chosen his son, who wasn't as good because he was the band director, and that was his kid. But he had picked her. Actually, he had made it even more fair. He had done a blind chair test by having them both go into the band storage room where they could set up, and the band kids could still hear them. The class would vote anonymously for them after each one played the same passage or solo. After all, you wouldn't want to see your best friend pick someone else, right? This worked out well for all, and a fair assessment was done, and the number picked who won took the higher chair in the section they sat. Everyone then knew who had won, and Kristin had won that day when she competed for Mikey's chair. Bob nodded approval, and the solo was then hers. She respected that method and didn't want to let him or the band down, so she worked very hard and practiced every day. Bob had earned her respect and she stopped laughing when the other kids made fun of his name or the placard on his office door, "B. Gross."

"Yes, you are!" Said the kids as they walked out of the band hall laughing. Bob knew and although it hurt his feelings, he knew the Gross family was a proud one. They had a long line of Gross family members who had done amazing things. He had a sister, Bertha Gross, who married a famous scientist, Tom Tunnecliffe and his other sister, Irma Ruby Gross, who had also married. But her husband, Bill White, had passed away when he tried to move the purple beast at the practice field. It was not a good day when that happened. The Texas sun was blazing at 105 degrees that day, yet they still had to practice their show. The mowing crew had moved the beast away from the grass field in order to mow but never moved it back. No other men were around, and Bill volunteered to try to get it back in place for rehearsal. It was too much for him, and if he had just waited, the band director, John Faraone, would have had some of the senior boys help him. When the kids arrived at the field to practice, Bill was lying on the field, clutching his chest. The paramedics arrived, but he was pronounced dead on arrival.

"Man, that was a bad day, Mr. G," Kristin said to Bob's sleeping body. "The only good thing it did was that it seemed to bring the band even closer together. I guess bad things happening sometimes does that, huh?" She leaned in to see if he was still breathing. He was.

"Whew, I guess this is a bad thing too. I actually think Mikey and I might even become friends after this. I wonder if you can even hear or understand what I am saying?" She waved her hand above his eyes back and forth to see if there was any reaction, yet only Presley followed her hand back and forth like she had a treat in it. The washcloth on his head was dripping a little, and some water trickled down his forehead and cheek. Presley was still thirsty, so he started licking Bob's face.

"Who-waah! Au fou, au fou!" Bob awoke startled. "What happened?" Bob looked around and sat up. He saw the dog by his side and Kristin sitting on his other side, leaning on the bed, smiling.

"Welcome back," she said. "Were you speaking another language just now?"

"What did I say?" Bob asked.

"You cried something then said, Au fou, au fou! Then sat up."

"That's weird. It means: The madman! The madman! in French. It's the same thing some lady shouted when Bolero was played for the first time at the Paris Opera in 1928. Man, I think I agree with her." Bob said.

"Where's Mikey? Sorry about getting all pedantic with the small details. We have to get everyone out of here," Bob said sternly.

Kristin said, "He split to go look for food and help."

Bob exclaimed. "What? Who does he think he is?! Oh boy, did he lock us in the room?"

Kristin nodded yes, "He said it would keep us safe."

Bob tried to look out the energy door to see if he could see him, but of course, he couldn't see anyone. "That kid. He's braver than a longtail cat in a rocking chair factory."

Footsteps were approaching.

Bob told Kristin, "Quick, get in the bed with Presley and cover up! I'm going to hide under it. Be quiet and pretend you are sleeping."

The door panel was entered, beep, beep, beep, beep and whoosh the door rose. Several hairy feet walked in and surrounded the bed, which Bob could see from under it. Then, some large hoofs clomped in and stood still at the foot of the bed.

"Gross one, I know you are here. Come out now, or I will start harming the children you watch over. It's time you meet him."

Bob gulped. He slid out from under the bed and put his arms up as the Yeti guards surrounded him with halberds.

"Alright, snow king. I know something rotten is in Denmark. Do what you want to me, but leave the kids out of it!" Bob said sternly.

"I promise you nothing. You are not in a position to request anything. Move him out. The master awaits!" Polybius ordered.

Bob said, "Who is the Master?

"You'll see soon enough. Just know that you'll be dying when you meet him." Polybius said, laughing.

Bob said, "Wait, what? Don't you mean he'll be dying to meet me? Whoa, now, can't we talk about this? Let's have a smoke, shall we? This is a joke, right?"

The guards marched Bob from the room as he kept trying to get out of it.

Polybius still remained at the bed, standing firm. He said in a booming voice, "Girl, I know you are not sleeping after that. Know this. He will not save you. The process has started, and the master will live again. It is foretold, and everything in the prophecy has been coming true. You are all insignificant and just food for the Gods. You may as well give in now and stop resisting. Nothing and nobody can save you. You are just a band of misfits, so get used to it." Then Polybius exited the room.

Kristin, still under the covers, was crying now and starting to sob. She was truly scared. Presley licked her face, streaming with tears and tried to cheer her up.

Kristin said shakily, "Oh, Presley, what are we going to do? What was he talking about? I want to go home."

CHAPTER EIGHT: Layla, you've got me on my knees

She took out a fresh drawing pad, tore out a large blank page and placed it on the desk in front of her. She then carefully used blue painter's tape to attach it by its edges to the desk so it wouldn't move. A huge set of Crayola crayons was opened near her with all of the colors anyone could ever want to use. It said it was the 'ultimate crayon collection,' with an amazing 152 colors. She started pulling out all of the different blues that she could find in the pack. They were blue, bluetiful, sky blue, periwinkle, pacific blue, robin's egg blue, and the favorites, midnight blue, navy blue and wild blue yonder. There were several others as well because she was determined to draw out a picture that was a blue-toned, geometric landscape. It actually looked like a pit made of ice walls that were hexagonal in shape and stacked to make the walls. She then started drawing a lot of children crying and lamenting that they were trapped and couldn't get out from the slippery ground and walls. They were actually trying to climb out and clawing at the walls to no avail. She began to laugh as she drew this trap of sorts.

She said, "Their quest will end nicely when they are trapped in the valley of ice."

We saw Irma White drawing in the Arts and Crafts room at the Bunker Hill Memory Care and Assisted Living facility where she lived. Others were also drawing at nearby tables, and an instructor/caregiver was walking around, offering assistance and making comments. "How lovely is that?! Great job! That's so pretty!" and other accolades to the residents in their art class. When the caregiver got to Irma's drawing, she stopped and became quiet.

She then said to Irma, "Um, wow, that is really, um, creative, Irma. You have a knack for interesting nature scenes, don't you?"

Irma looked at her, smiling evilly, and said, "It's the valley of ice. The most quintessential trap I could dream up. Do you think it will work?"

The caregiver said, "Um. Well. Are those kids in some sort of ice place? Why would you put so many kids there, and what did they do to deserve that?"

Irma said, "They are the cause of my husband's demise. They are a wicked bunch of heathens, and I will teach them a lesson of hubris."

The caregiver looked shocked and called out, "Nurse? Has Mrs. White gotten her afternoon happy pills?" Then slowly backed away from her and tended to another resident.

Irma then really got into the drawing and started coloring the sky, where she put black, ominous clouds all over, scribbling madly and shaking the table. She began to laugh and cackle even more now. "Hahahah! He will live again! He hungers! There is no escape! Hahahah!!

#

Mikey and Glitch made their way down the various tunnels and passageways, with Mikey telling Glitch to stop snowing and be still when Yeti guards were near. Glitch knew the place fairly well and was leading the way happily. He was so happy to be free from that horrible salt cell that was melting his wonderful snow. He clicked in a rhythm sometimes like a drummer who just can't stop drumming. Mikey noticed this and said, "Glitch, you like to make drumming noises and rhythms, huh? I bet you wish you had arms so you could hold drumsticks and play some mad paradiddles and vicious beats, huh?"

Glitch nodded yes, hung his head a little lower, and all his lights turned blue.

Mikey said, "Whoa, man, I didn't mean to give you the funk. It's all cool, my guy. I am sorry I mentioned arms. I really like what you are clicking and I bet I could play something cool along with it. I'm not really that good, though, but I would like to try – only if you are up to it- and want to, OK?"

Glitch returned to a nice bright yellow glow and slid around Mikey some more, then rubbed his head on Mikey's chest like a puppy would do.

Mikey said, "Ok, that settles it then. When we find some time and aren't somewhere we might get caught or killed, we'll give it a try!"

They approached a hallway where they could hear commotion around the corner and grunting by several Yetis. Mikey and Glitch stayed perfectly still in a small alcove and just listened. Soon, they saw Yetis coming down the hall carrying food trays and pitchers full of drinks. They were rather funny looking because they wore waiter-type clothing, yet they were still Yetis and very hairy.

Mikey said, "I guess the snow king likes to think he is all bougie and fancy, huh? Well, I know he is not a good guy. He can pretend all he wants, but he's just a big jerk!"

They both waited until the waiters were gone from sight, then Mikey said, "Now's our chance. This must be the way to the kitchen. Let's roll. No pun intended Glitch, my friend."

They turned the corner and actually saw a service elevator with a sign that said "To the kitchen- Authorized personnel only."

Mikey said, "Well, looks like we're going for a ride Mr. Jones." Imitating Short Round's voice and dialog from the Indiana Jones and the Temple of Doom movie. Glitch looked at him, not understanding and tilted his head like Presley was doing.

Mikey said, "Geez, man. It's a character from an Indiana Jones movie. Have you never seen a movie?"

Glitch shook his head back and forth with a no.

Mikey said, "Well, we're going to fix that one day too! I'll introduce you to my entire movie collection. I have the best movies! Anyway, it means we need to get on the elevator and go where they came from with that food. Let's go."

Mikey pressed the button for the elevator, and when the door opened, it was empty, so they got in. Mikey then went to press the down button but noticed below the button marked 'K', probably for 'kitchen,' there was a button that looked like a geometric skull below it.

Mikey said, "Now there's something you don't see every day, huh? That's one creepy button. I am hungry, but man, the temptation to press that sinister-looking button is too much for me to look at and not push! Shall we try it?"

Glitch stopped Mikey from pushing it by sliding in his way and blocking his finger from pushing it. He shook his head no, no, no, and his lights started flashing red like sirens. He clicked in an SOS pattern of three short clicks, three long clicks and three short clicks.

Mikey was startled and said, "Wow, not a good idea, huh? You know what's down there, right? You know where that leads."

Mikey then turned away from Glitch, crossed his arms defiantly and tilted his head up with a pouty lip. Then he said, "You know, I'm going to have to eventually go down there because it may be a way out of here. But I guess we will just skip it for now and go grab some grub."

Glitch calmed down, then turned yellow again with relief. As soon as he slid away, Mikey spun and pushed the evil-looking button, which turned blood red once it was selected.

Mikey said, "Too slow, Joe! I have to see what's down there, bro. Hey, that rhymes. Cool."

Glitch was worried, so he skirted to the back corner of the elevator and pointed his face in the corner cowering and shaking. His snow flurries had also stopped.

Mikey said sympathetically, "I am sorry, Glitch. I have to try to get us out of here. Please don't be upset with me. I know you are only looking out for us. It'll be alright, you'll see."

The door slid open to darkness. Mikey poked his head out of the elevator and tried to look around. Nothing, just a black void.

Mikey said," What is this? I can kind of see the ground. I'm going to have to have faith, I guess. This is also from another Indiana Jones movie, by the way. They called it, 'the leap of faith'." I have to just take a big step, and a path will miraculously be there. You'll see!" Mikey then put his right leg out in front and pointed his foot straight up to the top of the elevator with the intention of landing a big step forward- or he could fall to his death in utter blackness.

Mikey started to take this big step, so he leaned into it by raising his foot higher. Then, he started to put it down while leaning forward. He said, "Here goes something!" He closed his eyes, took a big breath, and held it. His foot was coming down, and there was no turning back.

#

Bob's eyesight was blurry, and he was disoriented. After blinking a few times, the blur started to clear up, but things still looked odd. He was upside down, looking at something glowing red and orange, yet shiny like glass.

A booming voice spoke, which shook him, "B. Gross. It's about time. I was beginning to think that my lackeys would never bring you face-to-face with me. Turn him, you fools."

Bob began to rotate right-side up and realized that he was strapped to something, and it was holding him in place. His hands and feet were bound to it, and he was attached to a disk and shackled on it like an X. As he stopped and was vertical once more, he saw a giant geometric red face looking right at him. It was so large in the glass cylinder that it looked like it could have easily eaten him as a small snack.

Bob said wearily, "Who be boo…um, who be you? What are you doing with me?"

The red face stared at him, then said, "I am the MCP, the master control program. But I am just borrowed so that I can speak to you in zone two from the real world."

Bob said, "The MCP, like from Tron? That's not real, man. Where the heck am I?"

The MCP said, "True, the MCP is not real except in movies, but it is very real where you are. I have found a way to use electronic signals, music and video games to connect the real world with the dream zone. You see, I know you, and you know me. Like I said, this is just a conduit for how I control and rule this realm. I have been waiting for this meeting a very long time, and I will have my revenge on you and your heathen band."

Bob asked, "What did I do to you? Who are you? What do you mean my band?"

The MCP said, "Bob, I am your sister… Irma Gross."

Bob looked horrified. "No, it can't be. What is going on? I don't believe it!"

#

Mikey's foot came down with a stomp, and he almost lost his balance. Sensor lights started springing on to light up the path in front of him, and the room lit up with blue lights in salient projections from the top of ledges and behind boulders. This place was a large cavern. There was something else, too, a platform where they were standing now, leading down to a track of sorts. This track looked like a monorail track one would see at Disney World. It went to the right and came from way ahead in the distance, where it went around a corner. Someone had engineered this cavern and built this elaborate monorail system. One stretch of the monorail train was parked at the bottom of the landing, looking like a silver bullet with windows and lights that came on in unison when the other lights came on.

Mikey said with a quiver in his voice, "Gee, I sure am glad I didn't die, haha. This doesn't look like a kitchen, either. I guess the snow king is trying to save electricity? What's up with the motion lights? Shall we see where that thing will take us?"

Glitch was still shaking his head in a "No, no, no."

Mikey saw this and said, "Ok, let's take the A train! C'mon, buddy!" He then started jumping and skipping down the platform to the train like he was going to be first in line for a rollercoaster ride.

Glitch didn't want to be left alone, so he hurriedly glided down the metal landing ramps to the train where Mikey was. As Mikey approached the train to look inside, the doors pneumatically slid open with a woosh, beckoning them to go in.

Mikey yelled, "Shotgun!" and ran inside. Glitch followed nervously, rotating his head around as he entered. He clicked nervously and frequently, as if he were saying, "This is not a good idea. I have a bad feeling about this."

The train's door whooshed shut, and it started to continue its original journey with Mikey and Glitch now as passengers. Mikey decided to change out of his PJs, and the backpack had clothes waiting for him.

Mikey told Glitch, "Hey man, I gotta change, so look the other way, ok, bro?" He then put on a tan t-shirt, some jeans, and a khaki long-sleeve shirt, on which he folded the sleeves. Mikey decided to put his headphones on and listen to his Walkman. *Foreplay/ Long Time* by the rock group Boston was playing on his cassette tape. The monorail glided silently along its elevated track, cutting through the dreamscape like a silver arrow. They rode for quite a while and saw some incredible sights from out of the train's panoramic windows. The landscape outside was a tapestry of colors and shapes that defied the waking world's logic. The music captured the scenery incredibly. They actually exited the caverns, went along harrowing cliffs, and saw incredible valleys and snowcapped mountain peaks. They passed by waterfalls that looked otherworldly and geometric-looking landscapes. There were even geometric clouds that seemed to float by. They went through a desert and right into a frozen wasteland made up of geometric, hexagonal pieces of ice that were as large as small homes. They passed over several straw hut villages and even went around some as well. They thought they saw some people, but as the train neared the villages, the people seemed to hide or vanish. Mikey thought, "Maybe there were no people there? I thought I saw some…maybe I am just seeing things?" The music was so good Mikey caught himself dancing a bit and let Glitch hear a bit, putting an ear of his headphones up to Glitch's head. He liked it and clicked to the beat, especially the clapping portion. They were both enjoying a nice musical moment. Mikey thought back when the words were sung, "It's been such a long time…" and he thought about home. He remembered his pop and him laughing and throwing cushions at each other in front of the TV. He remembered playing in a band concert and finishing, with the audience giving them a standing ovation. He remembers the marching band rehearsing on the practice field in the heat and then the same formation when they were under the stadium lights performing to a giant crowd cheering. Those were memories he would never forget, and he had taken those times all for granted until now. He realized those things were truly what he cherished and wished he could do them again. Was his fifteen minutes of fame over for good? Why were they here, and what was this all leading up to? For now, he was just going to see where this adventure led him and enjoy his music.

There was a large geodesic sphere ahead, just like the one at Disney's EPCOT in Florida, but three times larger, and the monorail was heading straight into it. It was a magical sight to behold.

The scenery transformed into a surreal wonderland as the monorail approached the large geodesic dome. Rolling hills of lavender and emerald stretched out as far as the eye could see, dotted with trees that shimmered with iridescent leaves. Rivers of liquid gold meandered through the valleys, their surfaces reflecting the sky's ever-changing hues.

The sky itself was a masterpiece, painted with swirling clouds of pink, orange, and violet. Stars twinkled even in the daylight, casting a gentle glow over the landscape. In the distance, towering mountains with peaks that seemed to touch the heavens were capped with snow that sparkled like diamonds.

As the monorail drew closer to the dome, the air grew thick with the scent of blooming flowers and the sound of distant, melodic chimes. The dome itself was a marvel of architecture, its crystalline structure refracting light into a kaleidoscope of colors. It stood as a beacon of beauty and mystery, inviting all who saw it to explore its secrets.

Mikey said, "I bet there is no Spaceship Earth attraction in that thing! We better get down low, away from the windows, and when it stops, be careful getting out. We shouldn't be seen, Ok Glitch? Turn your snow off, please. It will be weird if they see snow flurries all over the seats and rails in here, Bruh."

The monorail pulled in, and although Mikey and Glitch were hiding, Mikey tried to look out the window just a little. He saw sparks and Yetis all over the room, building something large, like a platform suspended on hundreds of cables. There were foremen and crates, lots of conduit and large cylinders full of glowing fluids. They even noticed Yeti scientists with white coats and clipboards examining the cylinders. There were blue, green and red fluids, and they seemed to swirl on their own like they were alive within the cylinders. The train slowed but didn't stop to exit in the large dome chamber. It slowed down and went to another location. Then, the monorail came to a gentle stop at a platform made of polished marble.

Mikey and Glitch waited and listened. Nobody was coming, so they slowly peeked out of the train and felt it was safe to exit. As they stepped onto the platform, they were greeted by the soft hum of the dome's energy and the warm embrace of its enchanting atmosphere.

In this dreamscape, time seemed to stand still, and every moment was filled with wonder and beauty. The journey to the crystal dome was not just a passage through Shen Yun but a voyage into the heart of imagination itself.

Gardens of bioluminescent plants glowed softly all around this room, illuminating pathways that wound through fields of flowers that changed color with every step. Waterfalls cascaded into crystal-clear pools, their surfaces rippling with the reflections of floating lanterns.

They exited and headed up the ramps as if they were exiting the ride.

Mikey headed for the elevator, but Glitch started freaking out, with the warning lights coming on once again and SOS clicking.

Mikey turned around to see what he was fussing about when he was grabbed by a large metallic hand on his shoulder. He was afraid to turn around and look at what grabbed him because he could now feel its presence right next to him and the tight grip on his shoulder. He could only stare up with fear because he could tell it was looming over him. He had been caught!

Mikey tried struggling away, but it was no use. The robot had him and grabbed him with both hands, holding him tightly. Mikey said, "Let go of me, you jerk!"

The robot picked him up, and Mikey's feet just dangled in the air. Glitch was freaking out but rushed up the platform anyway to attack this robot. He just bounced into the robot's legs over and over again, clicking furiously, which did nothing to the metal behemoth. The robot was no longer moving but was standing there locked in place with Mikey dangling in the air like a caught mackerel fish. Mikey thought that it was probably just waiting for backup to arrive, so he tried even harder to kick and wriggle, but that didn't work.

Then there was a sound, like a buzz, and the robot opened its hands and released Mikey, who landed on his butt on the ground. Glitch backed up and stopped attacking as well, going silent like he was turned off. Glitch's lights went dark. The robot's eyes that were glowing a bright yellow before now were a cold black. Both robots were now inanimate metal statues.

Mikey looked around and saw somebody approaching him from a secondary elevator. He turned and lifted himself to his knees but then stopped as a girl approached in a dark silhouette with the light shimmering behind her from the tunnels. He was stunned, and now he too was frozen, kneeling and looking at her walking to him like an angel savior.

As she got closer, he saw that she had long brown hair, was about his age, a teenager, and dressed in a jumpsuit, making her look like a hero from the *Fantastic Four* comic books. She was beautiful to Mikey. He thought, "Definitely a hero suit of some sort. That makes sense. She is the best-looking hero I have ever seen. Am I dreaming?"

She reached out her hand to help him up, and Mikey slowly raised his hand out to her and gently helped him to his feet.

She said softly, "Hello there. I am Layla. Who are you, and more importantly, why have you come here?"

CHAPTER NINE: The test

The monorail pulled up in the geodesic dome, and out came a dozen Yetis dressed in worker uniforms and construction hardhats of different colors. Some were blue, some were green, and some were red. One thing they all had in common was a patch above the left chest pocket with a sinister skull face and an evil grin. When they unloaded off the monorail, the workers with similar colored uniforms and hard hats went with each other in different directions from the unloading platform. Some had little shuttle carts that they got on and were driven further into the construction zone, where they got off and started to work on their section of this odd platform that seemed so important. Some welded, others connected cables, and some hooked up hoses to specific connectors in the side of the platform, which led down to the colored fluid containers that matched their uniforms. There was a leader in each section, and on the ground level, there was a computer station with several large screen monitors, a keyboard and, of course, a computer and an operator.

The computer monitors displayed open program windows filled with lines of code that were constantly compiling and flashing. Occasionally, the code would halt due to incorrect syntax. The computer worker would then input a correction, allowing the code to resume compiling.

On this evening, a special test was going to run. The red section was going to be utilized, so a foreman yelled out some wild language. Everyone in the other colored sections stopped working, and things grew silent. Warning lights came on around the inside dome and swirled lights around the chamber with a claxon blaring. This began together and was all being controlled by the computer operator for the red section, who was typing in the code and hitting the enter key.

A large bass tone reverberated through the geodesic cavern, and some of the Yeti workers stepped back. Others ran from their post to the outer boundaries in fear. A series of five red cylinders were already hooked up in a daisy chain configuration to a thick hose-like conduit that snaked itself up to the side of the platform where another Yeti was suspended with his hand on a lever. Whatever was in the red cylinders below was going to be injected into this red portion of the platform. A Yeti below gave a signal, and the computer worker typed something else and another tone was heard, but this time, a generator next to the red cylinders started running. Another signal was given, and the enter button caused the red liquid to start pulsing up the snake-like conduit to the top platform from the first cylinder. The Yeti there pulled the lever, and the ominous juice flowed into the platform. The cylinder below turned white when it was empty, and the second cylinder started to flow.

Electricity shot from the generator, and the ceiling of the dome glowed red. Like a jagged snake, electricity flowed down the cables suspended from the ceiling and down into the platform. The entire platform was engulfed in a surge of electricity, shocking and electrocuting several nearby workers. The room was filled with a charged atmosphere, illuminated by flashing red warning lights and chaos. The platform emitted a deep, rumbling growl and began to shake violently, as if an earthquake were happening.

When the final red cylinder was drained and turned white, the wind rushed into the chamber, along with all of the chaos that was going on already. Another Yeti guard by the monorail entrance pointed down the shaft and yelled something loudly in fear. He ran while other Yeti's armed with rifles and visors, which looked like VR headsets, dashed to the entrance, took a military stance, and started firing at something that was trying to enter.

A rush of parasitic draw bats came swirling into the wind-swept chamber in murmuration once again. The Yetis fired upon them and took many out, but there were too many, and they swept throughout the chamber, attacking the Yetis and those running away in terror. Some bit into the Yetis like vampire bats, and some grabbed the Yetis with their talons and flew them high above the platform, where they hovered, grasping their victims, wriggling and screaming in pain.

Then it happened. Everyone stood still as a loud voice said, "Beware, coward. I hunger!" The Yetis on the platform were shocked by electricity and lost their balance when the platform seemed to break apart into a giant, jagged chasm- like a hungry mouth opening to be fed. The wind from the chamber rushed into the opening like an air waterfall and began to pull in the Yetis like a giant vacuum. The bats above dropped their victims, who fell into the chasm screaming.

The bats dove down and attacked the other Yetis who were still alive, all while the chasm actually 'chewed' its victims and kept repeating, "I hunger!" The bats were now latching onto the Yetis and were draining them until their bodies withered horrifically, with nothing left but a husk of skin-wearing clothes. Those bats seemed to glow brighter when finished, and then they swooshed out of the dome and flew quickly through some of the tunnels. They had done this before. They exited through the energy doors like they were not there, as if coming out of a bat cave, and flew into the night sky, where they once again formed the ominous, evil skull shape against the full moon. Their direction then headed towards some of the villages nearby, searching for more victims to drain.

Inside, the platform stopped shaking, and things started to grow very quiet. Electricity stopped, the spinning red lights turned off, and the wind died out. All was quiet, yet a devastating scene was left to see. The claxon turned off even though the computer operator was dead already and wasn't able to do any computer inputting. From high above, watching from a window box that had a platform leading up to it, was Polybius, who had turned everything off from within.

He said to himself, "Good. Very good. He will soon live again." As he looked down on the platform, he could proudly see that the platform was a partially made evil skull face platform– yet only half was complete. Polybius laughed maniacally, "Hahaha. Run, cowards, run. He hungers, and he will live again. Very soon indeed."

#

Mikey, Glitch and this savior girl were now riding up a different elevator, apparently safe from the robot guards who had grabbed him earlier. Mikey was smitten and acting really nervous and kept staring at the girl and her skin-tight uniform.

Mikey said, "Um, hey, Layla. Thanks for turning Glitch back on. What was that thing that you used in the first place?"

Layla said, "It's something I made to help me roam around this place. I call it a driver disruptor. It only works on computer-type things, though. It doesn't help me much with those artificial Yetis."

Mikey said, "Artificial? What do you mean? They aren't real?"

"They are things made of code and snow. Similar to your robot here. You called him, er, Glitch?"

Mikey said, "Well, it seemed appropriate because he had that moniker in his hat band."

"I see. He was probably an early prototype for Polybius but wasn't mean nor nasty enough." She started to examine Glitch all around and up and down and Glitch's head followed her in a 360 turn. "He does have master code in him, but the snow part is glitchy at best. He doesn't look menacing, either. He actually looks like a sweetie."

"Polybius can be a tyrant. He treats all things living like we are pets beneath him. I came from a village where the void zone is now. He took me away from my parents, and because I had some computer skills, he kept me alive. I have been a working slave since that day, stuck here working on his code."

Mikey said, "Golly. Do you know what he is going to do to us?"

"You will either work for him or be drained of your life energy and stored in a canister based on how you dream. He is using that life energy to power himself, power this realm, and to power something else. He is building something horrible. Something that comes from nightmares."

What is he going to do with that?"

"He talks about serving the master and getting out of here, but I don't know where he is trying to go. I try to pretend that I am inept, so he thinks I don't know what's really going on most of the time." She then makes a silly face and pretends to type in the air,

"I'm just a dumb hacker girl." Then she smiled and winked at Mikey.

"Well, we are thankful for your perfect timing. I certainly don't think you're dumb!"

Layla smiled, saying, "Thanks. What was your name again?"

"I hadn't given it yet. My apologies." Mikey then stood straight up, brushed his shirt smooth, clicked his heels together, then put one arm out and bowed. "I am Michael Andrew Gross. So very glad to make your acquaintance." He remained bowed, then cautiously peered over his glasses to gauge her reaction.

"Um, OK. Nice to meet you, Michael Andrew Gross. May I call you Michael instead?"

"Certainly! But please, just call me Mikey. All of my friends do." Mikey relaxed, shaking off his formal stance and even stretching his arms to dispel the formality.

"Where did you come from, and why are you here? Said Layla.

"Boy, that is a great question, Layla. May I call you Layla? Or should I just call you mine?" Mikey grinned all stupidly.

Layla rolled her eyes and turned to look at the elevator floor light indicating their arrival. She said, "Layla is fine. Dude, you need to get out more."

The elevator doors hissed open, and Layla quickly led the way out, likely eager to escape Mikey's company. Even Glitch slid past Mikey, who was still grinning, and Glitch shook his head no, no, no. A bit of extra snow fell from Glitch's flurry and landed on Mikey's head with a soft sploosh. Mikey said, "A c'mon, man. Look at her dude. Can you blame me?"

The room was just off the elevator area, actually a cell, but with the door open. Layla entered the room and motioned for Mikey and Glitch to follow.

"But don't shut the cell door! It took me a while to hack that one open." They all followed her into the room, where she took a seat in a large computer chair facing multiple monitors, similar to the setup the computer operators had used in the dome.

"Sweet layout." Comments Mikey. "What are you running? An AMD Ryzen-nine? How about the graphic card? Is it an Nvidia RTX-4090? Those are so sweet. I am trying to build a cool gaming system myself with 4 Terabytes of storage, and I am making it liquid-cooled using a CoolerMaster MasterLiquid PL360 FLUX cooling system. It's going to be sweet! I have to save up for that GPU, though, that sucker is costly, Bro!"

Layla just stared at Mikey, who was a little too enthusiastic. "Um, yea, something like that." She typed a password into the computer keyboard, and the screens illuminated. Mikey could see the frozen robot standing by the elevator, its arms raised. There were other videos spread around on the different monitors. She must have hacked into the security camera feeds. She could see a lot of things from inside the geodesic dome, which was all quiet now yet glitching itself like the feed was damaged. Mikey saw the throne room and the kitchen staff preparing food. There was a camera showing the front door entrance, and he caught a glimpse of the rooftop with its cables and wires.

Layla said, "I know before I went to save you, Polybius was in the dome about to run an experiment with that life force. I think he was going to use the red energy canisters, but the camera feed seems kind of broken now. Let me see what I can do to get a better look. Maybe the webcam on the computer controller will show us something? She clicked a few keys and hit enter. A full screenshot of a drained Yeti, like a deflated balloon with fur, was in his chair with a horrific scream on his flattened head. Layla gasped and turned her head away quickly.

Mikey said, "Whoa, just whoa. That's pretty twisted. What happened to that guy?"

Layla was breathing hard and trying to calm herself, but she couldn't help but start crying. She put her hands over her face and sobbed. "It's the same thing he did to my father when he sacked our village when I was younger. He sent those parasitic draw bats to attack, but the village couldn't fight them all off. It's how he used to get his energy. Now, they have to fight them off because he can no longer control them. They feed off the cables and wires when life energy flows through them. They can sense it like a shark senses blood in the water."

Mikey tried to console Layla, putting his hand on her shoulder. "I am sorry, Layla. You have been here for a while now, huh?"

She nodded yes.

"What can I do to help? I hate to see you crying. I am so sorry for your loss. That must have been terrible. I just can't imagine." Said Mikey.

Layla said, "It's why I have to be here, so I can figure out a way to stop him. He needs to pay for his crimes, and I want to get back to my mom one day…if she is still alive."

Mikey said, "Whatever I can do to help you, I will. But I know my pop can help us if we can help get us out of here. Can you show me the insides of the rooms?"

Layla said, "Yes, I can see inside some of them. But only if they are in front of the monitor."

Mikey said, "I don't remember seeing any monitors in there. Just a desk and a light. There was the bed, a bathroom and a single window."

Layla said, "That's the monitor! It's not a window but a screen with a fake image on it. They recess it in the wall a bit so nobody thinks about messing with it. You'd have to be either really smart or a real dummy to mess with it and discover it's not an actual window."

Mikey put his hand on his chin in a thinking position and said, "Yep, that would be my pop. That's how he figured that out. We are often very lucky sometimes, and I don't know if that means we're smart, or if we are really dumb, but things often go our way anyhow. It's weird. I can't explain it. My pop says it's the Gross curse."

Mikey then went on to explain how a long time ago, his great, great, great grandfather was an archaeologist and bumbled upon an undiscovered Inca tomb. He unknowingly took some sacred artifacts and nearly escaped with his life. The tomb was booby-trapped, and he didn't so much escape, than fall out of the tomb- by accident, before it sealed him in forever. He brought back several magical items that he wanted the museum to have, but he kept a few items and brought them home. One item was a mummified monkey paw. Apparently, it had a spell placed on it by an old Muslim Fakir, a very holy man. He wanted to show that fate ruled people's lives and that those who interfered with it did so at their sorrow. It would grant three wishes to the man who held it, and his great, great, great grandfather made those three wishes. He doesn't know what the first wish was, but the second was to enchant his backpack to help him produce what he required when it was deemed necessary. It was passed down through the years, and Mikey's pop gave it to him to keep him safe. The wish backfired on the man, though, because once the backpack was enchanted, he lost the use of his arms. Luckily, it only happened to him and no other family members throughout the years.

Mikey said, "Dude, it would so suck to not have any arms, right? How could I play my oboe? I really feel for folks who are missing limbs. I want to be able to help people like that one day and give them bionic legs and arms. You know, make them superhumans!"

Layla then looked at his backpack cautiously and asked him, "What was his third wish?"

Mikey said, "They say in the family that he wished for a happy life. But that there was always a price to pay, so the monkey paw made it so that other members of his family had a bad life instead."

"Wow, said Layla. That is so creepy."

"I know, right? But it has helped us since I started school. My backpack has been very helpful, but I try not to use its magic too much. Once, I tried to ask for a lot of things, but it just stopped working for a week! I think it felt the things I wished for were not deemed necessary." As Mikey made his quotes with his fingers, "So, I am careful when using it, so it will always work. It's funny, though, and it only gives me things that are necessary. For example, if I wished for money, it would produce a newspaper with a Help Wanted ad circled. Like, there you go, kid, here's a job that will make you money right away! So, it's not an exact science. But most of the time, it really does help me."

Now Layla was thinking. "Maybe we can use it to help us. We will see."

She then pulled up Bob's room on the monitor, but it was crooked and empty.

Mikey asked, "Why is it crooked?"

Layla said, "It's probably because he messed with it, I suppose." Then smiled at him.

"But my pop wasn't in there; he was in Kristin and Presley's room down the hall."

"Ok, let me search some more." She clicked up several feeds of different children having nightmares, but when she finally found Kristin's room, they saw her and Presley sitting on the bed, and now she was crying.

"Oh no," said Mikey. "What happened to Pop? Can you find him?"

"I'll try," she said, and clicked away some more. Up popped a feed showing Bob hanging upside down in front of a whirling red and orange cylinder made of glass. What little hair he had on his head was dangling and blowing from the whirling colors. He was tied to a round platform mounted on the wall across from the cylinder.

Layla looked sad and told Mikey, "I'm so sorry. They have him. He's in with the master control program. We're in trouble now."

CHAPTER TEN: Stardust

The villagers saw the lights of the monorail above the cliff face speeding towards them. In a hurry, they all started hiding and shutting their doors. Many had secret rooms built inside their floors, and some industrious workers had makeshift bunkers where their entire families could hide safely. Windows were closed, and storm shutters latched up. All candlelight was blown out and extinguished. They couldn't afford to have any attention from the 'code walkers' as they called them. They had discovered that the Yetis, under the rule of the snow king, were not all real creatures. The leaders were, but most of his Yetis were nothing more than magical snow and computer code somehow meshed together, using dark magic. They were controlled by Polybius, who had them do horrific things. Afterall, they were programmed to do them, and a program is only as good or bad as its creator.

The villagers had tried to live a relatively normal life here in this zone, but others were seemingly sent here. Some are for crimes they committed or to right past wrongdoings. Mostly, though, they were good people and felt that this was a sort of purgatory where they needed to do something right in order to move on or get back to their 'real' lives. So, they all pitched in and tried to create a decent life for themselves. Some even had families, and there was even a crude school building. None of them knew how long they would be around, but they knew it was important to have a civilization regardless of the circumstances.

Regardless of who they were or how they got there, they all knew to stay away from the mountain entrances. Besides the entranceways being guarded by scary robots, if the snow king saw them, they would be captured and drained of their life energy for his odd experiments. There was enough of that happening frequently anyway, especially when those electric bats came hunting. So, they avoided the mountain at all costs.

The monorail zipped by and headed into the frozen areas. The villagers named it the Valley of ice. It actually used to be where Polybius was setup, and he had called it Zone one. But bitter cold and horrible ice storms destroyed the original castle there, and the cables he used froze and broke too often. It was initially perfect because it was remote, and nobody bothered to come there, but the weather was just too much for his experiments. He moved into the mountain nearby and named it zone two.

The valley wasn't void of life. There were many creatures still there, and once the snow king left, some of his experiments were found, and odd things began to occur. One such occurrence was when a colony of penguins got into some of his chemicals left behind, and some electric cables gave a few a good jolt. Something happened to a few who actually received the gift of human speech. Of course, they didn't just know how to speak because they didn't know words. They were just penguins. But when the village fishermen wandered into their frozen zone to ice fish, they heard the men speaking and often imitated what they said. This caused fear among the villagers, and rumors of ghosts spread throughout the valley.

The valley of ice, a strange fusion of natural formations and human engineering, resembled a geometric ice wonderland. Massive bore diggers, their hexagonal drill bits heated at the edges, bit into towering icebergs. With precision, they extracted perfectly shaped ice hexagons, each one carefully stacked to form the grand ice fortress that once dominated the landscape. The hexagon was the shape of choice—it fit together flawlessly, creating a sturdy, interconnected structure. But time, as it does, wore away at the once-impressive castle. Its walls crumbled, and even its deeply buried sub-basements were not spared, eventually collapsing and leaving behind a vast rift—a deep, icy valley where the talking penguins made their home.

The valley itself was a fragile balance. On the outskirts, the ice began to melt, as it bordered the scorching desert zone, a place of harsh heat despite its proximity to the frozen expanse. From the melting ice caps, a raging river cut through the desert, a stark reminder of the forces of nature that constantly reshaped the land. For the penguins, life was good on their side of the valley, though they always remained cautious, aware of the dangers near the edge of their zone. The water currents there were treacherous, swirling violently with a hidden undertow that could snatch anything—or anyone—unlucky enough to get too close.

And one day, tragedy struck. A young penguin, carefree and playful, wandered too close to the water's edge, and in an instant, the powerful current dragged him under. His family watched in horror, flapping their wings in helpless desperation. They tried to save him, but without arms or hands, without opposable thumbs, they had no way to grasp or hold on. It was a cruel irony—these penguins had evolved the gift of speech, yet they remained physically ill-equipped to act in a moment of crisis. The power of language without the matching evolutionary tools to truly use it seemed like a bitter joke, one that the forces of nature had played upon them.

One night, the penguin washed up on a desert bank where a young girl in that zone found and rescued him back to health. They became more than a girl and her pet penguin- they became real friends. Once she discovered that he could imitate words quite easily, she started teaching him many more. She realized that he actually understood them and started asking for things like fish and water. He eventually called her by her name, Layla. She had found him by the banks of the river, partially drowned under the stars. He was out of the water now, but because he was initially wet, the desert sand had caked on him and caused him to sparkle under the moon. She just had to name him Stardust because that's what he had looked like.

Her village was attacked. Dozens of parasitic draw bats came one night like blazing red streaks in the sky, and after destroying many huts and feeding on many villagers, the snow king marched in with his Yeti army and took many captives back. Her father had saved her and his wife by hiding them in a bunker. He stayed out, resisted, and fought the Yetis but wasn't strong enough. To force the others out of hiding and compel them to surrender, Polybius made a ruthless display of her father's fate. He paraded him before them, a living example of the consequences they would face if they refused to give up.

He called upon his Parasitic draw bats, which swirled around her dad and all bit into him at once in a horrifying frenzy. They drained his life force in front of the captors, and those who were hiding came out. Her mother told Layla to stay hidden in the hopes that they wouldn't go looking for her if she gave herself up. But Layla loved her mom too much and knew that her father was dead, so she pushed her mom out of the way inside the bunker and closed the door behind her, giving herself up instead. She could not lose both of them. She was shackled and taken to his mountain keep, where the snow king learned of her intuitive skills with computer technology. He kept her alive and put her to work, programming his devices and eventually having her work on some of the biggest projects, like the MCP. She knew one day she would learn enough to get out of there, but she also wanted revenge for her father, so she bided her time. One day she would get her revenge.

#

"Golly, that was quite a story, Layla. I had no idea," Mikey said, his voice softer than usual after hearing Layla share her story in her own way. His eyes widened, reflecting both surprise and empathy. There was a brief pause as he struggled to find the right words, the weight of her experiences sinking in.

"I can't believe you've gone through all of that," he continued, his voice thick with emotion. "I am so, so sorry for your loss, Layla. I just... I wish there was something I could do to help you now." His words hung in the air, filled with genuine concern and a helplessness that came from wanting to fix what couldn't be fixed.

Layla said, "Thank you, Mikey. I appreciate that. If you really want to help, please help me take down Polybius. You have already caused him some trouble, so can you continue doing that?"

"But, of course, malady!" Mikey bowed. "I specialize in trouble. At least that's what my pop says."

Mikey then said, "Hey, you mentioned you had a talking penguin, um, Stardust? Where is he?"

Layla said, "Would you like to meet him? I have to keep him hidden. Otherwise, he may get experimented on or worse."

"I would love too, but I am sort of worried about my dad. Can we help him first?"

Layla said gently, "Of course, we can help your pop, Mikey. But you are in luck because SD is near where your dad is being held."

Mikey said, "SD, huh? I like it. I have to ask another favor, though. I am so hungryyyy." Mikey's stomach growled loudly. Rrrraaahhrrr.

Layla looked surprised at how loud it was. "I have some sandwiches in my refrigerator over there." She pointed to a corner appliance with some drawings posted on it with magnets. "Help yourself."

Mikey rushed over to the refrigerator, eager to open it, but something caught his eye. Pausing, he gazed at the colorful drawings covering the door, his attention drawn to one in particular. It was simple yet deeply emotional—a picture of a man, a woman, and a small girl, all holding hands, their robes a vibrant array of colors. Beneath it, in a child's handwriting, were the words: "Mom, me, and Dad. R.I.P. Papa."

His heart tightened painfully, the cheerful hunger that had driven him moments before now replaced by a heavy sadness. The weight of the drawing hit him like a tidal wave. Mikey's hands dropped to his sides; his body frozen in place. His appetite vanished completely. He stood there, unmoving, staring at the simple yet powerful tribute, unable to speak or even think clearly. The silence around him felt louder than any words could be.

Layla said, "Just open the door. They're right inside."

Mikey turned to look back at Layla, and his eyes showed swelling tears. "Layla." He tried to compose himself. "We have to stop the snow king. And you know what? We are going to find your Mom, too. I promise."

Layla smiled. "Thank you, Mikey. I know you may have those intentions now, but you don't know how dangerous Polybius is. The creatures he has made to help him fight, and the army he is building, it's a lot. He has massive plans, and I think he is preparing for a war. What can we actually do against that?"

Mikey said, "Well, I think we can help. I've evaded the Yeti guards so far."

Layla said, "Except for the robot guard."

Mikey said, "Well, I didn't know about them. Those Maximillian dudes won't catch me again now that I know about them."

Layla questioned, "Maximillian dudes? Why did you call them that?"

"Because some of them are like the Maximillian robot from the movie *The Black Hole*. Have you seen it?" He watched for her expression hopefully.

Layla said, "What's a movie? I haven't seen what that is."

Mikey lost it. "What?! OMG, another person who doesn't know what a movie is! What do you guys do for entertainment anyway? Sheesh."

Layla said, "We would play Tides, Temse, and I really liked Tabliant. But I don't know of a game called Movie."

Mikey said, "No, no. A movie isn't a game. It's something you watch for entertainment. To have fun. Well, it can also be scary or make you cry, too, now that I think about it. AHA! It's like your computer monitors and what you see on them but recorded. That way, you can play them back and watch them again. You'll have to show me some of your games later, OK?"

Layla said, "Hmm. That movie thing sounds like something that could be useful. We only see what is shown on the monitors. I wonder how I could make a movie? I would like to discuss this more with you so that I can try a few things."

"Let's eat, go get into some mischief, then save my dad." Mikey opened the refrigerator, took out a few sandwiches, and started unwrapping them and eating happily. "Wow, this is the best sandwich I have ever eaten. The meat tastes different. What is it, chicken?"

"It's Goa meat. There are herds of them in the meadows, but they're really fast and hard to catch. I hate that they kill them, but I refuse to eat the manufactured food that the snow king makes. I think some of it is made from the people he has drained and killed," said Layla.

Mikey stopped chewing and said, "Did I eat people the other day? BRUH. That's not cool, snow king. Yucky poo poo." Mikey made a face. Then he continued eating anyway. "Goa meat, huh? I don't know what that is, but it's rather tasty."

The mood in the room was now more pleasant. They were safe and had a plan started. They were hopeful and fairly happy. Things were looking better. Little did they know someone from the shadows lay in wait, silently observing their every action on a camera on the ceiling.

A Yeti guard grunted in their own language towards Polybius, who was also watching, but in English, it translated too, "Sir, shall we go get them?"

"No. Let them come to us. They want revenge? Let them dig two graves."

CHAPTER ELEVEN: Ode to Joy

The Palantir globe glowed with activity, casting a shimmering light around the darkened room. A man dressed like a wizard with a long robe and hoodie looked intensely into it. He took both of his hands and waved them quickly over the glass orb like he was messing up its hair that it didn't have. "Enough! That is all I need to see for now. The fools don't have any idea of what they are getting into." The Palantir went blank and still. The man then reached out his hand, and a long, knobby walking stick floated through the air from a corner where it was standing and landed in his grasp. He stood up and threw his cowl back. It was the same wizard that was helping the military men fight Polybius and his Yetis.

"That child must learn to use that artifact backpack to his advantage." He said to himself. "From this realm, I can only do so much." He then stood still, thinking and using his empty hand, brushing his mustache and beard from his chin down to his chest as a nervous gesture.

"Nay. Me thinks I may have to interfere in this melee. Perhaps I can send a magical medley to the small, gross one and instill some fortitude? Aye, that will do." He abruptly turned and made a waving motion at the doorway, which flew open from his magical gesture. He marched out of the room and into a larger space that was dark. He raised his staff, and the room's lighting started coming on. There were lights in the ceiling and at the end leading to a stairway. But there were chairs and metal music-stands in front of him arranged in a semi-circle with several rows of seats. The music stands had lights connected to them, which also came on during his staff's movement. An elevated podium was in the middle of the arc facing the chairs. This was a concert formation.

He was about to conduct something magical. Each chair had an instrument sitting on it or on an instrument holder by it. He stepped up on the podium and sent his staff floating away to the back of the room while he stood with both arms extended and holding. When the staff landed softly in the back with the percussion equipment, he slowly reached his right arm back over his right shoulder and reached into his back collar. He grabbed something and slowly pulled it from its hiding place, following the reverse motion he had done to get it. It was a conductor's baton. When it was out and matching his other outstretched arm, he tapped the baton on the podium twice and raised it back up. Quickly, the instruments all magically rose into a playing position and froze, awaiting further directions. He gave a downbeat by circling his hands outward and back as if rowing, then he continued a steady beat with his right arm and baton, then as the music began to increase in volume, he plunged his baton downward, and the first chord struck. The music and conducting continued violently and then smoothly. He was conducting the fourth movement, or *Finale: Ode to Joy from Beethoven's 9th Symphony*. The string sections played in unison, and we eventually began to hear a choir. They were singing in German, but our conductor yelled out the words like an incantation as he conducted. "Good and evil alike follow in her trail of roses!" Later, he called out, "She gave us kisses, and the vine, and a friend faithful to death." Finally, as the music was feverous, "Go on, brothers, your way. Joyful, like a hero to victory. Do you see the creator world? Seek him above the starry canopy! Above stars. Must. He. Dwell!" The room exploded into chaos as swirling wind and shimmering magic dust filled the air. Bright lights of red, green, blue, and yellow illuminated different corners of the space, casting dramatic shadows over the flailing wizard. The colors pulsed in rhythm, each flash highlighting his frantic movements as he struggled to contain the arcane energy spiraling out of control. With a sudden, powerful pull, the whirlwind of lights and dust was sucked into the wizard's baton, condensing into a radiant glow. The baton shimmered bright yellow, casting a warm yet eerie glow across the room as the symphony came to a sudden, breathtaking stop. Silence settled, and the magic hung in the air, electric and alive.

The wizard leaned on the podium, tired from his conducting and spell casting, "Now to send this onward to the dream realm." He looked over at the room he had come from and saw the cold, lifeless Palantir globe on the table. He made a casting gesture with the baton like he was throwing a dagger. The magic dust and colors shot across the room into the glass orb that drank the magic happily. It shook a bit, then went inert once again. "Use this magic wisely, gross one. It is your only hope for now." The lights dimmed once again. Like the cooling lights, he, too, felt the need to rest.

#

Mikey, Layla, and Glitch stepped out of the elevator and cautiously looked around before going further. "Layla, you know this place better than we do. What's the next move, boss?" Mikey said quietly.

"We have to try and avoid the robot guards and not get seen on the camera feeds. There are some blind spots that I know how to get around, and I will bring my driver disruptor for the guards. If we run into any Yetis, that could be a problem." Layla said and held up the disruptor like a torch.

Mikey started to crouch low and started singing music again. "Dum de de de dum, dum dum dum, dum de de de dum, dum, dum, dum, de dumm da de dumm…" Mikey stopped and saw Layla and Glitch looking at him, trying to figure him out.

"What are you doing?" queried Layla.

"It's the *James Bond theme*. You know, written by Monty Norman and John Barry?" James Bond was the British secret agent who has all of the cool action movies and always gets the babes." Mikey stayed low but raised his hands intertwined together with his pointer fingers and thumbs out, making a hand gun. He then thought he would add some history to the music and said, "Even though Monty sued John Barry for stealing his James Bond chord, I still consider him cool."

Glitch popped a few times and looked up at Layla.

"He lost the lawsuit, but his chord is still so cool! It's the E minor major 9, based on the E melodic minor scale. It's 1, 2, flat 3, 4, 5, natural 6, major 7. I call it my film noir chord. I love it so much! It's so cool sounding." He put his clenched hands up to his chest. "I'm trying to get into the mood. Is that OK with you two? You know what? We could sure use some of those James Bond gadgets right about now."

Mikey started looking in his magic backpack and Layla said, "If you have an invisibility cloak in there, that could really help."

Mikey looked up at her with a grimace, then said, "I wonder what the pack will give us. It is a dire need, you know?" He pulled his hand out of the backpack and faced the front side of it, holding it in both hands. He spoke directly to the grimacing face on the backpack, "Backpack, can you help us find my dad like you did Glitch? Is there anything you can give us to help?" He then dug into the backpack and felt around.

Mikey said, "I got something!" He then pulled out something slowly, something made of brass and very shiny…and long. It kept coming from the backpack, which looked rather silly to Layla and

Glitch because how could this come from such a small backpack? It was a slide trombone!

Mikey said, "What the? How in the world is this thing going to help us? I play woodwinds remember- you, crazy backpack! My embouchure is made for woodwinds. WOODWINDS, sheesh!" Mikey looked around in frustration as if there were cameras and he was being punked.

There was an inscription in the bell that read in fancy cursive: "Play and slide. Enemies run and divide." Mikey said OK, I guess I'll try if we run into any, but man, this thing is going to be a bear to carry. The mouthpiece better be a Bach 6.5 AL because I am considered a beginner. I better check out the shank size, too. You know what they say about mouthpieces…it's like a wand choosing the wizard kind of thing. It has to be the right one for me and the right situation." He looked, and it was a Shilke 51D. Mikey said, "Dang, man! That thing is for low notes. Geez, I better loosen up the ole lips. He began to buzz and flap them, causing spit to go everywhere. Layla and Glitch backed up and away from him. "Sorry! I told you I don't play brass instruments. I am just doing what I see those guys do when they warm up. Sheesh. Give me a break, man. Anyone have some Carmex or Blistex DCT?"

Layla and Glitch looked at each other, confused. Mikey was talking in a language different from theirs. She said, "Um no. What are those?"

Mikey said, "Lip protector, so I don't split my lip trying to play this beast of an instrument." He then reached into the backpack again and pulled out a small tube of *Carmex* lip protector. "Thanks, backpack! My lips will thank you, sir!" He then applied a lot of Carmex to his pursed lips and made smacking noises with them several times. "Ok, now for the hard part."

Mikey jiggled the slide on the trombone back and forth quickly to loosen up (like he knew what he was doing), placed the horn up to his mouth, and buzzed into the large mouthpiece to make a note. BUHHHHH,

"Um, wow, that was a horrible sound," said Layla.

"Gee, thanks. Let's hope I don't have to use the slide. What is this supposed to do again?"

"Make your enemies run and divide."

"Well, I think they'll do that when they hear my playing, I suppose. Ah, Let's go."

They all headed out carefully, hugging the walls as much as possible and following Layla. Glitch clicked several times, agreeing that the note sounded horrible, but Mikey ignored him. Glitch wanted to be sure Mikey heard his laughing and clicking, so he slid right up to him and clicked in a laughing manner.

Mikey looked down at him while crouching forward, hugging to a corner wall and peeking around, "Laugh it up, snowball." Obviously, a reference to *Star Wars* and what Han Solo said to Chewbacca when he laughed at him, too, but Layla and Glitch had no idea what he was talking about or referencing.

Mikey actually saw some Yeti guards ahead working on some scaffolding over the walking area they needed to pass under. "Layla, do we have to go this way?"

"Yes, I am afraid it is the only direct path to the MCP room."

Mikey looked around the entire area and saw some grills on the walls and grates on the floor. "Hmm, I might have an idea about these guys. I don't see any robot guards, so we just have to get by those Yetis." Mikey pulled the horn up to his lips, ready to make a run towards them. Layla grabbed him by the shoulder and held him back.

"Wait. What if this apparatus doesn't do anything to them? They'll capture us, and it's over."

"You're right. But I have to believe that it will work. The backpack has always helped me when I needed it. There was this time in sixth grade when a kid named Pedro decided he didn't like me and decided to fight me afterschool. He started pushing me around as a crowd grew around me, cheering him on. Man, what is up with kids nowadays, right? Anyway, I didn't want to fight him, but he pushed me down to the ground, and my backpack fell off. It opened, and thousands of bubbles came out of it. The entire crowd was immersed in bubbles, and Pedro couldn't see me crawling away under people's legs. It saved me. Pedro thought it was so weird that he didn't mess with me anymore, either. So, I have to trust that if the backpack gave me a slide trombone so I could go all ham on my enemies, then I have to believe it will work. Don't ever stop believing." Mikey then pointed up with one finger as if he had an idea. "I need music for this, and it should be appropriate for this situation." He pulled out his Walkman and looked at the cassette in it. "Ah, number three, by *Journey*." He then pushed the fast forward button, listening to the tape play quickly and making squeaking noises as it wound forward. A pause in the noise made Mikey press the stop button. "There it is. My inspiration for this moment! *Don't stop believing*." He put the headphones on, looked at Glitch and Layla, and said, "Ok, here goes something. If it works, get past the Yetis and head to that wall by that grate's far side. I have a brilliant idea." He started the song and got super inspired.

Mikey took a few deep breathes and let the air out. He jiggled the trombone slide again and darted around the corner towards the Yetis, ready to play some loud notes directly at them.

Several Yeti workers stopped and looked at Mikey coming around the corner with a strange brass and tube thing up to his face. Was it a weapon? Who was this guy, and why is he in this forbidden area? We need to capture him and take him before the king. They stopped what they were doing and scrambled to get off the scaffolding and walkway to pursue Mikey.

"BUUUUHHH!" Mikey blew the horn at them. One strong note which actually stopped them where they stood. They were bewildered, confused, and frozen in place.

Mikey was also surprised and lowered the horn in disbelief. He stopped running and stood in confusion. He yelled back, "It worked! It actually worked!" The Yetis seemed to thaw and wake up from the stupor, so Mikey then tried a glissando on the trombone. This was a BAAWUPP sound and the Yetis reacted differently to this one. They actually bent and moved like puppets, going side to side or bending over and standing up like the sound. It was very comical to see Mikey controlling them with trombone sounds. The Yetis had no control over their bodies when that trombone played.

The sky flashed a bright yellow, and everyone looked up at the heavens in curiosity. A small light like a star grew ever brighter, and even Mikey stared up at it in wonder. "What is that?" The problem was that the Yetis were thawing, and not all were paying attention to the light from above. The light then turned blue, and everyone heard and felt a sonic blast. Mikey almost lost his footing since one hand gripped his backpack strap, and the other had the trombone. Before he could wonder what had happened, a blue lightning bolt cracked from the sky where the light was and nailed Mikey right in the backpack! It knocked him down to the ground, and he felt it getting very hot. He immediately took it off and wondered just what happened. "Whoa, dude. Are you ok, backpack?" Mikey said with true care in his voice.

The backpack was moving like something was inside of it, and because its flap configuration made it look like a face, it looked like it was chewing something. Even the Yetis stopped and were watching in curiosity. Mikey went over to it, and the backpack looked directly back at him. It opened its mouth and a solid beam of music notes in every color mixed in a solid energy beam shot out of the backpack's mouth and directly into Mikey's chest. It hit him directly and seemed to grab him and lift him in the air as the music stream poured into him. He actually lifted off the ground and was suspended, with his arms outstretched and feet now together, pointing down at the ground. He looked like a messiah. He was still holding the trombone in his right hand, and he was awash with a blue glow. When the beam stopped, he floated gently to the ground, and the blue glow around him slowly faded like a fire that had just extinguished.

Layla ran over to him, "Mikey, are you ok?"

Mikey looked up at her and said, "I've never felt better in my life. I feel like I AM music. I know how to play anything, and it's dying to come out of me." Mikey now had blue glowing eyes.

The Yetis were done watching and had started scrambling to attack.

Mikey felt confident, so he thought he would try something. He just knew the notes somehow and knew how to play the trombone at an expert level, so he played the *Empire Strikes Back* theme by composer John Williams…BA BA BAA, BUH BUH BAA BUH BA BAA, and the Yetis seemed to file in a line and stand at attention for him. "Whaaaaaa? This is so cool! Oh, this is going to be fun!" Exclaimed Mikey. "C'mon, guys! Let's get past these clowns." He waved back to Layla and Glitch, who were hiding behind the wall yet watching in amazement.

As the Yetis would 'thaw' and wake up, they would start getting angry and trying to approach Mikey, but he would then start playing the trombone and controlling them like puppets. It bought time for Layla and Glitch to get by and over to the other side of the area, by the wall where he wanted them to go.

When they were safe through the 'Yeti gauntlet,' as Mikey would remember it, he eventually joined them at a wall area with a large grate in the floor and a panel with slats on the wall. He was playing some sort of jazz trombone music and walking, and it was all funny again like he was at a Louisiana wake and had just come from Bourbon Street. He told them, "Ok, now for my plan. We pull the grate here and go in through the air conditioning shaft totally unseen. Brilliant huh?" He pointed to the slatted panel in the wall. He then had to play some more to keep the Yetis away, so he asked Layla to pull the grate open.

She tugged and tugged, and it finally opened, but not to an opening like he had hoped. It was a giant circuit board! "No, that's not fair! Why does this always happen to me?" exclaimed Mikey.

Layla said, "What about the big grate here on the floor?"

"Well, ok. I guess it will have to do. Why is the wall a circuit board anyway? This whole place still reminds me of being inside a computer. What gives man?"

Layla got down and tried the grate. It opened up on one side and swung open to them. There was a ladder inside going down. Mikey said, "I'll keep playing until we all get down, OK? Then I will need Glitch to ice this baby over solid."

Mikey then started playing some Tommy Dorsey trombone music because it just flowed from him now with his new found music powers. He played *"I'm getting sentimental over you."* A rather slow and simple trombone piece, and he would pause every now and then and yell at the Yetis, "I am not a brass player. But how do you like this, huh?" He was getting a bit stressed as there were a lot of Yetis. At one point, more Yetis came from around a corner, and Mikey felt the need to play more action-packed music. So, like the scene in the *Aliens* movie by James Cameron, Mikey started yelling and pointing the trombone at them as he played, "You want some of this?" BAA WUP BA BA BAA, "Oh yea? How about you?" BUH WUP BA BA BAA "You want some too, ok, here you go!" BA BA BAA BUH BUH BAA BUH BA BAA. He now felt powerful, just like a space marine from the movie. Mikey reached into his pocket and grabbed his clip-on sunglasses. He clipped them on and started playing the *Peter Gunn theme* by Henry Mancini. The Yetis couldn't do anything but bobble and shake, and some even marched off the ledges, with a few jumping into the water. Mikey smiled at Layla and Glitch, "This is so cool," he said. "Who is the man?" Mikey then flipped up the sunglasses clip in a cool manner and smiled.

Layla rolled her eyes, then climbed down the ladder and had Glitch slide into her open arm. Then, she climbed down and carried him. Mikey blew a couple of trombone glissandos and went down in a hurry, grabbing the gate and swinging it closed as he lowered himself as well. When he got to the bottom of the ladder and hopped off, he played loudly up at the gate grill and told Glitch to make it ice. "Give it all you got, Glitch my man! Ice storm, ice storm, ice storm!"

Glitch produced such a storm that they were all bewildered. It was rather terrifying, and Mikey backed away, holding onto Layla, where they both took shelter by the far wall. Wind in the tunnel swelled up, and everything started to ice up with a crawling freeze that spread from Glitch and emanated outwards like tentacles. Swirling snow flurries appeared outside the grate, and a hail storm formed. Large hail pelted the Yetis and the grate. The entire area was getting pulverized by thousands of icy bullets coming from above. Glitch had done it and they were safe for now. The grate was frozen shut.

Bob was lowered to the ground, and two Yetis unhooked him from the disk and marched him out of the room with his fetters jingling. The MCP was still not working, and Bob couldn't believe what it told him. Was it really his sister speaking through that thing? He still had a lot of questions, but he knew these Yetis wouldn't have the answers, so he remained quiet and just marched along the halls as the motion lights came on and illuminated their path.

Bob decided to sing "Oh We Oh. Ooh Oh. Oh, We Oh, Ooh Oh" from *the Wizard of Oz* movie when the guards captured the heroes. This seemed to be appropriate for the situation, and the Yetis ignored his singing anyway.

He thought about Mikey and his band kids. What could they have possibly done to have his sister so mad at them? Why was she denigrating his band, and did it have something to do with her husband's death? Was it because she couldn't take being alone afterwards and eventually had to go into assisted living? He felt bad for her, and he felt bad that he hadn't been a better brother. He felt a bit like he deserved a horrible fate because he wasn't more attentive, and it led to this situation.

The Yetis took him to a room not far from the MCP room and pushed him in, turning on the force field and locking him inside.

Bob yelled at them, "Is this how you treat guests?! I want pancakes and two sunny side-up eggs in the morning, with two strips of bacon. And don't forget my coffee, you snow jerks!" He sat on the bed and took in his situation, pondering what to do. He felt completely maladjusted. He said softly to himself, "This is hopeless. What am I going to do? I have to talk some sense into my sister. That's what I have to do. But what in the world is she doing this for?"

#

Kristin pet Presley on the head and combed the fur of his head over Presley's eyes- then laughed, "Silly puppy. I've gone and messed up your perfect dew, haven't I?" Presley shook his head and got his curly locks to spring back where they stood at attention again. He was nice and poofy, as if he had just come back from the groomers.

"What are we going to do, little one? They left us here, and that horrible snow king scared the bejeebers out of me. I think we need to go find Mikey because hanging around here isn't going to do anyone any good. You with me?" Presley tilted his head like usual, meaning he didn't understand what was being said.

"Good. Let's gear up for an adventure." She started looking around the room and in the cabinets for items that could help them. She found some small bowls that Presley could eat and drink from. She grabbed a handful of utensils and folded up the blankets from the bed. There was a bag of peanuts and some water bottles, so she threw those all in a pile on an open sheet on the bed, then gathered up the corners and bunched everything up in a hobo bundle. She couldn't find anything to tie it closed with, so she took off her scrunchie from her hair and tied it to the sack closed. There were still a lot of extra sheet ends hanging out of the top part, so she had the idea to twist them until they looked like rope and then tie them back to the scrunchie. It made a pseudo backpack!

"Girl power," she said convincingly to Presley, who just wagged his tail happily. She then put on her coat and slung the makeshift backpack over her arms and onto her back. The

118

silverware jingled as she adjusted it to fit better, but she was now ready- or as ready as she could be. This was a bizarre situation; all she knew was that she just wanted to return home. Get away from the snow, from this bizarre castle, and the freaky Yeti people. She had friends in the band, but she wanted to return to her family too. She thought about her mom at school and wondered if she was worried about her or if she even missed her. Afterall, she was the main counselor and didn't have much time for her "perfect" daughter. To Kristin, it seemed that she always had to be the shining example of a perfect student. God forbid that she got a 'B' or wasn't in the honors and AP classes. Then, somehow, she said out loud, "Plus, I am expected to be first chair, like that's not a problem. No pressure, right? It's expected. Man, I hate my life."

Presley looked perplexed as they carefully left the room.

"Sorry to vent like that, little guy." She peered around the corner, and then they both headed out the same way Mikey had left. "We'll find him, I am sure."

#

Mikey, Layla, and Glitch were making their way through the underground tunnels, and it wasn't going easy. First, there was no light, so they had Glitch lead and use his eyes as beams. Plus, the floor was gone, and water was flowing in some parts. There was also this green slime everywhere as if it had been flushed into these tunnels on purpose.

Mikey said, "Bruh, this green slime is everywhere. I wonder what it is from?"

Layla said, "Its residual essence. It's bad stuff. Whatever you do, don't touch it."

"Wait a minute," Mikey said. "What do you mean essence? Like the *Dark Crystal* movie-type essence? Skeksis and Gelflings type essence? That movie gave me the heebie-jeebies."

"Um, I don't know what that is, but it is the nightmares that are pulled from the rest of the essences," said Layla.

"So, nightmare juice?" Said Mikey.

"Yes, they can produce some very bad nightmares, and that's why I said don't touch it. I have seen some of the snow king's victims go mad when this stuff was first discovered."

Mikey looked shocked.

Layla then said, "Polybius sucks the life from you while you are dreaming, but sometimes, he gets you when you are having a nice dream, so that essence is tainted and won't work for his plans. It won't power anything around here, either. I heard once that he gets his power from the life-force essence as well, but if he ever had that yellow stuff, he would probably explode. So, he ordered it all be thrown out here in these sewer lines. The water in here is supposed to carry it all outside of the castle."

Mikey asked, "So, the bad essence. You said it powers this place and gives him power. Does it give the Yeti's power too?"

"No. They are made from snow and computer code. They're not really alive. Polybius created them to build this place, be security and help him with his HWLA program. It's why they can't really be hurt by much," said Layla.

"Well, what can hurt them other than my incredible trombone playing?"

Layla said, "You ask a lot of questions."

"Yes, I have been told I am very annoying," said Mikey smiling. "So, what is the HWLA program? What else are we going to do while we look for my pop in these nasty tunnels and nightmare slime?"

"Alright. Good point. The HWLA stands for he will live again, and I don't know much else, but I have seen some computer feeds in that large dome area, and it seems really big. He has been working on that thing for a long time. Whatever it is, it seems to be powered by the essence as well, so I think that is what he is using your friends for."

"Oh boy. That dude is not nuts. He's crazy!" Mikey said by imitating Short Round in the Indiana Jones movie *The Temple of Doom.*

"Again, I have no idea what you are talking about, but yes, Polybius is not a good guy. I am lucky that he leaves me alone to work because he knows I can't get away, and my computer skills are helping him run this place."

Glitch sounded some warning clicks and beeps. He turned on his police lights and stopped. Layla and Mikey looked ahead and saw an entire room filled with boxes and boxes of old equipment, old tubes for essence storage, and lots of wooden crates.

Mikey asked Glitch, "What's the hubbub, bub? Why the alarm, my snowy friend?"

Glitched aimed his lights at the wooden crates.

Mikey said, "Well, what's in those, I wonder? Why does Glitch think they are dangerous?" He approached one, found a piece of metal on the floor, and jammed it in the lid side. He pried it open and said, "Zooey, mama! These are hand grenades, my friends."

Layla said, "I remember seeing those used when they attacked my village when I was younger. They exploded and caused many deaths."

"Again, so sorry about that, Layla, but these bad boys may just help our cause now," said Mikey. "My plan is getting dark, and I am liking it more and more!" He took one carefully out and examined it cautiously. "Wait, this one seems empty of gunpowder or fragments, and look, this is just a layer. Underneath are gas grenade canisters." Mikey lifted the corner of the wood layer and showed them the second layer beneath it.

Layla was still standing cautiously away from Mikey.

Mikey said, "You know, these empties give me an idea. Do you think we can scrape up some of that green goo and not touch it? I think we can use it in these empty grenades." Mikey looked around more. What about using these empty canisters to help get the goo off the walls? Let's do it."

They took the containers and went around scraping and collecting goo essence in the tubes, eventually collecting enough to fill one tube completely. "That's all that will fit in this tube," said Layla.

Mikey said, "Ok, I found a bag of dry gunpowder in the corner, so we just have to mix a ratio of gunpowder to goo so that the timer pin will ignite the gunpowder and vaporize the goo in the blast. Anyone know what a good ratio would be?"

Layla said, "Or we use the gas grenade canisters and put the goo in the containment canister until full and use those kinds of gas grenades instead."

Mikey looked at her and said, "Yea, that's what I meant. Great minds think alike, right?" He gave Layla a big grin. She rolled her eyes, "Ok, Ace, let's get this going. Those Yetis are going to find other ways down here."

Mikey said, "Speaking of great minds, mine is starting to hurt." He rubbed his eyes. "Wow, something isn't right, guys. I think I better lie down for a sec." He almost fell off the chair but made it to the ground. Layla rushed to his side. "Mikey, what's wrong? Just lie here for a few minutes and get some rest. We're here."

Mikey closed his eyes and went completely limp. Layla looked at Glitch and said, "Glitch, I am not sure what's going on. Maybe we should give ourselves up and get him some help?" Glitch clicked and shook his head no, no, no. "Ok, then watch after him while I scout ahead. I think this way leads to underneath the MCP room. Maybe I can get him some water and see how close they are to finding us." Glitch popped approval.

Layla headed further down the tunnels and had to avoid open water mains spewing, lanes of green goo crossing her path, and poor maintenance of the tunnels leading to fallen beams, lots of rats, and other strange creatures. The worst room was riddled with giant spider webs, which she avoided carefully and quietly. She had seen those kinds of spiders before, and they fed off of unsuspecting Yeti guards, but only at night.

She rounded a tunnel corner and saw lights flashing ahead, so an exit must be approaching. She got closer and saw that the tunnel was filled to the top with crates, which blocked the entrance completely. The lights she saw came from the cracks between the stacked crates. They must have stored them here, not remembering that it was a tunnel. Over time it just kept getting piled on, so everyone forgot this was an exit or entrance. Good for her. She got close to the crates and peered through the cracks between them. Then, she saw rows of SGI Onyx mainframe computers that spanned from the floor to the ceiling. Rows and rows of them filled up and lined the room. Layla said to herself, "I thought SGI only produced a deskside and rackmount model. These I have never seen. I bet that's what feeds the MCP."

She carefully pushed some of the crates to the side so she could squeeze by and enter the room. It seemed devoid of anyone else, so she felt it was safe. As she looked around the room at the blinking systems and colorful displays, she eventually turned back to the tunnel and the crates. She then noticed what the crates had written on them. "Explosives."

#

Mikey awoke in a hospital bed, but not at the castle. He was somewhere else now. He was comfortable, but he had a bandage wrapped on his head and an IV with sodium chloride attached to his arm. He looked around and wondered how he ended up here and where was here?

There was a soft knock at the door, and a nurse came in slowly. "Hello there. Mikey Gross? How are you feeling now, slugger?"

Mikey said, "Um fine, I guess, but I don't remember where 'here' is. What's going on?"

"Well, you were found on the ground in a rainstorm. You must have tripped on the median and hit your head. You were out cold when they found you. You're one lucky guy."

"Yea, lucky. But I have to get home to my pop. Did anyone call him?"

"Ahh, well. We have tried to get a hold of him, but he hasn't answered. So, we were going to keep you here until we hear from him. Do you have someone else maybe, who we can call? Your head seems fine, and there is no real reason to keep you any longer unless you can't get anyone to pick you up. I just can't send you out of here without a parent or guardian signing off on it."

"I get it. Well, the only other person is my aunt, but she is in the home where you found me."

"No, we can't release you to her unless she can make it down here somehow. Want us to call her?" The nurse went to get some bandages and then took the IV out of his arm while she spoke to him.

"No, not yet. My pop will be here. I know it. If I can hang here for a little while, would that be OK?" The nurse put her thumb on the IV needle and gently pulled out the IV with the other hand and placed some gauze and a bandage on his arm. "Hold this, please." She put Mikey's hand on the gauze while she put a bandage on top.

"A couple of hours is fine, but you can't stay here overnight. We have other patients who might need the room and bed, OK? There, you're all fixed up."

"Fair enough. Please try him again."

"Will do. By the way, your clothes and that weird backpack are in the closet with your other belongings. You may get dressed if you like."

"Thank you."

The nurse left to go try and call again, but Mikey got out of bed and rummaged through the closet for his clothes. "What the heck is going on? One minute, I am in this mystical place called Shen

Yun and fighting Yeti soldiers made of snow and code, then the next, I'm back here in El Paso in a hospital bed with a serious headache from hell." Mikey got everything on and carefully snuck out of the hospital wearing his backpack, and was seen only once by a janitor who was mopping. Mikey approached the hall where 'Tim" the janitor was working while singing the *mission impossible theme* to himself and crouching below the windows as he passed by. Mikey almost ran into him but stopped and said, "Yo, how are you, sir? I'm just looking for the vending machines, my man. Carry on. You're doing a great job. Um, have a nice day, Bro."

He wasn't too far away from his aunt's assisted living complex, so he thought he might just go 'hang with his aunt' for a bit until he could figure this all out. He headed there immediately.

#

Layla was working on something and spent quite a lot of time in that explosives area. "Ok, that ought to do it," she said to herself proudly. "Wait until I tell Mikey what I have prepared. I better get back to him with this water and see how he is doing." She went back into the twisted hallways to find him.

Mikey's body was still out like a light here, and Glitch stood by him the entire time Layla was gone. He chased away a few rats, but nothing serious. Mikey was still safe yet passed out completely.

Layla showed up to Glitch's happiness. She held his head and tried to get some water into his mouth. He seemed to swallow a few gulps, so she was satisfied. "Glitch, we're not too far from where his dad was held, and I found some things that will help us keep the Yeti guards away, but we have to get on the other side of the tunnels to make it happen." She looked around the room a bit more. "Aha, I think I can build a sliding sling that can attack for you. Do you think you could pull him along if I attach it to you?"

Glitch popped and clicked like "Whatever." At least it wasn't a no.

For the next thirty minutes, Layla worked to fill about a dozen gas grenades up with the green essence goo and build a make-shift sling that consisted of two metal poles that attached to Glitch on either side of him and had a blanket sling tied tightly between them. It also had a seat belt to hold him in place. At the last moment, she found a pelican case with wheels, so she took them off and attached them to the bottom of his sling so it wouldn't have to slide. Now, it would roll instead. It seemed very effective. Layla got Mikey on the rolling gurney and strapped him to it, and with Glitch leading the way, they rolled Mikey towards the room Layla found.

CHAPTER THIRTEEN: The discovery

Mikey entered the assisted care facility and signed in like he always did. He still had the bandage on his head, though, so the front desk lady asked, "Son, are you ok?"

Mikey replied, "Living the dream, ma'am, living the dream." He then gave her the two pointer-finger gun hands and pretended to shoot her with both – one after the other, and gave her a wink. He had just put on his headphones and was listening to Bon Jovi's *Living on a Prayer*, so he be-bopped to the tune as he walked down the hallways to his aunt's room. He often stopped at many doorways and said, "Hello!" Because it always seemed to be the right thing to do, and he felt they might not get that many visitors. He got to his aunt's room and came in singing, "Oh, oh. I'll take you there. Oh, oh. Living on a prayer."

Standing in front of her makeshift gallery, she kept her back to him when he came in.

"Hey, Auntie, how's it hanging?" Mikey said joyfully.

She said sternly, "Ah yes, your dubious child-like ways caused me to wait since time immemorial."

"Sheesh Aunt White. I was just here, and then I fell down and ended up in the hospital."

She turned slowly and gazed at him from toe to head. "I see."

Mikey said, "I then got out of there and came right back here. I can't get ahold of my pop. Has he called you? I'm a little worried. Plus, I have been having these weird dreams. Do you get those sometimes as well?"

She said, "You are being too loquacious. Calm yourself, boy."

Mikey said, "Man, I really like your big words, Auntie. You must have been a really good English teacher in your day."

She ignored his questions, except for the one about his dreams, "What have you dreamed about, if I may query?"

Mikey thought and then said, "You know, sometimes your paintings seem to come to life in my dreams. They're so vivid. Pop always said I had a great imagination. "I dreamt that I was in bed drawing, and then I got really weak and sick, but Pop saved me. It was some sort of magic headphones I was wearing and music that was going all ham on my head."

Irma said, "Perfect. Um, I mean, oh really? Were there other people in your dream?"

"Yes, the whole band from Kinish-Tech was there, and pop too. It all seemed so real."

Irma grinned and hurriedly returned to the drawings on the wall. She said softly, "You do know that your so-called band ruined my life, right?"

"Whoa there, Auntie White. How did they do that? Why would you say that?"

"Because it's true. The heathens caused my Bill's demise, and I ended up here in this god-forsaken mouth to hell."

Mikey was stunned and quiet. "I didn't know how you felt. But the band didn't do anything to your husband. Not that I know about. What do you mean?" Mikey's head was starting to hurt a bit again.

"He had a heart attack because he was helping the band, and nobody helped him. So, they are all guilty and should pay for their sins. And they will all pay dearly." She began to actually cry a little. "They did this to me, and it's not fair. This entire city will pay, too. You'll see soon enough."

Mikey saw her tears and the quiver in her voice, and he said caringly, "Oh, Auntie. I know the band kids, and everyone is very sad about what happened to Bill. Remember when we had his funeral? They all came to it because they cared and wanted to support you too."

Irma said, "They were there to gloat, and then the city put me here in this place."

"No, you have that mixed up Auntie. They saw how troubled you were and that you needed some help. I mean, after all, your husband was gone. It would be hard for anyone to deal with that sort of thing. I still miss him too. He was really nice to me and used to push me on the swing every time we came over. When I was really little, I remember him letting me bang on the piano, and that made a lot of noise. But he was really cool with it and let me." He felt his head again. "You know what, maybe I should have stayed at the hospital. My head is starting to hurt again. Maybe I should go back?"

Irma said, "We have bifurcating opinions, but your point of view has given me some pause. I still don't agree with you, but I can hear that you are earnest in your words. I will forgive you for now." She looked for a painting on the wall, took one down, and handed it to Mikey.

"Before you go, please take this one. I call it the valley of ice. My gift to you and the band kids."

Mikey looked at it, then put it in his backpack. "Thanks. I know you work hard on these, so I will take care of them. I am getting quite a collection of them. Maybe I should start my own art wall, too?" He now squinted and gritted his teeth because of the pain. "Ok, I'd better run to the doc. I am so sorry for you, Auntie. Please try to look on the bright side of things more often, okay?"

She held out her hand, and Mikey softly kissed it, "Later gator." He then headed back to the hospital again. Mikey thought that she would benefit from some happy music. He was going to make her a mix tape for sure. That made him feel happy because he had a solution. As soon as he got to the hospital, he went up to the emergency triage window and said, "Hi, I was just here, but I split too soon. Can I have my bed back? I need to see the doc because my head is killing me, Yo." He then passed out at the window, and chaos ensued, with interns and nurses getting him placed on a gurney and rolled to the back as the emergency doors swung closed upon his exit through them.

#

Mikey awoke to lights whooshing by and a lot of bouncing. It was like he was going backwards, but he wasn't walking. He was pretty confused. He looked ahead and saw Layla walking towards him. Was he being pulled?

"Oh good, you're awake!" Layla said happily. "Want some water?" She gave him a bottled water to drink. He was thirsty and downed the entire thing.

"What's going on? Where am I now?" Mikey said, rubbing his eyes.

"I have a surprise for you. To answer your questions, you are being pulled by Glitch because I couldn't carry you, and we are still running from the Yetis. We are still in the tunnels heading toward where your father is being held, but I also have a bigger surprise than that." She smiled slyly.

"Do tell." Mikey looked behind him and saw Glitch carrying him like a rikshaw package. Then, he looked at the belt holding him in. "Wait, I think I can walk, ok? Glitch ole buddy, you can stop and let me get off this, cool?" Glitch stopped, and Mikey un-seat-belted himself and then stood up. He patted Glitch on the head, "Thanks, friend, and thanks, Layla. I don't know what happened to me. It's like I went somewhere else and don't know which one is dreaming. I think I am going crazy."

Mikey then looked around and asked, "What happened to the magic trombone? Did I lose it?"

Layla said, "When you passed out, it seemed to disintegrate into a magic dust. It was very pretty to watch."

"Well, I hope we don't need it. What are we going to do when we run into more Yetis?"

Layla smiled, "That's the surprise. I found some things and I think we can hinder them chasing us for a while, but we have to get on the other side of this room ahead over there." She pointed at the opening that was now shining brighter than it did before.

Mikey nodded and said, "Cool, I can hardly wait to see."

They got to the room, and Layla explained that she had found another exit ladder in the room but also found a lot of explosives. The ladder came out right in the monorail tunnel above them, and she had taken the explosives and rigged them to blow up the track. That way, they couldn't be easily followed. She just had to set the timer and get back down below before they all went off. She said she had gone down the tunnel a good hundred feet and planted them all along the rail on both sides. They were all tethered together, and the first explosion would then set up a daisy chain-like explosion for the rest.

Mikey was very impressed but said, "What about getting out of this dome and back to the castle? How will we get back if we blow up the monorail system?"

She said that was another surprise and would show him soon enough. All that was left was for her to climb the ladder and head down to the first charge. Mikey said he would also climb up and watch from the opening to ensure she gets back ok.

"Good luck, Layla." Said Mikey as she jogged down the monorail tunnel and around the corner. Mikey stood watching, then decided to put on his headphones and cue *Dirty Deeds Done Dirt Cheap* by AC/DC. It seemed appropriate. The first explosion was heard and made everything shake a little. Layla jogged around the corner and then started to walk back super confidently. In Mikey's mind, he saw her in slow motion as explosions from either side of the tunnel cascaded debris, fireballs, and smoke behind her, lighting up her superhero outfit. Mikey thought it was the coolest thing ever.

"There, that should slow them down," said Layla, smiling and dusting off her outfit of dust and debris.

Mikey opened and closed his mouth several times, trying to say something, but nothing came out. He was awe-struck.

"C'mon Mikey, let's go get your Dad," said Layla, who had to shake him a little on his shoulder to alert him.

"Oh yeah, sorry, I just couldn't believe how cool that was. You, are awesome," Mikey said with an excited inflection in his voice.

"I have my moments. Plus, I really want to get revenge for my family, so when I came across those explosives, I just knew I had to do something. This is helping me too- at least emotionally." Layla's gaze went down, and she looked a little sadder.

"I'm still really sorry for you, but I am really glad you are helping me. I don't know what we would have done if we hadn't run across you. I can't thank you enough," said Mikey.

Layla asked, "What would be a good movie line response to that?" Emphasizing the word movie with long "o's."

Mikey thought and said, "No problemo." He then went on to ramble, "It comes from a movie directed by James Cameron called *The Terminator II*. I think it's a superior movie to the first one, and that's rare when it comes to movie sequels. Usually, the sequels don't stand up as well. But there are exceptions, like the *Star Wars* trilogy, *Aliens, Mad Max*, and probably *Rambo*. Some would also argue that *Indiana Jones and the Temple of Doom* was a lot better than Raiders of the Lost Ark, but I found it very dark. However, it was more like the pulpy style of the old serials that inspired Steven Spielberg to make *Raiders of the Lost Ark* in the first place. So, I am not sure."

Layla said, "Wow. No problemo."

Mikey smiled and realized he was rambling on. He put his fingers to his mouth and pretended to zip them closed.

Layla now led the way, and she looked around at the signs and symbols on the walls and led them into one of the doorways. "I am pretty sure there is a way to come up under where your dad is being held. It's by the MCP room."

"What is the MCP?" Asked Mikey as they walked carefully.

"It's the real boss around here. I think it stands for the master control program. Polybius answers to it and does everything it tells him to. The MCP is why they are building something in that geosphere and why the snow king steals life essence from people." She looked concerned.

"I think whatever they are building is meant to do evil things. It's something new, and they just started working on it several months ago. I wasn't allowed near it even though I have been writing some code for it."

They came to a hallway and found another service elevator. The halls here were painted with red stripes and numbers, which were different from other halls they had been in, which were painted blue and some green. Even the lighting in this area was using red lights.

They got into the elevator and saw that they were already on the level with the scary skull symbol, so they pushed the button for one floor up.

"Remember, I have some of these goo grenades. I'll get one ready just in case we need it," said Layla.

"Man, I must have been out. I don't remember you making those. I am curious what they will do?" said Mikey, rubbing his head again.

The doors opened, and Mikey, Glitch, and Layla stood to the sides, just in case. They peeked their heads out when they didn't hear anything.

"Whew, OK, where is the boss now?" said Mikey to Layla.

She pointed to a sign on a room called 'Training.' "I think that room will be directly under the next-floor area where your dad is being held. We have to get in there.

Mikey said, "It's my dad, so let me try something. Let me have the gas grenade. I'm going in." He took his backpack off and started to look in it. He pulled out the yellow survival book and started thumbing through it. "Nope, nothing here to help. Bummer. Hey, backpack, can I get an outfit? How about a baseball cap and chain necklace with a giant clock on it?"

He reached in again and brought those items out. He smiled, put the chain over his neck, and put the hat on sideways. He then hiked his jeans down low on his waist and took the grenade in one hand. He said, "Watch me work," and walked all cool towards the training room. He opened the door and saw only two Yetis who were busy doing something on some machines against the walls. One looked at him when he came in, stopped doing whatever he was doing on the machine, and was curious.

Mikey said, "Yo, yo, my man. Do you know why I wear this clock? You know, it's because time is the most important element, and when we stop, time keeps going." He then pulled the pin on the grenade and tossed it in between both Yetis who were starting to come his way. Mikey turned and ran back through the door. He then leaned against it, trying to hold it shut. He then yelled, "Fire in the hole!" A small explosion and hissing were heard. In a moment after that, the two Yetis started moaning and screaming. At least one ran into the door Mikey was holding shut, causing it to bump at him and shake slightly. Things then got very still and quiet.

Mikey backed from the door, and Layla and Glitch came over to his side.

"We should check. It seems too quiet. Did it kill them?" Layla said concerned.

They opened the door slowly to see a room with green smoke dissipating on the floor and two Yetis in fetal positions, shaking yet sleeping. They kept twitching and moaning, but they weren't waking.

"Dang, what did it do to them?" Mikey asked. It looks like they are having nightmares.

"At least it worked, and it didn't kill them. I think they are just victims in this and controlled by Polybius and that MCP, so I don't want to hurt them. Not unless we have to." Said Layla.

Mikey said, "Man, this is cool. Nightmare grenades. I guess we don't want that stuff on us, right?" He then went to one of the Yetis and said in a gang-like voice, "If ya see that snow guy, tell him he owes me some money!" He then threw a gang hand symbol at the Yeti's face, whose eyes were closed and couldn't see it. "Tell him he owes Flavor Flav!" He then looked at Layla and Glitch, who both didn't understand what he was doing or referencing. Layla shook her head in disbelief and rolled her eyes.

"You are very weird. But that was effective, so…good job," said Layla. "Let's tie them together in case they wake up."

They both got the Yetis back-to-back and tied them with cables and a thin conduit that Layla pulled off the wall, which caused some sparks. Then, they all looked around at their surroundings. The room was rectangular with a long conference table in the center surrounded by ten chairs, and along the back and right walls were 6 machines standing almost eye level, which Mikey then realized what they were. The left wall was a large white board with various plans and scribbles from different colored erasable markers.

"OMG, those are video game consoles!" Mikey exclaimed and headed towards the ones in the back of the room. "They are all the same. This is what they call training? So weird."

"What is a video game?" Asked Layla.

Mikey said, "Where I come from there's not only movies that we watch for entertainment, but we also play a lot of videogames too. They're digital games that test your dexterity, as well as hand and eye coordination. All for fun. They can be quite challenging to master."

"Is that what they were testing- their eye and hand coordination?"

Mikey said, "I don't know, let's see what they were playing…" Mikey looked at the game screen and the animation demo screen. He stepped back and looked worried. Then he quickly ran to the next console to be sure. Again, he was worried and started shaking his head no. "Um, this is not good. Not good at all. I think I know what Polybius is building and why they are training using these game consoles." He shot a look of fear over at Layla and Glitch, and he had a really worried look on his face. He said shakily, "They are building a freakin' Sinistar."

Layla was fanning Mikey, who was now on the conference table lying down. He was mumbling "Ab abba abbaaba" in a catatonic state and staring at the ceiling.

"You're not freaking out again, are you Mikey?" Layla said caringly.

Mikey turned his head towards her, "You don't understand. That game, it's like the scariest arcade game ever made." He sat up to explain. "It came out in 1983, and it was called a cosmic horror video game. It's about a lone pilot in a spacecraft flying through a large region of space. You are the pilot and can see where you are using a mini-map at the top of the screen. Anyway, you are there shooting these drifting planetoids, which, when hit, release small, white crystals that you need to collect. When you get them, they turn into a 'Sinibomb," which is the weapon you need for defeating the end boss, Sinistar. He is an animated spacecraft with a demonic skull face. Just like the freaking button on the elevator, we saw! I knew I saw that somewhere else." He caught his breath and then did a "Whoo!" He continued, "If you hit those planetoids too much, they explode. The whole time you are collecting these things, there are these warrior ships who are trying to destroy you, but also mine for crystals, plus there are red enemy worker ships who can't hurt you, but they get in your way and try to steal the white crystals from you. It's very frustrating and hard to do. But that's not the scary part. The real scary part is while you are doing all of this, Sinistar is being built. It takes 20 crystals to create 20 pieces of a complete Sinistar. The good news is that it only takes 13 Sinibombs to destroy him. Oh, and there are 7 pieces that make up his scary face. Once that dude is built, he comes after you and tries to eat you! It still gives me nightmares remembering that game."

"How do you think this pertains to what is going on here?" Asked Layla.

"Well, we saw that dome room, and the Yetis working on something big. I think it was a Sinistar in real life!" Mikey looked more worried and said, "I think Polybius is using our life essence as the crystal power he needs to power Sinistar and make him function. He is trying to build a real-life Sinistar!" Mikey jumped off the table and started pacing back and forth. "What the heck, man? Why would he do that? What is he doing this for? Doesn't he realize how dangerous that would be? Why, why, why!" Mikey was having an emotional meltdown. He started hitting his head with the back of his fist, "I have to tell pops. We have to get everyone out of here. We have to run far away from this place! OMG, OMG."

image: Josef Axner

Layla put her hands on his shoulders, which stopped him. "Mikey, calm down. It will be OK. We can fix this, I promise." Her words were reassuring, and Mikey did calm down. In fact, he somewhat melted in place because she was touching him, and he now knew that he did have a big crush on her. He just gazed into her reassuring eyes.

"Ok. Sorry. I needed that," he said. "I don't know what he is going to do with Sinistar, but it's not good, and we need to warn everyone. We have to tell my dad and get the rest of the kids out of here."

Mikey then said, "Where is this room where they are keeping my dad? Up there?" He pointed to a ladder on the back wall.

"Yes, we need to climb that," said Layla.

"Last one up is a rotten egg," said Mikey as he bolted to the ladder and started climbing.

Layla said, "Hey, don't forget about Glitch. He can't climb."

Mikey looked down and said, "Right. Hey, I've got this. Why don't you take Glitch to the elevator and meet me up here? You have nightmare grenades, so you'll be ok, right?"

Layla said, "Ok. Just be careful, and don't get caught, please."

Mikey saluted her, said, "Hey. It's me," and continued the climb. He got to the top and unlatched the door. Then he pushed up on it slowly.

Layla and Glitch left the room and headed for the elevator.

Mikey lifted his head slowly into the opening and started to peer around. He softly said, "Pop? Are you there? Yo, Dad. Where are you, Bruh?"

He was grabbed by the back of his shirt and quickly pulled into the room.

He exclaimed, "What the?" As he was jerked up and into the room. He was put back down, standing on the floor, where he stood with his mouth agape. He couldn't believe his eyes.

A man's deep voice finally said just one stern word, "Gross."

#

Presley and Kristin cautiously went down the winding halls full of conduits with lit-up, blinking panels. There were odd symbols with a red-colored stripe that seemed to follow along the walls in this area. The one previously had been blue, so she wondered what that might mean. There seemed to be a slight wind that came from around the corner, and she thought that maybe it was a doorway outside. They headed there immediately with hope in her heart. She turned the corner, and it was a doorway to a large room that had giant-sized fans blowing. The wind was coming from those, and she thought, what a strange room, and why big fans? So strange for a castle. Was that their air conditioning?

"Whatevs," she said out loud. "Presley, this place is very weird, my little doggo friend. Would you know where your daddy went off, too? Do you have some sort of super sniffer, maybe?"

Presley gave her the tilted head "I don't know" look but wagged his tail.

"We should find some food because I don't think you'll want the salty peanuts I have. I can always eat those. But I am saving them for an emergency for sure." She then petted him kindly on the head. "You sure are a little poof-ball, aren't you? You are a very good puppy."

Presley liked that too and wanted more loving, so he popped his front legs up on her leg and had his little mouth open and panting.

"I know. I know. You are just the sweetest, but we must find Mikey and some food.

The large fans were blowing into tubes that exited the room at the back, and she wondered why they went that way. She thought she would check on it again later because her stomach was now growling from hunger.

"Let's search ahead a bit more and see if we can't find some chow." Presley's ears perked up, and he got excited as if his master just got home from work.

"What is it, boy? I said chow, and you knew that word, huh?"

Presley got more excited and started making cute, gurgly noises like soft growling or purring.

"I bet your master used that word for food, huh?" She then said sternly, like a dog order, "Presley, I want you to find the chow-chow, OK? Go find the chow-chow."

Presley got off her leg, did a 360 circle, and started sniffing the air.

Kristin laughed a little. "That's too cute. What a sweetie!"

Presley then bolted from the room down the hallway they hadn't gone to yet. Kristin scrambled after him. "Presley, not so fast, little dude."

After many winding hallways and passing more strange rooms, they narrowly escaped some Yeti guards when Kristin scooped up Presley in her hands and leaped into a doorway. This room was dark and very cold. It seemed to have some of the air that was coming from those huge fans, but not a whole lot, just enough to keep the temperature in the room very cool.

Kristin looked around, but everything was pretty dark, and there was an odd odor in the room, like fish and musk. Not really a good smell, and kind of like a fish tank.

"Ew, what's that smell?" Kristin said, covering her nose and mouth with her hand.

A voice from the dark said, "Yo, babe- turn the lights on, and you'll see!"

Kristin was shocked and said, "Scuse me? Who is that?"

The voice replied, "It's me, Abercrombie Stardust in the flesh. Your prince charming doll cakes."

Kristin shook her head and felt the wall for a switch. When she found it, she turned it on. The room lit up, cages at the back end, and large blocks of ice stacked all around. She looked around the cages to see where the voice was coming from, but she only noticed some large penguins. "Awe, poor things. Polybius has them all caged up like that. Not cool. Hey, where are you, um, Abercrombie Stardust?"

"Down here, sis, you looked right at me with your baby blues."

Kristin looked again and knelt down to the level of the cages. "I don't get it. Where are you?"

A penguin jutted his head outside of the cage bars, "Right here, toots. Do me a solid, and get me outa here, whadayah say? I'll plant a big ole wet kiss on you if you help a fella out."

"Ew, again," said Kristin. "Why are you locked up, and can I address the elephant in the room, please? How is this possible? You are a talking penguin!"

"Yea, yea, I'm a miracle, yadda yadda…Look, it's a long story, and I'll be glad to tell you all about it if you just get me outa here." He had a serious Boston accent and dialect.

"How do I know you don't work for Polybius, and this is just a trap?"

"C'mon, babe. Do I look like I work for that snow king turd? Why would I be helping him if he has me in this dang cage and room?" He pleaded with his little flipper arms out at his side, facing up as hands opened. "Look, one day, I'm doing my thing in the Boston Zoo with my crew, and BOOM, all of a sudden, I get this aching headache, and I am down for the count on the ice. Then, I wakes up here you know? Badda-bing, and I'm in this cage and that snow jerk runs an experiment on me by locking me in a weird chair and putting something on my noggin. I get zotted and next thing I know, I'm flapping my lips like the humans do. I mean, I always thought about things and could only squawk really, but I was OK with it. It's what we do. I heard the snow king say something about a penguin stew, and I was like, oh heck no! Apparently, he gathered a bunch of us up and they got placed in here with me. But these dorks don't speak like I do. So, if you hadn't happened along, I'd be someone's dinner soon. So, again. CAN you please get me out of here?"

Kristin thought, and Presley went up to the cage, sniffing.

"Whoa, is thing going to hurt me?" Asked Abercrombie.

"No, Presley is a sweet puppy. You're safe, I suppose. I guess I will let you out but on one condition…"

"Name it, sweets," said Abercrombie.

"The babe, sweets, and toots-connotations have to stop. It's very wrong to call me those things. My name is Kristin, and I would prefer that you use my name from now on, OK? Oh, and you need to show me where to find some food."

"Deal, doll face. Is that OK to say?"

'No. It's Kristin."

"Ok, my humble apologies, er Kristin. It's just not too often that I find such a sophisticated and beautiful woman as yourself in my presence. I've just been around these squawking lady penguins, and they're driving me bonkers."

"I think I can understand. In a weird way, but ok, said Kristin. She looked around for the keys and found a rusty loop keychain with several loose metal skeleton keys hanging loosely on it hanging on the wall. She took them down and tried several before she got the right one, and the cage unlocked.

Abercrombie went to the back of the cage and said, "Stand back once you open the door, please."

Kristin opened the door and swung it open, then stood aside. "Why?" she asked.

Abercrombie ran out of the cage, jumped through the air, and landed right on his penguin stomach. He slid across the floor and spun to face them, standing up with his arms out in a pose. "Boom baby, Abercrombie is back in action!"

He then said, "Who's hungry? Next stop, the kitchen."

#

Mikey stood still like he saw a ghost. He felt the cold chill of goosebumps and astonishment in his mind. He wasn't sure who he was looking at but was very surprised, so he stood there in shock.

"So, are you just going to stand there gaping at me, or are you going to tell me how you got here?" Said the man.

Mikey gulped and said "Faraone. How, um what, are, um, abba ab ab bahh…"

"Ok, Mike, this is a shock to you. I understand, but I have been here for a while now, and I am eager to get back. The psycho who runs this place has to be stopped. I've heard some things that distress me." Faraone started gathering some things together. "I've hoped that somebody would either open that trap door or they would come through the front, and I could take them out." Faraone started for the trap door with his bag of belongings.

"Wait, my friends are coming," said Mikey.

At that moment, Glitch and Layla appeared at the front energy door.

Faraone said, "Are these your friends, Mike?"

"Yessir."

"Well, they won't be able to get in. It's coded to some password," said Farone.

Mikey called out, "Layla, it's 8675."

She coded in the keys, and the energy field dropped.

Faraone looked very surprised, then said, "Tommy Tutone- why am I not surprised?"

Mikey smiled.

"Ok, nice to meet you all. Is that robot safe? I've seen more of those around, but they are not friendly."

"Who? Glitch? He's my buddy, he is safe," said Mikey. Glitch then showered some snowflakes down on Mikey. "See? He's cool, no pun intended." A small pile of snow formed on Mikey's head, which he shook off.

Faraone said, "I only trust two things in life: the power of music and a properly cooked steak. But I'll take your word on that for now. Now tell me why you are here and how you got here?"

Mikey said, "I'll tell you that, but I need to save my pop, and the other band kids are here too."

"What in the world? Why did you all come to this place- it's not good. I was kidnapped and brought here against my will. Why would you come here willingly? That Snow King is mad. He's been trying to get information out of me for a month, and the questions he has asked led me to think he's planning something nefarious."

Mikey reluctantly said, "Well, my pop was preparing the band for the Fiesta Texas Sweepstakes competition, and we somehow ended up here. There were these soldiers trying to kill us, and Polybius and his Yetis saved us and brought us here."

Faraone said, "Well, you've been duped. Those soldiers were from the Interdimensional Dream Team or IDT, and they were probably here to try and stop whatever Polybius has been doing and planning. They probably monitored his tests, and you guys probably got caught in the way when they came to stop him."

"The Interdimensional Dream team, what is that?" Asked Mikey.

"Look, I know you have questions, but I have to do a lot before I get out of here, and now it seems that I have to save your band and your father, too. So, let me explain as we move, ok?"

Mikey nodded yes as Farone looked down the hall.

"Ok, we need to move to a safer place. I might need to use that monorail system to get us out of the castle. I escaped once and made some friends in the nearby village. They can help us."

"About that," said Mikey. "We, um, broke the monorail system trying to get away."

"What do you mean, broke it?"

"We blew it up," said Layla. "We felt it would slow the Yetis down from finding us."

"Great. Just great. Ok, here's the problem. This whole place is coded to Polybius' DNA, and only he can open the doors to the outside. The only exception is the monorail system because it has to go to the dome where he is building something big. It comes and goes with construction workers and can pass through the energy shields freely. I was going to use the monorail to get out of here and get help. It's how I escaped last time. Otherwise, we need Polybius to open the energy doors, and I don't think he is going to willingly do that."

Mikey thought for a minute, then said, "What about a piece of Polybius?'

"Whoa, there, Rambo. That's pretty twisted young man. But I see your point and raise you an idea," said Faraone. "What if we got some of his hair? It would have to be enough for the reader to recognize him, but that might actually work."

Mikey said, "What about one of his horns? They grow back, right? So, it wouldn't be like we're maiming him. We're just borrowing something from him so we can get outside."

Faraone pondered this and said, "That's also twisted, but I like it. Let's think about it. It's our only choice right now while the monorail is dead." He pulled out a small spiral notebook from his bag which had a pencil attached to it with a string. He flipped through a few pages and took some notes. The cover said DCI Dot Book and was written with a black Sharpie.

Mikey started to tell him what was in the dome while he wrote. Faraone looked up at him and slowly formed a real serious expression. A bit of anger started to show, like a pot of water that had just reached 212 degrees.

"Sinistar?!" He exclaimed. "A real-life horrific, monster spaceship that eats everything around it? That's just nuts. If he is building it, I think he wants it to attack El Paso."

Mikey then told him about the essence and showed him the grenades they made.

"You have been busy, haven't you? I am impressed. Why didn't you put this kind of effort into your music playing, Mike?"

Mikey was embarrassed. "Sorry, sir. My pop says I am too much of a dreamer and not enough of a doer."

Faraone smiled and patted Mikey's shoulder. "It's cool kid. I was just teasing. I'm proud of you. I just meant that you can do whatever you put your mind to. And about your 'pop,' he means well and is only saying that you have to get involved with life. You can't succeed if you never try. Dreams are good, too. Without them, we wouldn't have anything to aspire to."

Mikey almost teared up. The words meant a lot to him; he felt like Faraone was a mentor and someone he could admire. Hearing him speak like this made his heart ache in an inspiring way. "Thank you, Mister Farone. I promise that I've gotten to be a better player. You should hear me play trombone."

"What? You are a double-reed player. When did you get the knowledge or chops to play a brass instrument? Wait, don't answer yet, I think I hear something coming. Hide."

They all hid in a darkened alcove as a robot sentinel walked by. When it was gone out of sight, Faraone said, "Those guys- you don't want to mess with. They are what was perfected after he experimented with robots like your friend Glitch here. There are also other variations too. Scary ones that he has in a storeroom. I thought they ran on code and some sort of magic, but it sounds like that essence also drives them."

"I helped to program those others. It's what kept me alive and here. I know what you are talking about. There are some really scary ones," said Layla.

"Hey, if you programmed them, can you re-program them?" Asked Faraone.

"Of course."

"I may have us another way out now, but first, we need to get everyone out of here, and I mean everyone. We might have to split up because I am going to need to stop this snow king tyrant, and that will distract him long enough for you all to get to safety."

Mikey said, "My trombone could control the Yetis, but it's gone now."

Faraone looked at him inquisitively, "What did you do to it? Where is it?"

"It disappeared. But I could probably get another from my backpack," said Mikey.

"Look, Ace, that's a nice story, but there's no way you have a trombone in that ugly-looking, small backpack of yours."

"No, really. It's magical and can produce things to help me, but only one thing at a time, or sometimes only for a while, and then they disappear when they aren't needed any longer. We got it from a Djin."

"Can you make me a master ninja costume and give me a Japanese Katana too?" Joked Faraone, not believing Mikey.

Mikey didn't think that was funny, so he took the backpack off and faced it. "You know what to do. Show him your magic." He then reached in and pulled out a complete man's black ninja costume, and slowly but dramatically guided out a long Japanese Katana sword inside a shiny black hilt, then handed it out to Mister Faraone like a Samurai warrior would do. He knelt on one knee and presented the sword out to Mister Faraone with his head bowed. Dramatic music played from the backpack, causing them all to look around until they realized it emanated from the backpack magically to set the mood.

"I am speechless, Mike. I was just messing with you and didn't believe what you were telling me. I mean, c'mon man. Who would have thought that could happen, right?" Said Faraone apologetically. "Did you say only one wish at a time?"

"Uh huh," nodded Mikey.

"How long will it last?" Asked Faraone.

"Dunno. Until it decides it's no longer needed or I am safe, I suppose."

"Well, I was being a little dramatic in my jest, but I can actually use these to help, so why not? I apologize, Mike. I will try to believe things a bit more in this world."

'Mister Faraone, why are you here too?" Asked Mikey.

"Well, kid, I was actually in the teacher's lounge gathering my coffee cup and special roast mix- then I was going to see the principal and thank him for the years I had worked there at the school and get my last paycheck. I had a teaching job waiting for me in Alpine, Texas, at the college, so I was just there to tie up loose ends because they had already hired your father to replace me. Some other faculty members were there chilling when one of them came up to me and said that she was glad I was leaving. I was a quote, 'murderer like the others, and I deserved horrible things to happen to me, and so did the rest of the band kids.' I was shocked and looked at her sternly. I told her, "Hey lady, you don't know what you are talking about, and I don't even know you. Why are you being a jerk to me?"

She said, "There cannot be darkness without light. There cannot be love without hate. Awake or asleep, life will bifurcate." He shook his head as he remembered this like a bad memory. "I remembered those words, but I told her, "You are crazy lady, and you shouldn't be teaching here. You shouldn't say things about people, and don't you dare say anything bad about the band kids. They are the brightest here in the school. You do realize that like 95 percent of the honors kids are in the musical arts somehow? How does that warrant having something happen to them? They are a shining light here at this school."

Faraone then said, after a small pause to catch his thoughts and calm down, "I then stormed out of there and went to Principal Kirtley's office. I told him what she had said, and he said he would deal with it. They had numerous complaints from parents about her, too. She was an Advanced Placement English teacher, named uh missus White, I believe."

Mikey was flabbergasted. His mouth dropped open.

Faraone continued, "I got in my truck and started to head out when I got this killer migraine headache. It wouldn't go away, so I sat in the parking lot for a little while, cranked up some *Fresh Aire* music, and hoped it would subside. But it didn't. I blacked out and found myself lying near a valley that looked like it was made of ice. I went looking for help and was eventually surrounded by these mechanical monster creatures, tied to one of them- a giant robot spider and marched back to this castle. Polybius threw me in a cell, and I have been here since. Except for the time I escaped. That's another story."

Mikey then nervously told Faraone, "Missus White is my aunt. She was fired that day, and we had to put her in assisted living months later. I still visit her and feel sorry for her. I didn't think she was a bad person; she was just different. She didn't used to be that way. Everything changed when her husband died."

"Mike, I had no idea. Sorry for calling her crazy, but she wasn't being very nice." Said Faraone.

"Yeah, I get it. She has been pretty weird for a while now. She also gave me these tripped-out drawings and some of them were disturbing to look at. I have some in my backpack. Do you want to see them?" Mikey showed several to Faraone.

"Mike, you do realize that these drawings look awfully familiar, don't you?" Asked Faraone.

"Kinda. I didn't really look at them too well. They weird me out sometimes, so I try and make light of them. You know, so as not to insult her. She is still my aunt, and I don't want to hurt her feelings."

"Look, here is that valley of ice, but look what she also drew. Kids are all trapped in it and trying to get out. Here is one of Polybius and Lightning, fighting the Dream Team. There's even one here of those electric bat things flying around the castle. Do you realize that she is drawing what you are living here?" Asked Faraone.

"I never put two and two together because I would get them when I went to sleep here, and I would dream that I was back at home. It happens all of the time," said Mikey.

Layla spoke up, "He just passed out a while ago, and we thought he was dead. Glitch and I had to carry him here until he woke up. It's very weird, I agree."

"Wait, let me try to understand," said Faraone. "When you go to sleep or pass out here, you wake up in the real world?"

"Yes, I think so," said Mikey. "I often don't remember much of the other place or this place, and I'm often confused."

"So, when I woke up here, I briefly saw someone that looked like me dissolve into a magic dust. The thing is, it was someone I had dreamt about before or been in a dream. He was me, but it was my idea of what I wanted to be," said Faraone.

Mikey looked perplexed. "What do you mean he was an idea of what you wanted to be? I was just here then there, but I didn't see anyone."

"Well, as you know, I am a conductor and music educator, right? Well, when I was young, I wanted to be a conductor more than anything. To control an entire band or orchestra with the flip of my hand or a baton, and have them produce emotions in people using the power of music. I saw Disney's *Fantasia*, and it really left a mark on me. It inspired me and I wanted to be just like the sorcerer in the film, Yen Sid. So, I imitated him and have always thought I wanted to be that guy when I got older. I know it's silly, but I personified myself after that animated character. But I also thought *the Lord of the Rings* novels were great, and I especially liked Gandalf. Why? Because he was a wizard, like Yen Sid, but I think he looked cooler in my mind. So, I what I saw was a mixture of the two wizards, but with my handsomely distinguished features. You know, strong chin, muscles, and astonishing good looks…" He smiled, then winked. "I dreamed about him, and he was me sometimes."

"You must be a dream walker, Mikey," said Layla who started pacing in a circle, then started tapping one foot on the ground and crossed her arms. "Mikey, why didn't you tell me? This changes everything. There are only a few dream walkers that I have ever heard about growing up. They usually have a special birthmark that proves their power on their shoulder. Do you have a birthmark there?"

Mikey backed away from them both and put his hands up in front of him warding them off. "Now, let's not be hasty, ok? I do have a birthmark on my right shoulder, but I'm not going to show it to you. It's embarrassing."

"What is it," Layla asks, about to take a step towards him.

"I'd rather not say."

"C'mon, it's important. Just show us quickly, then. We won't laugh."

"You promise? I really don't like it when people laugh at me."

"We promise, right?" Layla looked at Mister Faraone, who nodded approval to what she was saying.

"Ok," then Mikey lifted his sleeve on his right arm to reveal a birthmark that looked like…

"A BANANA?!" Exclaims Faraone, who then starts laughing. "Oh man, it looks like a tattoo that went bad and gave up." Wiping his eyes from laughter.

Layla also tried not to, but she snickered a little but was able to hold back her laughter. Glitch rolled in and stretched up to see it, too. He clicked and popped as if he agreed that it looked like a banana.

"You said you wouldn't laugh! You guys suck," said Mikey sadly and turning away from them. He quickly put his sleeve back down.

Faraone stopped laughing and reached out to Mikey. He placed his hands on his shoulders and said, "I'm sorry Mike. That took me by surprise and I was wrong to laugh, really."

He tried to lighten Mikey's mood by empathizing, "If it makes you feel better, I have been mocked for my big chin and long nose since I was a kid. At least you can cover up yours."

Mikey turned around and said," Yea, I can see that. You are right. I'm just a bit sensitive about it, that's all."

Faraone put his right hand in the air to swear, "I promise to never mock your yellow fruit birthmark ever again." Then he said, "Orange you glad I didn't say banana?" He smiled at Mikey, and Mikey gave him a smile back. Then Faraone said "Ok, I really do apologize if I hurt your feelings. Feel free to make a joke about my chin if you want. I owe you one."

Mikey then asked Layla, "What does a dream walker mean?"

"It means that they could be in the real world and the dream world at the same exact time. However, only one of the instances can be awake when they travel there. It's why you were passed out here, I bet, and we couldn't wake you. It's making sense now."

Mikey said, "But I don't remember much, if anything, about the other place when I dream or wake up."

"You will eventually. It takes conscious practice. You need a dream master to train you. We had one in our village, but I was honestly a bit frightened of him growing up."

Faraone said, "Let's think about this and these drawings, but first, I need to change, and we need to do some hero stuff." He rubbed the ninja costume material between his fingers. "Nice. Real master ninja polyurethane material. I am really impressed. Because there is a lady present, I am going to duck in this room and get this on for my mission. You guys keep watch."

He went into the room and shut the door. He emerged in the black ninja suit and katana sword sticking up over his left shoulder, ready to be grabbed and used. He was very menacing looking. The backpack played some sort of brass and orchestra music reminiscent of a James Horner fanfare. They all looked at Mikey wearing the backpack and where the music was coming from.

Mikey shrugged his shoulders, "I dunno. It sometimes does that. Like a soundtrack for life, I suppose. I usually have to hum my own music. You're lucky. I guess it likes you?"

Faraone said, "Well, it was a good entrance fanfare, so I like it too. This won't, like, just disappear on me, will it? Because My clothes are stashed in the room there. If this costume disappears, I'll be wearing nothing but my birthday suit."

Mikey shrugged. "I don't know, boss. It stays until the backpack thinks it's been used enough. That's all I can tell you. It's a magic artifact and does what it wants. But it always seems to help."

Faraone then tells them to go back into the room where they will devise a plan to save the others and stop the Snow King. "Take those drawings out, I want to analyze all of them. We'll find a weakness and exploit it, I promise."

CHAPTER FIFTEEN: A voice in the dark

Polybius sat on his throne thinking. He had just gotten news that the monorail was blown up and his Yeti guards had not caught Mikey and the others yet. He knew he was going to have to answer to the MCP. He jumped out of his thrown quickly and headed down the hallway at a hastened pace. He ordered some more Yetis he ran into the hallway to search another level, and ordered some down to try and do repairs to the monorail system, but he knew that was probably useless right now. He passed the two Yeti commander guards at the elevator, went in and selected the floor for the MCP.

He exited the elevator and the motion lights lit his way as he walked with a mission. He entered the MCP room and knelt on the digital grid below him while he faced the mighty face of the MCP.

"You disappoint me. How can some children elude you and your forces? Have I not given you ample resources to govern how you want? What do you have to say for yourself?" A booming MCP voice said.

"It's not my fault," said Polybius. "They got help, and they are tricker than I thought."

Abruptly, Polybius is lifted in the air and pushed back violently against the wall behind him, where he is stuck flat against the wall. The entire room was filled with a bright red light. A digital panel behind him scanned up and down his body while he was held place to the wall. It gave him pain, and he cried out in agony. As the light scanned him, you could see his skeletal structure show and fade as the light passed that part of his body.

"Shall I de-rez you?" asks the MCP.

Polybius was in pain and tried to talk, yet the pain made it difficult. "Mmm, mm…MOM, please stop."

"Don't call me that. You're not allowed. Not until you can do something worthwhile. Have I not provided a realm to rule over? Have I not given you powers beyond your wildest dreams? Are my intentions nebulous to you? All you have to do now is finish Sinistar so that he can breach the dream void and come into the real world. This computer interface is now 6,219 times smarter than before. Once you power up Sinistar you will transfer the AI from the MCP into him and then- only then, will you probably make me proud enough so that you may call me mom."

Polybius had a tear roll down his cheek. "I, I will muh, make you proud. I puh, promise."

The MCP released him, and he crumpled to the floor, catching his breath.

"You are too forgiving, just like your father was. Look what happened to him. You have to be strong and demanding, Jim otherwise people will walk all over you. When they do bad things to you, you must retaliate against them. You must crush their light and masticate their fear. It's what Sinistar will do to El Paso. Then, he will strike at Fort Bliss and gain control of the Patriot missiles stored there. No one will stop him, not even the Pentagon! Do not fail me like Dillinger did."

Polybius can barely do it, but he gets himself up on his feet.

The MCP said sternly, "Do we have an understanding?"

"Yes, MCP. I understand what to do."

"You had better. End of line." Then the MCP tube starts to spin once again, totally ignoring Polybius at this point.

Bob woke up in a totally dark room except for a small window in the door emitting some light. He realized that he was chained to the floor and if not for the cushion given to him, there was nothing else in the room that was made up of cold stone.

Bob yelled, "Hey! What are you doing? You can't keep me locked up in here. I have rights, you know. There's an army coming to rescue me, and you are all going to be sorry." He thought to himself about how he got here and the magical way they just appeared. Something had to have caused that. Then he thought about why those soldiers were attacking the Yetis. Were they the good guys, and he just didn't realize it? Maybe so. What about what they were doing to the children and that energy-draining headphones thing? What was that all about? Something was going on here, and it wasn't good. He also wondered where Mikey and the other kids were. After all, they were his responsibility, and here he was, chained up in a cold, dark room…helpless. Now, he has learned that the MCP is actually his sister Irma, who is controlling Polybius. But to what end? What did she mean about revenge? Was this all only about Bill's death…was she crazy? He had to get out of there, but how? He would wait until someone came for him again, and he was going to have to try something…anything to get free.

#

The small misfit team of Mikey, Layla, Glitch, and a new Master Ninja- mister Faraone, band director extraordinaire, had a plan and decided to split up to accomplish it. Faraone was going after Bob and the children while Layla, Mikey and Glitch try to find the other robots like Glitch to see if Layla can hack them to help. All while avoiding the Yeti guards and the sentry robots and traps.

"Did you see mister Faraone climb over that wall like he was a bug? How can he do that?" Asked Layla to Mikey. "Was he always that athletic?"

"I saw him, and I know it was the suit that was helping him. When he mocked the backpack's powers, I sort of thought about a master ninja outfit with all of the powers that come with being a master ninja. I remembered those Chuck Norris movies like *the Octogon* and *the American Ninja*. They always had cool stuff like smoke bombs and cool daggers, and those ninja throwing stars…so cool! Whoever wore that suit would have those powers bestowed upon them." Mikey was looking up and smiling.

Layla said, "Where are you, Mikey? Come back down here with us, will ya? We have some searching to do. We need those machines if we are going to go up against the Snow King and his army."

Mikey said, "I wish the backpack could have given us something, too, because we are going to need all the help we can get." Mikey thought for a minute. "Hey, you know what I am thinking? I know we have to find those machines, but there is something that has been bugging me."

"What has?" asked Layla.

"Since I got here, this castle doesn't seem to be a castle. I mean, look at those cables on the walls, and the pipes…and look at those circuits on the wall over there. Even the panels are not panels; they are more like resistors and transformers for electronic equipment. Like a big computer board would have!" He smiled and was proud of himself. "That's it! This entire castle is a circuit board for a giant computer system. Look over there; those are inductors, and those over there are giant diodes, and those giving off electricity are capacitors. Now, this is making some sense."

Layla said, "I think you are right. I have been here for so long that I just thought these things were normal. I am usually using the computer and writing code, but I have never thought about what makes it all work."

Mikey said, "This can work for us because I have built computers before. If I remember how they are laid out on a computer motherboard, I may be able to guess where things will be. It's worth a shot, right?"

"That's brilliant, Mikey!" Layla reached over and put her hands on Mikey's shoulders, then leaned over and gave Mikey a small kiss on his forehead.

Mikey was awestruck and stood shocked. Layla then said, "Ok, where to computer genius?" Then she started walking. "You should lead the way, Mikey, c'mon."

Mikey was still frozen, so Glitch ran into him, bumping him a few times, and clicked at him. Mikey still didn't budge, so Glitch caused a small snowstorm over him, and a mini lightning bold came from a small cloud and zotted Mikey in the bottom.

"Woo hoo! What was that for? Geez." Mikey exclaimed.

Glitch nudged him towards Layla's direction again.

"I got it, I'm fine. I'm going." Then he started walking but leaned over to Glitch while they walked and said softly, "I'm also in love," and smiled at Glitch, who jumped up and down a couple of times and popped and clicked for him. As they walked further down the hall, Glitch had his storm go back over Mikey, but this time, it formed a mini rainbow, which made Mikey smile.

He looked back at Glitch, "Slay."

Mikey caught up to Layla and said, "Ok, if those lines are cables that connect the relays, then around the corner, we should find the CMOS battery and fuses. He pointed as they went around the corner, "There! Those are PCI slots, so behind them, we'll find the CPU, but I am not sure if the RAM chips will be on one side or the other. We'll see."

Layla asked, "What is RAM?"

"RAM," said Mikey, "is short for random-access memory. It's the short-term memory of the PC. It's where the data is stored and the CPU uses it to run your open files and programs. It's very important."

"I thought it was a beast that we used to hunt on the plains," said Layla.

"Well, it is that, too, if it's not the acronym. They have big horns and use those for butting. Did you know that a regular-sized ram can actually knock out a bull?" Asked Mikey.

"I don't know what a bull is, but I believe you," said Layla.

"A bull is like a big cow with horns, too. But their skulls are not made for sudden blunt force trauma like ram's are." Layla looked confused. "I digress," said Mikey. The ram I am talking about is computer storage."

Layla then said, "If it is storage, then wouldn't it make sense that the snow king is also using it for storage?"

"Brilliant," said Mikey. "I bet that's where the robots are stored. We just need to find the ram!" Mikey was proud and pulled ahead to lead the party. "I wonder if mister Faraone is doing as well as we are?"

#

An explosion threw several Yeti guards into the air and then to the floor. Green smoke bombs got set off, and Yetis were scrambling everywhere. Chaos had ensued. In the smoke, a black figure was fighting several Yetis and sentry robots at once and dispelled them all. He tucked and rolled and used the katana sword masterfully, slicing the Yetis like practice dummies. Sentry robots that have been embedded in the wall charging up came to life and were attacking. Sparks flew everywhere as he used his gleaming katana blade on them masterfully. A few got some Chinese throwing stars between the eyes and short-circuited. One Yeti managed to push the alarm button just before it got its hand cut off by Faraone's blade. Only the hand remained on the button.

"Dang, I was too careless. This suit has many surprises. I'll give my thanks to little Gross later. I need to get out of here before reinforcements arrive." Faraone pulled out another smoke bomb. Just as many surrounded him, he threw it down to the ground, and a blast of green smoke enveloped him, and he disappeared. The Yetis looked confused. He appeared above them, climbing to another story and onto a walking path, which they didn't notice. He saw many rooms with wooden doors ahead. Maybe Mikey's dad and the children were being locked up in them? "Well, let's go take a little look," he said and smiled to himself.

He found a small black tube in a pocket and some darts next to it. He loaded up one at a time, and these blow darts took out the guards by the rooms. Thwip! Thwip! Thwip! They are targeted right in their necks. They fell to the ground, and Faraone approached them carefully.

He heard some yelling from one of the rooms, "You can't keep me in here forever, you know! This place is surrounded by now. Just wait until I get out. You'll be hearing from my lawyers. Remember the Geneva Conference rules for prisoners. You are going to be in big trouble, mister snow king!"

Bob finally calmed down after yelling a bit. It's still really dark in the room, and his little window of light was obscured for a few seconds. "Hey, you can't turn out all of the lights, buddy. That's not cool," he said.

The door splintered into two vertical halves because a blade had entered it from top to bottom and was kicked in.

Bob cowered because of the door blast and then looked slowly towards the new light streaming into the room. A silhouetted figure was standing there in the doorway in a super hero pose with both fists on his hips. The ribbons on his mask were billowing in the breeze from the hallway.

A deep man's voice said, "Miss me?"

Bob's eyes focused more, and said to the figure, "Who are you? You sound familiar..."

The figure approached Bob, and the katana raised to strike.

Bob yells, "No!!!"

The chains on his hands were broken by the blade's swiftness. Two strikes, and they are off Bob's hands. Bob cowered; afraid he was next.

The voice said, "Gross, you haven't changed a bit. Are you teaching those Clarke studies like I told you to do? Are you tuning the band to a concert F- also like I instructed before I left? I bet you aren't."

Bob's mouth was agape. "Faraone? Is that you, John? Wha...how?"

"Oh, it's me, alright. You want to get out of here and see your kid?"

"I really want to get out of here. You have no idea. Thank you, thank you!"

Faraone helped him to his feet, and they both exited the room and into the hallway, where green smoke was still in the air, and a mixture of a dozen Yeti guards and humanoid robots were vanquished. It looked like a war zone. Some robots were still spurting sparks and twitching.

Bob said, "Where are we going now? How are we going to get out of here?"

Faraone said, "We're going to find your boy, and he is going to have transportation ready for us- if everything has gone according to plan."

"My boy? You are talking about Mikey, right? My kid, the foible?" Said Bob.

"You have to believe in the kids, Bob. That's a big fault you have. Your kid is a good kid, so trust him to do the right thing. He may be a dreamer, but always remember, we are the music-makers, and we are the dreamers of dreams…we are the movers and shakers of the world for ever, it seems."

"Wow," said Bob. "That's very poetic. You are very wise indeed."

Faraone smiled under his mask and said, "Bob, that's from a poem called *Ode*, by Arthur O'Shaughnessy. It's not my wisdom, but I do live by it. Now let's go find the kids."

"There's more than one?" Asked Bob.

Faraone pushed Bob to the ground, leaped in the air doing a somersault, and landed on top of a sentry robot that just came embedded in the wall towards them. As quick as he had landed on it, he was off. He had placed two small discs on the back of the robot's neck. They erupted with 1,000 volts of electrical current, incapacitating the robot in place and then exploding his head right off, causing the robot to go inactive and slump to the ground with a metallic thud.

"Oh, we have a real lively crew, bub. Wait and see," Faraone said nonchalantly as he picked Bob off the ground.

"Golly, said Bob."

CHAPTER SIXTEEN: Red One makes an appearance

Layla, Mikey, and Glitch made it around the PCI slots and saw where the RAM was stored. They had to avoid one trap that was set by the Yetis, a trap door that Glitch noticed by scanning ahead. To disable it, he started an ice storm over it and froze it so that it wouldn't fall open on them. Several sentry robots were avoided, and about a dozen Yeti guards missed them completely by hiding in a thin alcove with Glitch at the bottom, Mikey, and Layla standing on each other's shoulders. That was Mikey's idea, and he was rather proud of that maneuver, although the others felt it was silly. They got down, and when it was clear, they headed for the doors where the RAM storage was located.

Mikey said, "I don't know about you, but I feel trapped in the movie *Westworld*. Too many humanoid robots for my liking."

A large DO NOT ENTER sign was on the doors, which also had a number keypad on them like the cells.

Mikey said, "Let me do the honors," and he punched in the 8675 code, and the doors made a metallic clanging noise as if a large bolt was suddenly pulled back, striking another metal bar.

"Hmm," said Mikey, "Must be a real secure door."

Layla and Mikey each pulled a door open.

The lights started flicking on, and the room of horrors slowly revealed itself to them. They saw all manner of giant insect robots, from metallic centipedes to grasshoppers and even scorpions. The creatures were not moving but were still menacing to see. Glitch clicked, and they saw several snowman-like robots like Glitch, but they were different in size and missing part of their globe shapes. They were more snow than metal, and there was no snow on them.

One even had metallic arms, which made Glitch jealous. The entire room looked like a metallic bug museum with some half-eaten metallic snowmen thrown in for fun. It was creepy being in there if you didn't like bugs. Mikey certainly did not.

"Bruh, this place creeps me out, man," said Mikey. "They are kind of cool looking but also scary. I wonder why he has these just stored like this? Thank goodness he isn't using them to come after us. I couldn't handle that, bro!"

Layla finally spoke and said, "These are the prototypes I remember working on. But none seemed to fill Polybius's needs. Finally, one day, he came up with that Yeti-type beast, which was a mixture of creatures. When we got it working using the code, Polybius ordered us to put it on the throne and leave it. You do know Polybius is just a man, right? That Yeti suit is what we built for him."

"Wait, what?" said Mikey. "The snow king is a dude just like me?"

"Well, not just like you. He is older and was sort of dorky looking like you- no offense."

"None taken."

"The suit he wears now is a disguise made of magic and computer code. He gets stronger when he sits on his throne. It's how he rules here. Nobody dares challenge him now."

"But these things do work, right?"

"Oh yeah, we just have to start them up. We may have to charge them, though. It looks like they've not been used in a while. I think Polybius was using the essence to power them, but they were originally designed to be charged up. They can plug into different parts of the castle to feed. There are power junctions all over the castle."

Mikey asked, "How did Polybius get inside the snow king outfit? Is it something we can do as well? You know, so we can use these things?"

"I like the way you think, Mikey," said Layla.

She went on to explain the boarding process which wouldn't work unless each mind was accepted by the robot, and the person could physically fit inside the strange cockpit for that creature. There was also some pain involved because your mind must be connected to the computer to run the robot. This involves two small needles that pierce the gyrus temporalis inferior right behind the ear, and they connect directly with the cerebellum, which maintains your balance, posture, coordination, and fine motor skills. It will allow you to be one with the robot and use your mind to control its movement and special skills.

Mikey said, "That's gas. Very cool indeed, except for the needles part. I hate needles."

"It is the only way, I am afraid," said Layla.

"Well, we should pick our poison then. What would be necessary to strike fear in our enemies and give us a great way to get out of here?"

Layla said, "Polybius wanted something strong but small enough to be believable. We don't need to do that. We can go big, but it will also require more energy to fuel it up." She went around and started plugging many of them in to begin charging.

Mikey thought and looked around a bit at the different creatures. He saw a giant praying mantis, a giant spider, an armored pill bug, which he pointed out to Glitch, and a cockroach that looked menacing. He said, "I think I am settling on the giant scorpion."

Layla said, "Good choice. It has a stinger attack, which may come in handy. I'll juice that one up. I think I am going with the praying mantis. Those giant claws look scary. I bet they can do some serious damage if we get in a melee."

Glitch went up to the giant pill bug, with its armor shiny and glistening, and clicked and popped approval.

"Glitch, I may have to hook you up once inside with some cables and leads because you don't have a brain to poke into, alright?"

Glitch jumped up and down a few times to say that he approved.

Mikey then said, "What about the others? There are not enough robots for the entire band and my dad. What about Faraone? Did he want us to acquire enough transportation for everyone?"

"No," said a deep voice at the doorway. "I just need some muscle support to get us all out of the castle."

They all turned, startled to see Faraone as the master ninja, and then Bob popped out from behind him.

"Hey, kiddo. How goes it?" Said Bob.

"OMG!" Exclaimed Mikey, who ran to his dad and jumped on him, hugging him in happiness.

It was a heartwarming moment, and Layla felt a bit sad though. She was still thinking that maybe one day she would have the same reunion with her mom. She still had hope.

"Pop, I have so much to tell you. Did you know that I am a dream walker?" He pulled up his sleeve to show his dad his banana birthmark. Bob strained close to see it and was about to ask about it. But Mikey continued, "Oh, and guess what? I can play music really well now. Something came from the sky and struck me and gave me musical powers. Oh, and we made nightmare grenades. It was so clutch, and..." said Mikey in a hurry.

"Whoa there, little man, slow down," said Bob. "I have news for you all too. But let's share as we get out of here. First, what the heck are those scary things behind you all?"

"We're going to use them to get out of here," said Mikey proudly.

"Good job, kid," said Faraone. "I'm impressed."

Bob said to Mikey quietly, "He doesn't get impressed, so take that as a huge compliment. Hey, do you still have my yellow survival book in your backpack?"

Mikey took the backpack off and felt inside, "Here you go, Pop."

Bob flipped through the pages and said out loud, "How to survive a tornado, how to survive a shark attack, how to escape from quicksand, how to make an underwater escape, how to survive a duel...nope, nothing in here to help, sorry." He put the book back in the backpack.

Faraone said, "It's cool, Bob. We figured out a plan, assuming the kid found these things and that we could get them to work. Layla says she can get them going so we can continue with the plan." He looked around at how the robots were connected. Layla, I need a power source for one more.

She handed him a cord, and he went to the back of the room and behind the insects. There was noise when he went out of sight, then clanging, and a metal bar dropping noise. He yelled to them because they couldn't see what he was doing, "Layla, get them loaded up. Put Bob in one that's ready to work, and I'll join you all in a minute." An electronic whurring noise was heard, and then a low bass chord was struck with one note, like something powered on.

Layla looked around at the creatures and pointed Bob at a large metal caterpillar, "This one is ready to work, Bob."

"What? A caterpillar? That's not fair! What about something scarier?"

"Nope, nothing is ready, sir. It's that or nothing."

"Sheesh, Ok, I guess it's better than nothing." Bob climbed in the open door.

Layla told him nonchalantly to take a sitting position at the front and hold perfectly still, there were needles that needed to pierce his skull and go into his brain.

"Whaaaa?!" Cried Bob. "What are you talking about? That sounds insane. Can't we just drive these things?"

"It's how you drive them. The initial poke hurts, but then you won't feel it. It's the only way."

"I'm going to regret this," said Bob, who then climbed in and went to the front of the caterpillar's head.

Layla yelled instructions, "When you get situated, push the blue synching button, NOT the red emergency only button, and hold perfectly still. You may want to close your eyes and grip the armrests. It was going to hurt. She heard Bob wriggling in the leather chair and making himself as comfortable as possible. Then she told Mikey and Glitch to do the same in their robots. She treated Glitch like he was a person, which Glitch appreciated.

They followed orders and then heard Bob yell, "Zooie Momma!" Then Mikey got needled, "Waaaa, owie!" He screamed. Layla went into Glitch's pill bug and got him connected and interfaced just fine as well. She then got into hers and prepared for the poke.

"OW!" She yelled as well, although it was muffled inside the praying mantis's head.

It was pretty fancy how the system could scan your body and determine with an X-ray exactly where to poke your skull with precision. The robotic arms worked in unison on each side of the chair and leveled up and down, back and forth, until it knew exactly where to pierce your skull.

The creatures all started to come to life, and the eyes lit up with a soft glow. Probably like headlights, Mikey thought.

Their first steps were awkward, and they crashed into other creatures and almost toppled themselves. There was a green button in each that said below it, "Disconnect charging," which they all pushed, and the power cords popped and snaked back into their self-winding cabinet spaces. They started to head for the front of the room and marvel at each other. Bobs was rather comical in that it would inch forward by stretching out. Then its legs would crawl forward to match its location, moving it forward. They were impressed and knew these would help protect them. They heard Faraone's creature from the back, which was now powered up, and saw the light of its eyes glowing in the darkness of the back of the room. They turned and watched as his creature leapt in the air and landed in front of them all. It gave out a loud roar. He was driving a mechanical Voltron lion. The red one, to be exact.

They were stunned in place once again. Bob said, "Hey, no fair! How come we didn't get one of those?"

Through the loudspeaker in the mechanical lion, Faraone said, "Because I knew there was only one here. I had seen it before, but I didn't know what happened to it until I saw this place. I just figured it was back there because it wasn't an insect." Faraone then said to encourage them all, "You all look great! It will all work out."

Here they were: a majestic robot lion, a menacing scorpion, a giant pill bug, a scary praying mantis, and a caterpillar made of metal. Mikey put on his Walkman headphones and found *Magic Carpet Ride* by Steppenwolf. He felt it was appropriate since it was also the music played in the movie *Star Trek: First Contact* when they launched the first human constructed warp-capable vessel.

Faraone's lion said, "I'll lead the way. Remember, we have to free the kids so try to avoid fighting the Yetis and sentry robots if you can help it. The band kids come first…they always come first."

His lion burst through the doors and bounded down the hallway. The others drunkenly followed, running into the walls as they exited and still bumping into each other. Eventually, they got the hang of driving their creatures.

Mikey said, "Hey Pop, I'll stay a bit behind to protect you because yours seems slowest of all. The rest of you follow Faraone. We'll be ok."

Bob's caterpillar had to creep forward so many steps, and then its backend would catch up from the stretch and ultimately arc and then push the front forward again. It was not a fast movement, and Bob complained to himself while in his caterpillar cockpit. Nobody heard him complaining. Realizing they were far behind the others, Mikey thought they might try to find Kristin and Presley. After all, they hadn't seen them in a while, and Mikey was missing Presley.

"Pop, I need to go get Presley, my dog, and help Kristin," Mikey said through his loudspeaker.

Bob agreed and said, "I am not sure they will be in the same room because Polybius captured me there, and I would think that she was caught, too. We should find them, though, I agree."

Mikey said, "I'll lead the way. I am pretty sure I remember where they were."

Bob inched up behind as they both heard crashing, explosions, and, for the first time, rapid gunfire. A claxon was sounding once again in the hallways. The battle had begun.

Bob said, "Golly."

#

Kristin heard explosions and rapid gunfire. "Uh-oh, something is going down. We need to find safety before it reaches us. Let's find a hiding space." She pointed at a room with the lights off inside. "That should do. Nobody is in there, c'mon."

It was a storage room, and the walls were storing sentry robots, who were facing out and halfway in the wall at equal intervals. They were not active, but they had cords connecting them to the wall batteries and other electronic parts near each of their standing beds.

"Ay yi yi," said Kristin quietly. "Could we have picked a worse room? If these things wake up, we're doomed."

The explosions and gunfire got closer, and eventually, the door to the room they were hiding in was destroyed in an explosion, and what looked like a giant metal tail tore through the wall where the door was. Several Yetis wearing bullet sashes and touting weapons that looked similar to modified AR-15s came backing into the room they were hiding in, firing back at something coming in after them. Kristin held Presley close and kept them down behind a table at the fall end, away from the door. Abercrombie was also cowering by her, and when he got close enough, she pulled him into her chest as well, holding him tight.

One Yeti guard decided to turn and head to the back where she was, so she closed her eyes tightly and expected the worst. In came a giant robotic scorpion, crab crawling to the sides, moving erratically and running into everything, but effectively hitting the Yetis and pummeling them both. The one heading towards Kristin and the gang actually got grabbed by the pinchers and was cut in half. No blood, just a spray of water and sparks.

The scorpion hit the table as it turned and slammed it against the wall with its tail as it turned to leave. There crouched Kristin, a puppy, and a giant emperor penguin huddled together.

Mikey was driving the scorpion and didn't notice them at first, but as he tried to get back through the destroyed doorway, he saw them at the back of the room. He turned back into the room and started to approach them.

"Oh no!" Kristin yelled as Abercrombie pulled away and ran to the side, facing the scorpion. He put his fins up like a prize fighter, "Yo, knucklehead. Bug brain, over here, you louse!"

Mikey was confused but turned to face the giant penguin. He was then trying to turn off the scorpion and let Kristin know it was him inside, so he was a bit distracted and ignored the penguin.

Abercrombie charged and did a slide on his stomach under the scorpion. He knocked out a few of its legs, causing it to fall to the side a bit. He then jumped on top of the scorpion while grabbing one of its giant pinchers. He pulled with all of his weight towards the other side and actually caused the scorpion robot to flip upside down. It was a sight to behold.

Mikey called out on the intercom system once he was on his back, "Yo, Dawg. I'm here to help! Kristin, it's me, Mikey! Call off your attack, penguin!"

Kristin let her breath out- she had been holding it for a while- and said, "Mikey? What the…how can this be? What's going on?"

The scorpion's legs were twiddling in the air, and it was rocking side to side to no avail.

Mikey said, "Can you turn me right side up, please? I can't get out because the cockpit door is on the back."

Kristin told Abercrombie to please flip it over again, and he did so. Kristin then said, "Ok, Mikey, do you mind telling me what is going on here? Oh, and please come out of that hideous robot, please, it's giving me the willies."

The hatch on the back mechanically slid open, and Mikey exited and plopped to the floor with both feet and a ta-da pose while he smiled and then waived his arms in front of the scorpion robot like he was a game show model showing off the big prize. "Ha! What do you think? Pretty cool, huh? I named it Sting after Bilbo's sword in the movie *The Hobbit*. It seemed appropriate.

Explosions occurred outside, and more gunfire. It was no time to chit-chat.

Mikey said, "I was actually coming to save you and Presley." Presley heard his name and started wagging his tail madly. He wriggled out of Kristin's arms and ran up to Mikey. He then leaped up into his arms and started licking his face happily. "Who is the mighty Quinn here, the penguin?"

Abercrombie then spoke back, "Yo meatball, the name is Abercrombie. Boston born and bred. Next time you come a blazin' in like that, and we don't know you, I'll knock your lights out, OK? Who are you anyway?"

Mikey was shocked, "It talks?! I guess I shouldn't be surprised in this place. Strange things are happening here."

Abercrombie said, "Watch it with the 'it' reference kid. That's warning one."

Mikey said, "Sorry, um, Abercrombie. No disrespect, seriously. My apologies."

"It's all right, kid. You don't know nothing. Ole blue eyes can fill you in."

Kristin said, "It's quite the story."

The room shook with another explosion. Mikey said, "We have to get out of here, but we need to find the rest of the band. Do you know where they are?"

Outside the room, an intercom said, "Mikey, where are you?" It was Layla's voice emanating from the robotic praying mantis. She was searching one room at a time while fending off robot sentries and Yetis with assault rifles.

"We gotta go now. The others need my scorpion help. We're fighting the snow king's forces and trying to get out of here. I found my dad! C'mon, I'll protect you all. Follow me." He jumped back up on the scorpion's back and climbed in the door. They all heard an "OUCH! I hate this part!" coming from inside as Mikey got plugged into the scorpion's AI computer brain. The scorpion came back to life, and they all left out of the door in a single line behind Mikey. Abercrombie stood by Presley, but Kristin still kept an eye on them both. The hall ahead was still war-free, so they went that way.

The red lion was leaping from wall to ledge to wall, taking out Yetis and sentry robots alike with slashes of its claws. It took several rounds of gunfire, but it eventually smacked those Yetis into a wall and actually bit one in half…water and sparks gushing from its mouth. Faraone noticed that Layla was missing, and he was fighting on his own. He turned back to find her and the others.

Layla saw the scorpion ahead and called out again, "Mikey, behind you. Where did you go?" Then she saw Abercrombie and Presley, then Kristin. "Hey, who are you all? Friend or foe?" She approached Abercrombie, who stood in front of Presley, ready to tangle in a brawl to protect him. Mikey turned around and saw her mantis approaching with talons up.

"NO! Friendlies, they are friendlies, Layla!" Mikey yelled through his intercom.

Layla lowered her talons and said, "Good thing. We need all the help we can get." Layla squinted at the penguin, "SD? Is that you?!"

Abercrombie stretched his neck up and said, "Layla? Are you in that big bug thing?"

Layla said, "Yes, it's me Stardust. I am so glad to see you out!"

Kristin smiled and jokingly said, "Hey, Stardust."

Abercrombie said, "Hey now, it's either SD or Abercrombie, OK? Not that foo-foo name, please. I prefer Abercrombie."

Mikey came back towards them and said, "Thank goodness. Everything is going to be all right now!"

Lightning coursed down the hallway and struck Layla's praying mantis, engulfing it in electric crackles. Sparks exploded from the robot, crashing it into a wall. Smoke sinewed out from the crevices, and it lay there lifeless. A bass voice shook the air, "Yes, everything is going to be all right." It was Polybius. To Mikey's horror, he was coming straight at them.

CHAPTER SEVENTEEN: The battle

Bob had tried to catch up to everyone but was really lagging behind in his caterpillar robot. He was getting better at it, but he thought he could probably jog faster than this thing. However, it was protection. He just had to follow the debris on the floor and the bullet holes in the walls to know which way to go. At one point, he saw many robots coming from around a corner in front of him and going away down the hallway after his kid and Layla. They totally ignored him and didn't even really see him. Then he stopped and stood still. Polybius came from the hall on the right and pointed to the Yetis, who came from the left. He motioned to them to all go down the hall, and several robots marched that way as well. Polybius followed. Bob was actually behind them all, unbeknownst to them all. He looked for any kind of weapons but had none. Only the big red button with the sign that said Emergency ONLY up above his head's up display and viewport window. As Polybius got further down the hall, Bob decided to follow. He had to inch past debris and short-circuiting wires and conduit, broken walls and small fires, and dead Yetis with destroyed robots, some of which were still twitching and sparking. He told himself, "Slow and steady wins the race."

\#

Polybius marched angrily down the hallway, but not in a hurry like his Yetis and robots that he sent ahead. He walked with a reasoned pace and grew angrier as he saw the carnage in front of him and on the sides as he marched down the halls. "They'll pay for this," he muttered. "It's time to release Sinistar, and they won't be able to stop him. Mom will finally be proud of me." He heard gunfire and explosions ahead and knew he would eventually get into the melee. He looked forward to it. These kids had given him the essence he needed to power the castle, to give him more power, and to power up his cosmic horror robot, Sinistar. There was no stopping him now, and he would not have some kids ruin this moment for him. He rounded the corner and only saw a glimpse of the praying mantis entering a room. He stopped and watched. "That was my creation, but it wasn't strong enough. I'll defeat it easily." He heard screams and gunfire, and after a minute, it came out and then looked like it was running to attack more of his troops down the hall. But then it stopped and lowered its talons. It stood there, unknowing that it was being watched, and he wasn't going to let this moment pass by. This was war, after all. He heard Mikey say, "Everything is going to be all right now!" He then said out loud, "Yes, everything is going to be all right." He powered up his electric charge and sent the currents from his fingertips directly at the giant silver mantis. It landed a deadly blow and tossed it up against a wall, which seemed to destroy it. It looked dead. He headed towards the others there.

Mikey yelled, "NOOOO! You monster! You'll pay for that!" He started to attack Polybius, but the snow king ducked out of the way and the scorpion's tail attack missed completely. The battle continued down the hall while Kristin ran to the Mantis robot to see if Layla was ok. She told Abercrombie to come with her. He forced the door open on her robot, and she was in there unconscious. They got her out while Mikey and Polybius fought, which was a good distraction. She was barely breathing, but she was still alive. They then pulled her into a room and found a hole in the next wall, and into the next, so they could make their way past the battle by going through the broken walls. Mikey wasn't fairing too well against Polybius, who was really just toying with him. Polybius often just brushed his attacks aside and mocked him, saying, "Is that all you have got? C'mon, give me a fight. You owe me that much for what you've done."

Mikey was frustrated and only landed a few blows, which seemed to get Polybius more angry and stronger. He called out, "Polybius, you have to let us all go. Why are you doing this? We thought you were good." Even Glitch got into the battle and rolled to hit Polybius several times in his silver pill bug robot, but Polybius smacked him away like a bug. He was a bug. He ping-ponged off the walls and around the corner every time he hit like he was in a pinball machine.

"You don't understand. This has to happen; this is my kingdom, my world, and the only place where I feel happy. I hate the regular world, and I hate the band. My mom told me that your band killed my dad, so now it's my turn to get revenge." Polybius bludgeoned Mikey's scorpion several times, and Mikey cried out in pain. Presley heard him, leapt from Kristin's arms, and ran back toward the fighting. Kristin called out, "No, Presley! Get back here, you crazy puppy!" While Polybius hammered on Mikey's scorpion, Presley ran and jumped up on some downed robots and launched onto Polybius's left shoulder. He crunched down on the snow king's antler and swung from it as Polybius tried to look at what was on him. Polybius swung violently and threw Presley off, but not without harm. Presley's bite had broken off a good piece of the snow king's antler in his mouth. He landed fairly gracefully and ran off towards Kristin with his trophy in his mouth.

Mikey said, "Leave my dog alone, you jerk!" He then looked around the scorpion cockpit for a weapon button but only saw a button above his head that said 'Black body,' which he didn't think meant much. He got shocked again by Polybius, which stalled his robot for a few seconds and shorted out his heads up display briefly. He decided to run away and take the fight away from wherever everyone was. Maybe he could lead Polybius away from everyone.

Polybius yelled, "You cannot escape!" Then he quoted Khan from *Star Trek: The Wrath of Khan*, "I'll chase you 'round the moons of Nibia and 'round the Antares Maelstrom and 'round perdition's flames before I give you up!"

Mikey said to himself, "Great, he's also a Trekkie. Figures." He noticed Polybius was starting to glow blue again, which meant he was powering up for another electricity strike. If he got a blast like Layla took, he was doomed. He thought about Luke Skywalker, when he turned off his navigating computer when attacking the Death Star in Star Wars, he thought maybe he should trust in the force as well. Would that work here in this realm? Then a voice said, "Use the button, kid." He looked around and saw the red lion approaching quickly. He closed his eyes and pushed the Black Body button. The Scorpion stopped and began to vibrate. A computer voice said to him, "Black body initiated. Thermal equilibrium has been reached. Emissivity is at one." Mikey noticed the silver panels on the scorpion turning black and dull, completely different from the shiny silver they were before.

He thought, "What will this do?"

Polybius said, "Now, young Skywalker. You will die." He then unleashed a mighty bolt of blue lightning from his fingertips, similar to Emperor Palpatine from *Return of the Jedi*. It hit Mikey's scorpion directly, and it did nothing but absorb the power! In fact, the power gauge Mikey had seen dwindling was getting charged up. This was actually helping! Mikey turned on his Walkman and played *Back in Black* by AC/DC.

Polybius looked stunned and angry. "That isn't fair."

"I'll show you fair," said Faraone's Red lion, who pounced down on top of Polybius. But the snow king shocked his robot away and caused great damage to it. Faraone told Mikey, "Attack him, he can't hurt you now."

Mikey hit him several times, and Polybius tried to shock him again, but it caused no damage. It was absorbed instantly allowing Mikey to get more hits in. Polybius screamed, "Turn that music off!" Mikey smiled, finally coming at Polybius and grabbing his hands with both pinchers. He then lifted Polybius up in the air and said, "This is for Layla, you scumbag." Polybius was spewing electricity everywhere, taking out walls and electrocutting the floor. Then Mikey plunged the spike from his tail into Polybius's chest. A giant explosion of light and sparks came from the blow and caused Mikey to drop him to the floor. His smoking body looked limp and unconscious.

The form of Polybius started to static and glitch, and all that lay there when it stopped short-circuiting was the form of a young man around the age of eighteen with an Edgar hair-cut and large glasses, wearing jeans and a brown t-shirt that was too small for him with white converse high-top sneakers.

Mikey looked down and squinted. Then he said, "Moody? Jim Moody? How in the world?" He was once again bewildered and couldn't believe his eyes. This was Jim Moody, Mrs. White's adopted son whose father, Bill, had passed away. Jim decided not to use either Gross or White as his last name and instead kept the original last name that was given to him by his birth father, whom he had never met. Now, it was starting to make sense to Mikey. Was this all because of a band accident? Sheesh. He thought he must be in some sort of nightmare.

Red one landed, and Faraone told Mikey, "We have to find the rest of the kids. I think they might be on some of the higher floors because I don't see anything down here where they could be kept. I'll scope it out and meet you all up there. Tell the others. Good job, kid." He leapt away.

Bob's caterpillar inched up, and Bob said, "Ok, let me at 'em. Where's the fight? What did I miss?" He then looked down at Jim on the ground. "Moody? That kid played saxophone, right? Where did he come from? I thought he had graduated already."

Mikey said, "He was the snow king pop."

"Whaaaa? Wow. I guess that makes sense now. His mom is the MCP. She was controlling him. He's not the boss. She is. Poor, disillusioned kid. Where's Faraone and the others?"

Glitch came barreling around the corner as a rolled-up pill bug, then stopped and unfurled to be by their side.

"Faraone went to look for the other kids on the upper floors, and I think Kristin, Presley, and Abercrombie took off that way down the hallway. OMG, LAYLA! Dad, he killed Layla!" Mikey's scorpion went over to the downed mantis robot smoldering with small fires on it in sparse places. He then saw the hatch was open at the top. Could it be? Could she have survived? "Dad, could she have gotten out of there? She had to have! I feel it. She has to be alive. Maybe the others helped her. We have to find her dad. We have to!"

"You got it, kid. I bet you're right. Let's go find the others."

#

White gazed into her Palantir in frustration. She tried looking at different angles, and her anger intensified. "Where is he?!" She paced the room with her hands behind her back. She stopped and thought. "I'm going to have to rectify this myself. That vacuous dolt has probably caused more havoc and disarray. We cannot waste any more time with him. It's time to launch and get my revenge." She floated a few spell books from the library of novels on the wall- they magically floated through the air and onto the table before her. She swished her hand, and they opened up where she wanted them to. "I'm going to have to use almost all of the essence to pull this off, but no matter. I'll have no more use of that kingdom after this." She looked into the books and grinned. "Yes, this will do nicely." She then went to a computer setup in the corner with a screensaver of the Sinistar logo bouncing around slowly on the screen. As soon as the mouse was moved, she put in her password and started typing on the keyboard frantically. After some enter commands, she reached for a gaming headset that was hanging on a small hook on the all. She put it on and then started typing some more. "Ok, now to connect to the dream zone…" She clicked on the computer and music by Prokofiev started playing. It was *Romeo and Juliet, No 13 Dance of the Knights*. Her eyes turned solid red, and code started swirling on the computer screen. She began twitching, and her face showed physical pain. The lights in the room flickered and then dimmed. Only the Palantir, her glowing red eyes and the computer screen emitted any light. The symbols and code on the computer screen seemed to dance with the music as they swirled around in a vortex. Then they came out from the computer and engulfed White, circling her like a swarm of bees. She was now connected, and her consciousness was in another realm. She spoke, "Snow King, what are you doing, you fool? Answer me, or there will be consequences."

#

Jim awoke slowly. He was lying face down on the ground and no longer had his protective Polybius code and powers, but he was alive. He slumped up slowly and was still quite dizzy. He felt like he had been smashed with a giant hammer, and all of his muscles were sore, and joints were aching. What had happened? He was supposed to be invulnerable. Nobody had been able to stop him before, nor had his lighting strike power. How did he lose so easily? His mom was going to be very angry at him. He was worried about that the most because her temper and mood changed so much since her husband passed away. She was just angry constantly.

More explosions could be heard in the distance, and the ground shook a little at each blast. Jim noticed the water nearby in a moat-like trench ripple and slosh as the blasts occurred. It wasn't water-it was really distilled water and biocide, which was added to help protect the walls from corrosion and prevent bacterial growth. He was good at building computer systems and had single-handedly figured out how to assemble this entire complex. He designed how it could power his Yeti army, create an energy source for the castle, and sustain the Polybius suit. It's how he became the leader here in this realm. He was banished here by his mother, who felt he was worthless and that maybe being here would 'grow him up,' as she stated. He was also truly hurt, especially after the death of his father. Didn't she realize that it really affected him more than she knew? He needed to mourn as well. He shut down and became quiet and introverted, and he just didn't feel like talking to people after his father's funeral. He needed that time to mourn and figure things out, but his mom wouldn't let him.

"Get off that computer and find a job. Stop mopping about, get off your butt, and go do something, Jim, or I'm going to do something, and you'll be sorry." She was always angry like that, but she held to her word, and he woke up here one day. Instructions then came to him from the computer he had with him. Still, he eventually gathered equipment and took advantage of the natural resources and rare earth minerals he found, and he built a better computer system. He discovered that magic in this realm could enhance things, so he used that to his advantage and figured out how to build things that seemed alive but were really local resources and computer code meshed together. The Yetis were the best example. He remembered them from his childhood, and because he was afraid of them, he thought the villagers would be as well. It's how he finally had the castle built- by scaring the local villagers into working or else! He also adopted the Yeti costume and figured out how to power it. He stumbled upon the discovery of essence when he was trying to extract electricity from some rare earth minerals, and a villager slipped and fell into the experiment pod. It killed the villager and left him as nothing but a skin husk. Because the extraction system also used both magic and computer code, it took the life force from the man and stored it instead. Upon investigating this odd gaseous liquid, he discovered that it could be used for combustion and conductivity. It also magically transferred a person's amygdala neural structure as a vaporized toxin that attacked another person's prefrontal cortex in their brain. It caused them to experience a bout of debilitating anxiety and then drew on the Hippocampus (the brain's home for memories) to make the person relive their worst nightmares. This sometimes triggered the Vagus nerve, which sometimes shut the person down completely, and they died. The accidental side effect was that it could also draw out the four neurochemicals of happiness instead: Dopamine, Serotonin, Oxytocin, and Endorphins. These feel-good essence chemicals were stored away because Jim didn't know how to dispose of them, and the last thing he wanted as a tyrannical ruler was a happy populace. Those chemicals were yellow in color and were building up quite a pile of canisters in the lower castle hallways and sewer areas. Waste management wasn't his strong point, so they were just placed down there and ignored.

Jim coughed and then rose to his feet, observing his torn clothing and burned scorch marks. He thought his eyebrows were singed off, too, as was the hair on his arms and legs. He straightened his large brown frame glasses, turned around, and began to limp back from where he came- the throne room. He needed his powers again.

#

Kristin held Layla's head as she lay on the floor and gave her some water to sip. She was awake now and starting to be more coherent. "What happened?" She asked.

Kristin said, "Well, Polybius shot you with a serious blast of lightning, and your mantis robot got blown up pretty bad with you in it. We got there just in time and got you out before more fire broke out. We snuck you out through the holes in the wall. How are you feeling now?"

"Like I've been crushed under an avalanche of snow, I suppose." She looked around a little. "Where are the others? Where's Mikey?" Presley heard her say Mikey, and he proudly jumped up on her, waging his tail and still brandishing the horn in his mouth.

"What is that boy?" She took it gently from his mouth and examined it from all sides. "Odd, this is part of Polybius, but it didn't de-rez when it broke off of him. We may be able to use that knowledge and this horn piece later." She gave it back to Presley. "Don't lose this boy, ok?" Presley took it happily and marched off proudly with his trophy in his mouth.

"Do you think that is a good idea?" Asked Kristin.

"It will be ok. I don't think he will lose it. He seems very smart."

Layla said, "I don't hear much going on out there now. Do you think we won?"

"I think because we got split up, the battle got bifurcated in different directions," said Kristin. "Mikey and the others may still need help, but we are powerless to help, really. I mean, what can we do?" Layla saw a computer terminal in the room.

"Girl, we can do plenty!" She said, smiling. She got up and went over to the terminal and powered it up. "That's more like it," she said, still grinning. "Watch me work." She started typing away and saw that the security was alerted and was ordered to head to this level. Another thing she noticed was that she had access to seal some doorways, so as Yeti guards marched that way, Layla typed some commands, and the doors shut in front of them. She laughed. Sentry robots began to power up, and she shut them down. "That should help our guys out." She then caught something on the top of the screen in a floating box. It had a countdown of ten minutes and counting down. The initials only said HWLA, and she knew what that stood for. She looked at Kristin and said, "We have to find the others and get out of here fast. I helped write the code for this thing. The countdown to Sinistar has begun. We only have ten minutes until he will live again." She pointed to each initial individually as she said he would live again.

Kristin asked, "What is Sinistar?"

Layla said, "It's a giant anthropomorphic spacecraft with a huge red and silver evil face with devil-like horns, and he has been in construction for quite some time now. I knew Polybius wanted to use it to transport an army to another place, but why? I don't know. I have heard rumors that it is in the giant dome, and it uses the essence that Polybius drains from people to power it up. I think I can get a camera feed on it…" She clicked more on the keyboard and some video screens appeared in floating windows. They saw in one window a battle area and her smoldering mantis robot. "Nobody is there now." Another window showed a wide shot of a hallway with multiple balconies on the side and large receptors on the floor. A giant red and white robotic lion was scaling it and leaping to the other levels back and forth like a parkour expert.

"That's a good guy, right?" asked Kristin.

"Yes, a very good guy." Said Layla. "I am glad he's on our side."

Another window was dark, so Layla typed some more, and the window lit up. She turned the lights on. They saw children in cages, dirty and sad. They were sitting around and looked weak. Another feed showed Yeti guards floating pods down a hallway towards the throne room. They could just make out that there were children in each pod. "What is he up to?"

"I think he is taking all of the kids into the throne room, probably to drain them all."

Layla found a video of the throne room and saw the snow king sitting on the throne and getting power from the cables coming from the ceiling and the floor. His throne was glowing, and so was he. This wasn't Jim Moody any longer. The Snow King was coming back.

CHAPTER EIGHTEEN: We can be Heros, just for one day

The snow king had powered up fully once again and was having the band kids brought into the throne room and hooked up to the cables. The Yetis were getting them all from a holding cell, putting them in their pods, and lining them up in the throne room. Polybius hadn't needed their life essence yet, since he had plenty to draw from already, but he was going to drain them before they left in Sinistar, so this was just pre-launch preparation. He also wanted to do this because he was angry and wanted revenge for being decimated by Mikey's scorpion robot.

"Let's see how you like it when I kill all of your friends and take their life essence for myself, Gross. I will not succumb to you fools, and I will make my mom happy again, you'll see. You will all see."

#

Layla watched the Snow King get off the throne and wander the room, giving orders and pointing. The Yetis were lining the pods up in a circle formation around the throne and connecting them to cables on the floor. There were approximately 50 pod locations, but only about half of the children were brought in. "There's still time," said Layla excitedly.

Kristin said, "Time for what?"

"To stop him and save the kids," Layla said. "I have an idea-an old hacker trick. If it works."

"You go, girl," said Kristin, smiling. "Where are the others?"

They then saw the scorpion and the other robots, minus the caterpillar lagging way behind, going up a ramp and into a large service elevator. "There. They're going up to the upper floors. I guess Polybius let them go? Weird."

"We need to tell them what he is doing." Said Kristin.

"I have to stay here and do this programming," said Layla, "You'll have to go warn them. Level 7, red zone." She pulled up a map that showed a path to the location. "Got it?"

"Got it," said Kristin. She headed out with Presley in her arms and Abercrombie following. "We'll warn them. Good luck with what you're doing, Layla. Nice meeting you, by the way. You're pretty rad. I hope we meet again."

"Thanks! Likewise, Kristin. Hey, before you go. Um, about Mikey. Are you two a thing?"

Kristin snorted, "No way. He's a dork." She saw Layla's expression change. "Um, I mean, he's an ok guy, I suppose, but no, we're not interested in each other, if that's what you mean." Abercrombie moved his head back and forth like he was watching a tennis tournament as each girl spoke.

Layla said, "Ok, thanks. I think I actually kind of like him. He makes me laugh."

"Yeah, he can be pretty silly, I suppose. Well, I wish you two the best! Cheers!" Kristin looked out the door cautiously and then waved goodbye. Abercrombie shook his head and followed her, then said, "Later on, girl. Make us all proud, will ya? Keep up the good work, Layla. See youse around. I'm glad you're not dead."

Layla said, "Me too. Hey, thanks for rescuing me. I owe you."

"Naw, you just do you. You would have done the same for me, right?"

"Right, I would have," said Layla. Abercrombie disappeared around the doorway.

Kristin talked to herself, trying to remember the map in her head. Some of the areas she had to go to were destroyed, so she improvised and had to climb over and through debris all while still staying out of sight from sentry robots and Yeti guards. She made good progress and actually saw Bob's caterpillar robot getting on the service elevator. She snuck on, too. Up they went, and she ran out way ahead of the caterpillar, who didn't even realize she was there with him. It was a frustratingly slow robot. She made it to the terrace where the others were gathered and about to split up.

"Wait!" She called out and put Presley down.

They all looked at her and stopped going anywhere. "Kristin," said Mikey on the speaker. "Where's Layla?" asked Mikey.

"She's ok. She is below trying to do something to help stop the snow king, or the countdown, I don't really know. She said that she is doing something that will help."

"Well, we're trying to help too. We need to find the rest of the children," exclaimed Mikey from the speakers.

Kristin said, "They're not here. We saw them all being loaded into the throne room. Polybius has been powered up again, and he is super angry."

The elevator door pinged and opened to reveal a giant silver centipede crawling its way out.

Faraone in the Red Lion said, "We need to get down there and stop him. We need a quick way down, any ideas?" They all looked over the high balcony, and then Mikey had an idea.

"Pop, what happens when a caterpillar cocoons itself?"

The speaker fumbled on with a little feedback and clicks, then Bob said," It turns into a chrysalis, son, then it eventually transforms into a butterfly."

Mikey asked, "Do you have a button in there that states a power?"

"Um, there's just an Emergency ONLY button, but that's it," said Bob.

Both Mikey and Faraone, in unison, yelled, "PUSH IT!" This was an emergency, and they both thought the same thing.

They all heard a low, resonant hum began to emanate from within the metallic behemoth. The ground trembled slightly, and the air grew thick with anticipation. Suddenly, the caterpillar's segments shifted and rotated, releasing a symphony of mechanical clicks and whirs. The transformation had begun.

The caterpillar's head, a formidable array of sensors and cameras, retracted slightly before rising, revealing a hidden compartment. From this compartment, a pair of gleaming, articulated wings unfolded with fluid grace, each wing composed of thousands of interlocking semi-transparent metal panels that caught the light in a dazzling display. The wings stretched wide, their span casting a shadow over the surrounding area.

As the wings unfurled, the caterpillar's body began to elongate and straighten. The segments, once tightly interlocked, now separated and expanded, revealing a complex network of circuitry and hydraulics. The caterpillar's legs, previously stubby and utilitarian, elongated and reconfigured into sleek, powerful limbs. The transformation was both awe-inspiring and terrifying.

With a final, thunderous clang, the transformation was complete. The giant metallic butterfly robot stood tall- its wings poised for flight. Its eyes, now glowing with an ethereal blue light, scanned the distance below with a sense of purpose. The once banal caterpillar had metamorphosed into a majestic and formidable guardian of the skies.

Mikey said, "Now that is clutch!"

In a dramatic flourish, the butterfly robot's wings beat once, twice, and then it lifted off the ground with a powerful gust of wind. The team below watched in stunned silence as the mechanical marvel ascended first into the air, then plunged straight down towards the lower level.

Mikey yelled, "Go get 'em, Pop!"

Faraone said, "We all need to get down there. Head for the elevator. Be ready to fight when we get there."

Bob and his robot soared and fluttered until it landed below. The doorway opened for Bob, and he got out. He glanced up from where he had come from, "Wow. Pretty cool."

He then started to jog towards the throne room. He was worried about the children even more and didn't want anything else to happen to them. He was actually pretty mad about this whole experience and felt the snow king should pay dearly for his misdeeds.

He saw two Yeti guards pushing a levitating child pod down the hallway towards the giant throne room. This was a chance to stop this child from getting harmed or worse. Bob started running at the Yetis, who immediately noticed him and turned to face him. Bob kept running while pointing up above the Yetis' heads and cried out, "Lookout! They're coming from the skies," which made the Yetis look up behind them. Then Bob leaped onto the floating child pod head first and straddled it as it careened into the doorway of the throne room. It started spinning as it bobbed and soared into the great room towards the other pods surrounding the snow king's throne. It slowed as it bumped into several of the pods and halted right at the feet of the snow king, who stood there menacingly and looking down at Bob.

Bob looked up at the snow king and grinned really large. "Um, stop what you're doing, Snow King." He got off the pod clumsily, almost falling. "By the powers vested in me as a Region 12 District 5A band director in the state of Texas, city of El Paso, I hereby place you under citizen's arrest for kidnapping and torture. Will you come willingly, or do we have to do this the hard way?"

Polybius slowly put his hand and one hoof out in front of him to feign arrest, then said, "You've got me gross. So, what's next, hmm? How do you expect to take me out of here, and how do you think we are going to go to your home dimension?" He paused while Bob pondered. "Well? I think I have a better idea, a much better idea." He swiftly pulled his hands back and turned quickly to dismiss Bob. He stepped up on a few of the steps towards the throne chair. "How about you surrender and then I will drain every last ounce of lifeforce from you and these pathetic children. Then I will have all the power I need to launch Sinistar, who will go to your dimension and then take revenge on your pathetic city of El Paso." He grinned evilly, "I think he might even be hungry enough to eat your soldiers at Fort Bliss Army base, and then I think he might head to the Pentagon- and then maybe the White House. What do you think of that plan instead?"

A giant hole in the far wall exploded open, followed by a blue plasma beam that hit the opposite wall and then stopped. A giant red lion robot leapt in and landed with a roar that echoed throughout the chamber. The speaker from it clearly said, "I think that plan sucks. I'm going to go with Bob's option one, snow jerk."

Bob said with a smile, "Faraone! Just in time."

Before he could turn to look at the robot clearly, Polybius grabbed Bob by the throat and pulled him into himself closely. "Stay back. I'm warning you."

Outside of the throne room, the others caught up and hadn't seen all of the commotion, but Mikey and Glitch arrived carrying Kristin (holding Presley) while Abercrombie rode inside his pill bug with Glitch. They stopped and weren't sure if they could go in or not.

Mikey decided to exit his scorpion once he saw his Dad being held and entered the room. "Hey! Let go of my pop!"

"The little gross one has gotten quite brave, "Polybius joked.

Faraone's robot started walking sideways along the wall but toward the snow king.

"Whoa there, kitty cat," said Polybius, who then squeezed Bob's throat harder and turned him in between the Red-one lion robot and himself. "Let's not do anything rash. I would hate to just end him here when he still has such delicious essence left in him. He's really no good to me dead, but I will make an exception."

Faraone stopped moving.

Mikey said, "Stop! You're hurting him. Jim. Yes, I know it's you, Jim. Please stop this madness. Why are you doing this? Just let us all go."

"You know what?" Asked Polybius to Mikey. "You can help me here, and maybe I will make this easier on you all."

Mikey's heart leapt, and he gasped a little because he saw Layla sneaking into the back of the room behind the throne through a panel.

"What is that?" asked Polybius.

"Nothing, "said Mikey. "I am just a bit overwhelmed right now, and I have to catch my breath."

Layla put her finger to her mouth to tell Mikey to shush about her. She crept closer to the throne and looked at the cables running to it.

Mikey tried to stall. "Ok, what do you need me to do? Just don't hurt my dad."

"That's more like it. I am a reasonable man. I just want what is owed to me, and I want to get out of here and go back home, just like you all do. Is that so wrong? We all want the same thing, so help me make that happen."

"What do you want me to do?" asked Mikey.

Layla has gotten to the back of the throne and can't be seen now.

"I want you to first get these cables," he motioned to the floor, and two panels opened up magically. Two tentacle-like cables snaked out of them into the air, and then they lay down calmly on the floor. "Grab those and hook them to that red lion robot's back legs." He pointed at Faraone's lion.

Mikey did as he said. He dragged them over to the robot, and they each grabbed and locked onto the back legs.

Faraone in the robot said, "Kid, what are you doing? Don't listen to him."

"I have to mister Faraone. Trust me, it will be ok."

"Now," belted out Polybius, "here are some for you and your dad." He waved his hand again over the floor, and two more sets writhed from the ground panels, and they lay dormant at Mikey's feet. "Put them on, now." Ordered Polybius.

"Wait. How do we know this won't kill us, and you'll just take off without us?"

"You don't, but I will tell you this. These leads are last in the chain, so if I get the power I need before the draining reaches you all, then I will stop it, and you all will live." He motioned above the throne, and a large display magically appeared with a meter that went from zero to HWLA with the level being already halfway full. "Here, you can watch and see how close you come to dying."

The snow king released Bob once Mikey's tentacles connected to his legs. "Now go take your medicine, Gross," Polybius said to Bob sarcastically.

Bob walked to the tentacles meant for him and connected them to his legs as he looked to Faraone and then at Mikey, who nodded yes in an imperceptibly small way, then winked.

Layla snuck away from the throne and back to the panel, where she went in and replaced the grate.

Bob said, "Jim, I know your mom is behind this all. You are just an unsuspecting pawn in this game. You still have time to redeem yourself. If you want to go back, help us, don't hurt us."

"It's too late for me. If I don't do this, my mom will never love me. She will hate me forever. She's the only family I have left. I have to do this."

The snow king marched up to his throne and sat down after unfurling his cape dramatically.

He looked at them all and said coldly, "Are we ready to begin?" He pressed his hand to an indented hand print that was glowing embedded on the throne's arm.

Mikey yelled at Bob when the lights started to dim, "OllowFay ymay eadlay," he said in Pig Latin. Then Mikey pretended to be in pain.

Outside of the castle, located in the heart of the frosted peaks, the wind started to howl like a mournful spirit. Inside stood the imposing throne of the snow king, which started to glow blue. The ancient palace, carved from the very essence of winter, shimmered outside under the moon's pale light. Its crystalline walls echoed with the ominous silence that precedes a storm.

Bound by the enchanted cables, our heroes lay helpless at the feet of the towering Yeti, the snow king. His fur, as white as the driven snow, glistened with an otherworldly sheen, and his one eye burned with a cold, malevolent fire. The air crackled with the raw power that emanated from his colossal form.

With a guttural roar reverberating through the icy caverns, the snow king raised his massive arms, invoking the ancient magic that would siphon the life force from his captives. The throne, an artifact of dark sorcery, began to pulse with the sinister blue light, drawing the energy from the heroes and the children through the cables.

But fate, it seemed, had other plans. Unbeknownst to the snow king, the throne's enchantment had been tampered with by the cunning hands of Layla. As the energy transfer commenced, the throne's glow shifted from blue to a blinding yellow, reversing the power flow.

The snow king's triumphant snarl twisted into a mask of horror as he felt his own strength being leeched away. His once formidable frame began to wither and short circuit. The mighty roar turned into a pained gasp. The throne, now a conduit of retribution, drained the very essence of the snow king, feeding it back to the heroes.

Their eyes flickered open, vitality returning to their weary bodies. The cables that once ensnared them fell away like brittle twigs. They stood, rejuvenated, as the Snow King collapsed to his knees, his power reduced to a mere whisper of what it once was. Even Red-one had a full power charge, and as it was released, it let out an enormous roar worthy of a Voltron lion.

At that moment, the ice palace seemed to sigh in relief. The oppressive weight of the Snow King's tyranny lifted. Now free and empowered, the heroes knew the battle was far from over, but the tide had turned in their favor. The Snow King's reign of terror was at an end, and the dawn of a new era began to break over the frozen horizon.

Bob stood looking around at the children who were now exiting their pods and hugging each other with happiness. They were ok. He said, "Mikey, what happened?"

Mikey ran to his dad and hugged him. He looked up and said, "Layla and I pulled the ole' *Superman 2* Fortress of Solitude reversal trick!"

Bob said, "I see. What was supposed to go to him instead took it from him and went to us. Very clever."

Faraone said, 'Not bad kid. I would give you an A if I were still teaching."

Layla came around through the doorway this time and hugged Mikey and then actually kissed him on the lips! "Thank you, Mikey, thank you."

Mikey was now bewildered and in heaven. His first real kiss. "Wow, thank you."

Things were looking up for him, and he was delighted.

They hadn't noticed the snow king because of the celebration, and as their celebratory attention faltered, the entire castle began to shake and rumble.

Jim started to laugh, and his laughter grew louder and more maniacal. "It's too late, you fools. You tricked me, but more than enough essence was already collected to launch Sinistar. Haha, you lose again!" He collapsed to the floor smiling and weakly said, "If Sisnistar doesn't kill you all, you will have to deal with my mom. She will be your black annis." Then he passed out.

They all ran out of the throne room and found the windows in the castle to view the dome in the distance. The tension, disappointment, and excitement of what was happening were palpable. The Yeti scientists, engineers, and our heroes alike held their breath, witnessing the culmination of years of relentless effort and innovation.

As the launch sequence finished, the geodesic dome's panels retracted, revealing the night sky adorned with countless stars. Sinistar, towering and evilly majestic, began to rise, its powerful engines roaring to life. The ground trembled as the giant robot ascended, breaking free from the confines of Shen Yun and soaring into the vast expanse of space. The shaking ground revived Jim, and his laughter echoed throughout the hallways. Sinistar was now loose. In the distance, they could hear the words booming through space: "Beware, I live! I hunger!"

CHAPTER NINETEEN: The Symphony

The castle of the Snow King lay in ruins. Its icy spires shattered and scattered across the frozen landscape. The lift-off of Sinistar and the demise of the Snow King's powers left little essence to power the castle's structure, so it had partly collapsed. It was continually falling apart little by little. The Yeti soldiers had all retreated from the castle in exodus.

Bob stood watching with clenched fists. Beside him, his son Mikey, the heroic band director John Faraone, the ever-curious Layla, the talking penguin Abercrombie, the weather-controlling robotic snowman Glitch, and the loyal puppy Presley surveyed the aftermath of their battle. The magical backpack, a gift from an ancient Jin, hummed softly on Mikey's back, ready to produce whatever he needed. Presley jumped into Mikey's arms with a worried puppy look.

Their victory over the Snow King was short-lived. Sinistar was soaring higher into the darkening sky. He kept repeating, "I hunger…"

As the colossal Sinistar robot soared through the sky, its engines roaring and eyes glowing with a menacing red light, the air around it began to shimmer. The heroes watched in awe and fear as the fabric of reality itself seemed to ripple and tear.

High above, the clouds parted, revealing a swirling vortex of colors and light. This was the dream realm portal, a gateway between worlds, opening in response to the Sinistar's approach. The portal pulsed with an otherworldly energy, its edges crackling with electric arcs that danced across the sky.

Sinistar, drawn by an unseen force, altered its course and headed straight for the portal. As it neared, the vortex expanded, its colors intensifying and swirling faster. The robot's massive form was silhouetted against the vibrant backdrop, creating an awe-inspiring and terrifying scene. It screamed, "I am Sinistar!"

From the ground, Bob Gross and his team could feel the pull of the portal, a strange sensation that tugged at their very souls. Mikey clutched his magical backpack tightly while Layla's eyes widened as she realized the magnitude of what was happening.

"We have to stop it!" Bob shouted- his voice filled with determination. "If that thing reaches the dream realm portal, it will enter the real world and wreak havoc. It could destroy El Paso and the Earth!"

Layla ran back into the castle throne room and got behind the computer that was behind the throne. Her fingers flew over the portable hacking device that she had plugged into the computer attached to the throne. "I've managed to hack into its systems, but it's heavily encrypted. We need more time."

Abercrombie waddled forward- his beak set in a determined line. "We don't have time, princess. We need to use our powers now. We need a Hail Mary touchdown pass."

Mikey looked at his father, then at the magical backpack. "Dad, what if I use dream walking? I can enter the Sinistar's mind and shut it down from the inside."

Bob nodded. "It's risky, but it's our best shot. Everyone, gather around."

The group formed a circle, holding hands around Mikey as he lay down and tried to sleep himself into the dream realm. Haunting music emanated from the backpack and swirled around them, lifting their spirits and guiding them into deep concentration. One by one, they also fell into a dream state, their consciousnesses merging and drifting towards Mikey. Mikey entered the dream state and entered into Sinistar.

Inside the robot's mind, Mikey found himself in a vast, mechanical landscape. Gears and circuits stretched as far as the eye could see, and the air buzzed with electricity. At the center of it all stood the core of the Sinistar, a pulsating orb of red energy.

"You need to reach the core and shut it down," Layla said, her voice echoing in the dreamscape. "I am dropping the shield…now," and a barrier that was surrounding the orb dissolved.

Glitch raised his metallic head to the sky, summoning a storm of snow and ice to hinder Sinistar's path and slow it down. The robot's movements became sluggish, but it continued its relentless advance towards the portal. That did seem to help slow its movements for a few minutes. The Sinistar robot was getting out of his reach, though, so it got weaker and weaker.

Mikey's dream persona charged forward, his small form darting and jumping through the maze of machinery. His magical backpack stood ready to assist him with tools and gadgets to aid his journey, but Mikey instead reached in and produced his friend, the oboe. He assembled it and kept it in his hand. He told it, "Be ready, my old friend."

As he approached the core, a figure materialized before him. It was Mrs. White, her red eyes glowing with malevolent power. "You think you can stop me?" she sneered. "I control the Sinistar now. Your world will be mine. I also control the dream portal where the laws of physics hold no sway." She waved her hand, and Mikey lifted off the ground and was pushed back away from the pulsating red orb. He spun a few times and flipped but didn't release his oboe.

Sinistar reached the edge of the vortex, and the portal seemed to come alive, tendrils of light reaching out to envelop the robot. The heroes caught glimpses of the real world beyond, where shifting shapes and colors blurred together—a surreal landscape of jagged buildings, the rugged peaks of the Franklin Mountains, and distant monuments in El Paso. Each flash was like a brief window into reality, where familiar landmarks seemed to twist and flicker, distorted by the strange, otherworldly force surrounding them.

Mikey landed and then stepped forward, his oboe at the ready. "We won't let you destroy our home. Music has the power to heal, to unite, and to defeat evil."

He began to play a powerful, uplifting tune, the notes cutting through the dreamscape with an intensity that seemed to vibrate the very air around him. The music surged from his oboe, rich and stunningly beautiful yet tinged with a haunting undercurrent. Each note echoed, weaving a melody that stirred the soul. As the sound swirled through the surreal landscape, it shimmered with an almost tangible energy. Mrs. White grimaced, her face contorting as she covered her ears in pain, the haunting resonance too much for her to bear. The power of the music was undeniable—and he was determined to wield it.

Faraone called out, and Mikey heard him within the dreamscape, "We've got this kid. We can help from here. Play your solo as if your life depended on it." Farone asked Bob, "Hey, does that magic backpack have anything that will help us?"

Bob said to the backpack, "If you can produce something that will save us all, now is the time we could really use it." He reached in and pulled out a glowing conducting baton. The small inscription on the baton's hilt said, "When light is needed to defeat the darkness, there is only one way. Use music to win the day." He then handed it to Faraone like a knight shows a king his sword, hilt first.

Faraone took the baton, which continued to glow brightly in front of his face as he read the inscription. "Ok, I've been working on something just for such an occasion. You never know when an insane witch is going to launch a menacing flying robot into space to attack the Earth for world dominance, right?" He winked at Layla, who shrugged her shoulders to physically say I suppose. He then looked around and said, "Here goes something." He started to conduct in the air at a non-existent orchestra. It was a symphony he had composed. The sounds of musical instruments began to fill the air from all parts of the castle chambers. The piece began slow and mysterious, then increased with an ostinato and more brass. Soon, an entire hundred-and-fifty-piece orchestra and full choir playing and singing could be heard. The others joined in singing with their voices, and the sounds of instruments throughout the chambers magically blended with them into harmony. The music grew louder and stronger until it reached the core of the Sinistar and harmonized with Mikey's playing. His symphony drew from famous composers and styles, yet were his own. There were heroic brass flourishes akin to John Williams, French horn runs, and counter melodies similar to James Horner, powerful, sweeping melodies from the string sections as good as John Barry, and musical motifs with electronic music mixed in and otherworldly noises created from musical machines and computers like Hans Zimmer would create. Such a powerful and growing tone-poem piece that took the listeners to different scenes and situations and slowly built to a climax movement.

Mrs. White screamed in rage as the energy orb began to flicker and dim. The gears and circuits around them started to slow, the entire structure shaking as the Sinistar's power waned. With one final, triumphant note, the core shattered, and the dreamscape dissolved.

Mrs. White's projection flickered violently, glitching as she raised her arms and lunged toward Mikey. Her form, unstable and distorted, passed straight through him, dissolving into a cloud of static. "I will build another, you fools!" she shrieked, her voice echoing in the air as her figure disintegrated into nothingness. Mikey stood frozen, heart pounding, trying to process what had just happened. His breath caught in his throat, but before he could react, his vision dimmed, and the world around him faded to black.

The portal pulsed one last time before collapsing in on itself, leaving only a faint shimmer in the sky as a reminder of the incredible event.

Mikey then awoke to find himself back in the castle ruins. His father grabbed and hugged him tightly. "You scared me, son."

Mikey said, "Bruh, anyone have a Monster drink or a Red Bull? I need an energy drink badly."

Sinistar, now lifeless, crashed back to the ground gloriously in the distance, its threat neutralized. Mikey, Bob, and his team had done it. They had saved the Earth.

The heroes looked towards the crash in stunned silence, the weight of their task pressing heavily upon them. They had stopped the Sinistar robot from entering the real world, but the battle was far from over.

They knew they had to find a way to close the portal for good and ensure that no other threats could pass through. Was it true that she might build another threat? They saw that the portal seemed to materialize and open from inside the Franklin mountains, where it would emerge onto the unsuspecting West Texas town of El Paso.

Bob turned to his team, determination in his eyes. "We need to find a way to seal that portal and protect our world. We also need to get the kids home. Let's get to work."

#

The old wizard felt a weight lifted off his chest. A relief and an ease that he hadn't felt in a long while. Something occurred, and he knew it was something good. He rushed over to his Palantir to eagerly bring it to life and gaze into its wonders. Eno Araf was the wizard's name, and he was the one who gave Mikey his musical powers and who had sent the Interdimensional Dream Team, or IDT, through the magical portal gate to fight Polybius. He whipped the small shawl off of the glowing ball of glass in a hurry and tossed it aside like he wouldn't have to use it again. He began to incantate and hum in a singing manner while he waved his hands on the top of the ball. He eventually waved them quickly like he was messing its hair up again, but it had no hair. He had done this before. An image came into his focus, and he gasped. "So, they did some good there. Very nice. Very nice, indeed. But the terror is not over yet. They must not lose sight of the witch and her evil plans. She still has total dominion over that dream realm, and I am sure she has put something in place to thwart them. I may be needed there instead, and my waking mortal counterpart may just have to trade places with me."

He placed his hand back on his beard once again and began to stroke it downward several times. "There is no choice. He is a formidable opponent to the evil that lies there, but my powers and knowledge may do the children more good now that Sinistar has been defeated. I must not tally." He dashed from the room and went into the band room once again. This time, he headed for the main band director's office. "I'll find what I need in here and make things right."

CHAPTER TWENTY: The Valley of Ice

The throne room was in disarray. It was cluttered with the floating pods the children were transported there in, and many columns and parts of the walls and ceiling were now littering the floor, broken symbols of a once great structure. Slowly, children were sorting their stuff and getting backpacks on, hopefully ready to go home now that the snow king was defeated and Sinistar had been stopped.

Layla was still at the computer console by the throne, and she saw something distressing. "Guys, there is something I am concerned about." They looked her way and came over to look. She pointed at the playback of what occurred when Sinistar almost breached the other 'real' dimension. "Look at the sky map. It's not one tear in space, but there is another. See, that one he headed for was El Paso and the Franklin mountains, but what is that other one? There are two altogether."

Faraone put his hand on his mouth and chin and thought. He started stroking his chin as if it was a beard. He then said, "Ok, it looks like White had a plan B. If Sinistar had missed one portal, he could have gone through the other one. Now the question is, where does that one come out? We're going to have to stop both of them somehow."

Mikey stared at the screen, then said, "This is too salty for me, Bruh. I thought this was over." He motioned to Presley, who jumped up in his arms happily. "Little dude, what are we gonna do now?"

Bob said, "The first thing we need to do is find a way to get these innocent band kids home. Then, we can deal with the witch and her plans. Mikey, you'll be going with them."

Mikey said, "Pop, I can't leave you here, besides I'm not really here, remember? I am dream-walking. I'm safe somewhere back at home."

Faraone said, "He's right. There are a few ways to enter the dream realm, and dream walking is a rare but great way to get here. The second way is to actually be transported here like you all did to get here."

Mikey said, "What's the third way?"

Faraone said. "To be switched with an entity here. They go to the real world, and you get to come here. It's a universe and physics thing…no two identical fermions can occupy the same quantum state simultaneously."

Mikey made a harsh face and said, "Wha? Dude, sorry, not sorry, but what does that mean in English?"

Faraone smiled. "It means that two identical things cannot be in the same place at the same time. It's called the Pauli Exclusion Principle in physics. Stay in school, don't do drugs."

Mikey said, "Got it. So, how did you get here?"

Faraone said as he turned away, "The third way."

Mikey said, "What was that, bro? You turned, and we couldn't hear that."

Faraone turned around and faced them all. "I said the third way, OK? I was replaced in the real world. I know because he was watching over me when I woke up, and then he disappeared."

Mikey said, "How do you know that he replaced you?"

"Because he was a personification of what I wanted to be in my dreams, and he sort of looks like me. It kind of freaked me out, to be honest. I've been stuck here since."

Bob said, "We thought you had taken a far-away teaching job somewhere else."

"Nope. I was here trying to find a way back. Sorry for the misinformation," said Faraone. I did have a gig teaching band up in Alpine for a little while, but I missed Kinish Tech and wanted to come back- then this happened."

"Must feel nice, you know, to be free again," said Mikey.

Faraone smiled kindly down at him, and before he could say anything, a look of horror flashed over his face. He began to dissolve into magical sparkling dust. He was gone.

They were all stunned and not sure what happened. Bob said, "What's going on?" He looked around, and the children, who were finally free and speaking to each other, also started to disappear into a cloud of magic dust. The earlier warmth and mood of their victory began to shift. One by one, the band kids started to vanish into the same shimmering, magical dust. Panic set in as the remaining kids realized what was happening. Their joyous celebration turned into a desperate attempt to hold onto each other, to stay grounded in the new reality they fought so hard to reclaim.

The room, once filled with triumphant music and cheering, now echoed with fear and confusion. The remaining band members huddled together; their eyes wide with terror. They didn't know why this was happening or how to stop it. Each disappearance left a haunting silence, a reminder of their fragile existence in this magical, unpredictable dream realm. The once-victorious throne room now felt like a trap, its technological beauty masking the unknown dangers that lurked within. Soon, all of the children had vanished, just like Faraone.

The heroes stood in stunned silence, their earlier sense of triumph quickly dissipating. Confusion clouded their faces as they exchanged glances, each silently wondering the same thing: What happened to Faraone and the children? Where had they gone? The tension in the room thickened as the computer console where Layla had been stationed flickered erratically. The screen scrambled into static, then slowly reformed, revealing the ominous presence of the MCP. Its glowing digital eyes locked onto them as its voice reverberated through the space, resonating from every direction.

"Fools," the MCP intoned, its voice cold and mechanical, "You hastened to celebrate an empty victory. Don't you realize that I control this realm? I should have de-rez'd all of you, but there is no jubilation in that. I want to see you all suffer for what you've done. You left me no choice but to strand the children here in this dream realm. That will distract you long enough so that I can launch my other Sinistar! Do you really think I put my trust in my loser kid? He is just as gullible as his father was, but no matter. I will persevere, and Sinistar will erupt from the Mouth to Hell while still accomplishing my goal. Try to stop me, please. You've been a bother but not a challenge. Let's see how you do now." The MCP then began to laugh, a sinister laugh that echoed throughout the castle, and then the MCP glitched off the screen as if nothing had happened.

They all looked at each other, and Mikey said, "That's just great. Game over, man!" A quote taken from the *Aliens* movie. "She is not a nice lady."

Bob said, "Ok, this is rough. But let's figure this out and find where the kids and Faraone went. Stranding them here? Where?"

Mikey's backpack started to speak, to everyone's surprise. "You must not dwell on who is naughty or nice. The children have been sent to the Valley of Ice."

Bob took out his pipe and placed it in his mouth, holding it there with his hand. It always helped him think. He said, "It's not lit, ok?" Looking sternly at Mikey. "Why did the backpack tell us that? It's never really spoken before."

The backpack said, "It is I, Eno Araf. Wizard Imperium at your service, my gross man. I am speaking through this enchanted bag. I have powers here that will prove helpful, but alas, your hero and my counterpart, John Faraone, has been sent home to the real world. We cannot exist in the same space. You will have to rely on my help now, but because I come from this realm, trust that my powers will serve you well. We have two tasks at hand. Some will have to rescue the children, and some will have to stop that evil robot. I can help with both, but can only do one at a time. Split into two groups. One group meet me on the rooftop, and the rest exit the front door to begin your mission. You decide. Use your heart and your head. Do not tally. We must go with haste! The fate of your world depends on it." The backpack stopped speaking and was inanimate once again.

Abercrombie the penguin waddled up with a swagger, his Bostonian accent cutting through the cold air. "Alright, folks, listen up! We got ourselves a situation here. We gotta save those band kids before they turn into popsicles."

Layla, the sharp-witted hacker, adjusted her computer monitor and tapped away on the computer keyboard. "I've pinpointed the coordinates of the Valley of Ice. Who's going there, and who is going after the second Sinistar?"

Abercrombie said, "Yo, I used to live in the Valley of Ice. It's been a long time, and I don't want to go back if I am honest. The place is treacherous and no place for kiddos."

Mikey, clutching his magical backpack, looked at his father, Bob, who was fumbling with a map he had. "Dad, you take the left group with Eno Araf to the Valley. I'll go with Layla, Glitch, Presley, and Abercrombie to the rooftop."

Abercrombie said, "I heard that computer voice also speak something about the mouth to hell. I have heard that mentioned before. I think it's a crater somewhere. Maybe Layla can find that on her computer gizmo there?"

Layla said, "Let me do a search. Yes, here it is. It's a massive crater in Siberia known as the 'Mouth to Hell.' There is a dream realm version here in the void zone. And it seems to be rapidly swallowing the land around it. It seems to be connecting directly to El Paso. That crater is omitting a lot of instability and fluctuations. I can save the directions to it on my watch. It's not that far."

"Right," said Mikey. I stopped Sinistar before, and I'll do it again. I have Layla, Abercrombie, my magic backpack, and Presley. I'll be unstoppable!"

Bob said, "Whoa, kid. I think Kristin and I will need Presley on our mission to find the other kids since we don't have Abercrombie."

Abercrombie put his head down and said, "Sorry."

Bob continued, "We could use his sniffer to help find them once we get there. I saw the map on the computer. The Valley of Ice is a large area. Are you OK with that?"

Mikey was hesitant but agreed. "Sure, pop. I get it. He's a good puppy, and I know he really likes Kristin." He picked up Presley and gave him a big hug. "You be good and do what they say, OK? I'll see you shortly, little buddy." Presley wagged his tail and gave Mikey some puppy licks on his face. Then Mikey remembered something. He reached into the backpack and pulled out the drawings. He thumbed through them and pulled one out specifically. "Aha! Here it is. Check this out y'all." It was the drawing that his aunt had given to him in the real world. "This looked familiar. I noticed that these drawings my aunt gave me are all things that have happened or are going to happen. Is she just messing with me? Maybe she wants me to figure them out- like a game? Well, if I had more, we might know what is going to happen next. I wish it had shown me that there was a second Sinistar. Oh well. This drawing shows them in a frozen, geometric landscape – and they are not happy. You guys need to hurry."

The heroes all hugged each other and wished each other good luck, then went in different directions- towards the front exit and some to the rooftop.

Mikey, Layla, Abercrombie, and Glitch reached the rooftop of the castle. Eno Araf, the enigmatic wizard, materialized on the roof and told them to stand very still. He then summoned the giant parasitic draw bats with a wave of his hand. "Fear not, for the bats are swift and sure. We shall reach the Mouth to Hell crater in no time as long as you all hang on tightly."

Several giant bats came swooping around them from the wizard's magical calling. They still had electrical currents surging through them.

"Eno?" called Mikey. "Won't they electrocute us?"

"They will indeed. So, use the magic bag to help you. Hurry, I cannot hold them around much longer."

Mikey reached into the backpack and pulled out several grounding wristbands like the ones computer technicians use when they work on computers so they don't short the components out. He passed them out and helped Glitch put his on around his neck. "Hope these bands work, or this will be a very short adventure!"

Eno said, "When I draw them near, grab their talons, and they will grip your wrists."

Mikey nodded, trying to look confident. "Right, right. We'll fly on those giant bats. Just… don't look down."

Mikey said, "What about Glitch? He doesn't have arms?"

Eno waved his hand, and Glitch magically had snowman arms materialize. "Now he does young gross."

Glitch jumped up and down and clicked with joy, then proudly raised his new arms in the air, eager to use them but also in celebration.

As Mikey Layla, Abercrombie, and Glitch took to the skies, Abercrombie turned to Glitch, the robotic snowman. "Hey, Glitch, you ready to roll? We got an evil robot to stop."

Glitch's mechanical eyes glowed with determination. He clicked and popped happily.

The bats all grabbed them, and they lifted high into the air. Eno floated up with them until they were all airborne.

Eno said, "I have seen Layla's map and given the directions to the bats. They will take you there with zeal, so fear not and yoke together. Your problems will start once you get there, not sooner. Good luck, and I will see you when you arrive, or at least a vision of me. May your music always be crisp and clear, heroes." He then magically disappeared, leaving just magic dust floating behind.

Meanwhile, Bob, Presley, and Kristin reached the front door to the castle. It was still a blazing energy shield. Eno appeared outside and started trying to cast spells to turn it off, but it was pointless, and they all failed.

"Aye, there is some dark magic here. I am not sure how to get you out of there. Perhaps you go to the rooftop, and I will summon more bats to bring you down?"

Bob said, "Try saying FRIEND. It was in a movie I saw."

Kristin said, "Wait, only Polybius could open the doors, right? What about a piece of him, would that do?" She reached into her pocket and pulled out Presley's souvenir, which he had broken off of Polybius during the battle- his left horn. She then touched the biometric hand scanner with it, and lights scanned it up and down, and then the energy door turned off. A countdown above the doorway activated as before.

Proud of herself, she marched first through the doorway happily. Presley trotted behind her, followed by Bob. Eno was very impressed.

"Science is also considered by many cultures a form of magic as well. Kristin, I can tell that you are studied and versed in those skills. Good job, young witch."

#

Mikey and crew soared through the twilight sky, carried by the powerful wings of the giant parasitic draw bats. They gazed down upon a breathtaking dream world landscape. Below them stretched an expansive, otherworldly terrain, bathed in the soft, ethereal glow of bioluminescent flora.

The giant craters they were soaring towards were a marvel to behold, their edges lined with towering crystal formations that shimmered in a spectrum of colors, reflecting the ambient light. Their crater's depths were filled with a lush, verdant forest, where trees with iridescent leaves swayed gently in an unseen breeze. Streams of liquid light weaved through the forest, creating a network of glowing rivers that converged into a radiant lake at the crater's center.

Surrounding the craters, the land was dotted with floating islands, each one home to unique ecosystems and fantastical creatures. Some islands were covered in fields of luminescent flowers, while others hosted ancient ruins that hinted at a long-lost civilization. The sky above was a canvas of swirling nebulae and distant stars, casting a magical, ever-changing light over the entire scene.

As the giant bats descended, the heroes could see the intricate details of this dream world more clearly: the delicate patterns on the wings of fluttering insects, the soft hum of the glowing rivers, and the gentle rustle of the iridescent leaves. It was a place of

226

wonder and mystery, inviting them to explore their secrets and uncover the stories hidden within this enchanting landscape.

But one crater was not like the rest. It even looked evil. As our heroes approached this sinister crater from the air, a palpable sense of dread filled their hearts. Unlike the other vibrant and enchanting landscapes, this crater exuded a malevolent aura. Its jagged edges were shrouded in a thick, swirling mist that seemed to whisper dark secrets and ominous warnings.

The ground around the crater was barren and cracked, devoid of the lush vegetation seen elsewhere. Instead, twisted, blackened trees with gnarled branches reached out like skeletal hands, casting eerie shadows in the dim light. The air was heavy with the stench of decay, and the faint sound of distant, mournful wails could be heard echoing from the depths.

Peering into the crater, our heroes saw a churning, inky blackness that seemed to absorb all light. The surface of the dark pool was disturbed by occasional ripples, as if something monstrous lurked just beneath, waiting to emerge. Strange, glowing red eyes flickered in the darkness, watching their every move with malevolent intent. Could this be the new Sinistar?

The atmosphere was oppressive, and an unnatural chill seeped into their bones, making it difficult to breathe. The very ground seemed to pulse with sinister energy, and the heroes could feel a malevolent force tugging at their minds, trying to lure them closer to the edge.

This crater was a place of nightmares, a stark contrast to the beauty and wonder of the surrounding landscape. It was a dark, foreboding reminder that not all is as it seems in this dream world and that danger could lurk even in the most enchanting of places.

The giant bats circled and then set each of the heroes down in a grass clearing, away from the edge of the menacing crater, which was appropriately named Hell Crater by the locals in Shen Yun.

#

On the other side of Shen Yun, the skies shimmered with hues of lavender and gold. The wizard Eno, Bob, Presley the Puppy, and Kristin embarked on a quest through a dreamscape terrain. Their mission was to find the Valley of Ice, where Bob's band kids had been mysteriously teleported, trapped in a frozen prison with no easy way out.

As they journeyed through the surreal landscape, they encountered floating islands, rivers of liquid silver, and forests where the trees whispered secrets. Presley, with his keen sense of smell, led the way, sniffing the air and wagging his tail with excitement. Kristin, clutching the clarinet she took from her makeshift backpack, played melodies that kept their spirits high while Bob and Eno strategized their next steps.

After days of travel, they finally reached the edge of the Valley of Ice. The sight before them was both breathtaking and daunting – towering geometric icy walls and a ground covered in a thick layer of frost. The air was frigid, and the valley seemed impenetrable.

Bob asked Eno, "What are we going to do? Everything is so icy. How are we going to get down there and get them up?" The children below were still trying to find ways out but were not doing well.

Eno, with his deep knowledge of the ancient lore of Shen Yun, remembered a legend about the Firemares – mythical horses whose hooves could ignite flames capable of melting even the toughest ice. Determined to save the band kids, Eno led the group to a hidden cave where the Firemares were said to reside.

Inside the cave, they found the majestic creatures, their hooves glowing with an intense, fiery light. The hooves were actually emitting fire.

Upon seeing them, Bob said, "Whoa, these horses are straight from the movie *Krull*. Mikey loved that movie because the music was composed by his favorite musician, *James Horner*. Unfortunate to the world, Mr. Horner passed away in a plane crash. So sad."

With a gentle touch and a few whispered words, Eno convinced the Firemares to help them. The horses, sensing the urgency of their mission, agreed and followed the group back to the Valley of Ice. Eno also summoned two great eagles to fly into the valley and locate the children. Presley had gotten them there, but the eagles had to lead them down into the icy pit where the children were trapped and on the verge of giving up hope. The band members were huddled together. "We're here to rescue you!" Bob announced, though his voice wavered.

Eno Araf cast a warming spell, and the band members cheered as they were lifted onto the Firemares. "Let's get you all back home," the wizard said with a smile. Bob's band kids, who had been shivering in the cold, were overjoyed to see their rescuers. Eno had mounted one mare and led the way to give the children directions on how to hold on and ride the Firemares out. There were enough mares for each child.

As the Firemares galloped across the icy terrain, their hooves left trails of fire, melting the ice and creating a watery path. The once impenetrable walls began to crumble, and the ground thawed, revealing a way out.

With the giant eagles leading the way, Eno, Bob, Kristin, and Presley guided the band kids out of the valley, riding on the Firemares. The journey back was filled with laughter and relief as the group celebrated their escape from the icy prison. Thanks to the bravery of Eno, the loyalty of Presley, the determination of Kristin, and the wisdom of Bob, the band kids were finally safe, and the legend of the Firemares lived on in the hearts of all who witnessed their fiery rescue. Eno then told Bob that he had to go help his son and the others so he bid farewell for now.

#

Faraone woke up in his truck. He rubbed his brow and eyes under his glasses and then readjusted his New York Yankees baseball cap. "I guess I'm back. That was a trip I won't forget." He looked around outside where he was, then started the truck up, which roared awake with a mighty engine. He then reached above his visor and selected a CD ROM to play from the multitude of choices he had in a carrying device that was attached to the visor. He let the disc slide into the radio CD slot and then cranked up the volume. The electronic notes from *"Toccata"* from the 1979 *Mannheim Steamroller* album *Fresh Aire III* began to play. He knew he had to do something quick and sped off in a hurry because he had some people to see.

At the next stop- light he reached back behind the passenger's seat and felt around. "There it is," he said to himself, then pulled out a baseball cap. He took his NY Yankees hat off and tossed it on the empty seat. He then fit the new cap on his head, adjusting it until it was just right to his liking. The letters embroidered on it were the initials IDT written above a red orb symbol with a digital quarter note in the center and a musical fermata symbol directly above it. He peeled his truck out on the green light. He had to get where he was going pretty quickly. It was time to help save the world…again.

CHAPTER TWENTY-ONE: The Black Crater

The city of El Paso woke up to a beautiful sunrise. The city came alive with the sounds of daily life. The streets began to fill with people heading to work, children going to school, and the aroma of freshly brewed coffee wafted through the air. The Franklin Mountains stood tall and silent, witnessing the start of another vibrant day in this remarkable city. El Paso, Texas, is a city of stunning contrasts and vibrant life. Nestled at the foothills of the majestic Franklin Mountains, it offers breathtaking views and a rich tapestry of cultures. The Franklin Mountains, with their rugged beauty and ancient geological formations, provide a dramatic backdrop to all of the sides of the city. El Paso is a melting pot of cultures where the influences of Mexican, Native American, and American traditions blend seamlessly. This cultural diversity is reflected in the city's festivals, cuisine, and daily life, creating a unique and welcoming atmosphere. The city is renowned for its glorious sunsets and sunrises, and when the sun dips below the horizon, the sky transforms into a canvas of vivid reds, pinks, and oranges, casting a warm glow over the desert landscape. At dawn, the first light of day illuminates the mountains, creating a serene and awe-inspiring scene. The city enjoys warm weather year-round, making it an ideal place for outdoor activities which the city's residents take full advantage of, with hiking, biking, and exploring the natural beauty of the surrounding desert and mountains.

Fort Bliss, one of the largest military installations in the United States, is a proud part of El Paso's identity, and the presence of Fort Bliss brings a sense of pride and patriotism to the city, as well as a strong community of military families. That is why Sinistar targeted it. If he had stopped their military there, he would have been almost impossible to defeat because the next closest military presence in one direction was White Sands Missile Base, and in the other direction, Fort Hood in Killeen, Texas, which is near Austin, the state capital.

There was a secret cave entrance off Trans Mountain Road that he aimed for. He drove along the road, with the Franklin Mountains towering majestically on either side, their rugged cliffs casting long shadows in the early light. As he wound through the curves, his sharp eyes caught sight of a barely visible dirt trail branching off to the right, nearly concealed by desert shrubs and rocks. This unmarked path was the first clue to the hidden cave. Steering his truck onto the uneven trail, he bumped over rocky ground, the path narrowing with each turn. After a mile of rough driving, the way forward was blocked by a massive boulder. Now, the true challenge awaited.

To access the cave, he had to locate a hidden lever disguised as a cactus. Pulling the lever caused the boulder to shift, revealing a narrow entrance just wide enough for a person to squeeze through. Inside, a series of ancient symbols were etched into the walls, glowing faintly in the dim light. Navigating through the cave required solving a series of puzzles, and the first puzzle involved aligning the symbols in a specific order to unlock a hidden door. Once through, he found himself in a cavern with a deep chasm and only a rickety wooden bridge spanning the gap, swaying precariously with each step he took. On the other side, a waterfall cascaded down the rocks, concealing the final entrance. To reveal it, he had to find and press a sequence of pressure plates hidden among the rocks. This made the waterfall part, unveiling a metallic door with a biometric scanner. Only members of the Interdimensional Dream Team could access this door, as it required a unique retinal scan. Once inside the doors, the cave transformed into a high-tech base equipped with advanced technology and monitoring systems. This was the headquarters of the Interdimensional Dream Team, who vigilantly protect the world from threats emerging from the dream realm. The base here was a blend of natural beauty and cutting-edge technology, a testament to the team's dedication and ingenuity. They knew he was coming once he left the road, and they tracked him every step of the way. The white ninja greeted him as he entered the control room, "Greetings John, welcome back."

#

The heroes stood at the edge of the ominous crater; the air thick with tension. The ground trembled as Sinistar began to emerge, its metallic form glowing with malevolent energy. The dream realm around them flickered, hinting at the fragile boundary between dreams and reality. Sinistar roared "I Live!" This brought goosebumps to our heroes, who all stepped backwards shakily. The air then became electric, and a flash of brilliant light appeared by the heroes. It was Eno. "I told you not to worry. I would come to assist you, young gross one."

Mikey said, "Dude, my last name is Gross, but I'm not. Sheesh. Was that a magical chord that played when you appeared?"

Eno said, "My humblest apologies, young man. I am not keen on the pleasantries you share in the other world. I try to stay away from most people, and only the music is true. But the IDT soldiers did take me, although I had done nothing to harm them. They forced me to use my magic to open a dream gate. As you know, they were not successful at stopping Polybius, unfortunately. And yes, Mike, when I appear, sometimes a musical chord is heard, but sometimes it does not. When I am really fortunate, a choir sings as well. It's very pleasant."

"That's really cool, bro. But can you help us now? This crater is about to give birth to a Sinistar robot."

Eno thought and then pulled out his magic baton. He said, "Sinistar's power is tied to the dream realm. I will use a powerful binding spell to anchor Sinistar here within the dream realm. It is temporary, but it will prevent it from crossing into the real world. However, this spell requires a rare item found only at the heart of the crater. Someone is going to have to go inside to get it."

Mikey and Abercrombie volunteered because they could both navigate the dream realm with ease and would venture into the crater to find the rare item while Eno prepared the spell.

Mikey asked, "What are we looking for exactly?"

Eno stated, "Look for an item made of granite, with a silver and gold angel at the top holding a music lyre above its head. I believe there is some writing on an attached golden plate. Bring this object back to me."

Glitch, the robot snowman, with his icy abilities, created a barrier of frost around the crater to slow Sinistar's emergence. This would buy time for Mikey and Abercrombie to complete their mission.

They were both lowered by repelling ropes that the backpack produced for them, and Glitch navigated them down using his new mechanical arms and some servo motors inside of him.

Abercrombie and his knowledge of the dream realm guided Mikey through the treacherous landscape of the crater. They encountered various dream creatures and obstacles, but the penguin's wisdom and Mikey's resourcefulness in playing his oboe helped them overcome these challenges. They both stayed tethered while they explored. Some enemies were these snake-like worms that attacked from both sides, but Mikey's playing hypnotized them like a snake charmer, and he had them tie each other in a big knot. At one perilous point, Mikey's playing made large boulders float so they could walk across. This music power he had was really helping them.

On the top side of the crater, Glitch and Eno were attacked by a dozen flying robotic sentries sent from the Snow King's castle, but Glitch used his snowstorm strength to fend off the minions Sinistar summoned. Eno helped, of course, destroying them one at a time by shooting a blue laser of music notes at them from his wand as Glitch froze them. They exploded in a symphony of chords and musical instrument sounds.

Mikey and Abercrombie saw blue lightning flashes in the darkness above them as the ropes slipped every now and then, worrying them that they might fall to their doom. But Glitch and Eno were successful in thwarting the robots.

Mikey saw the item they were searching for and said, "I should have known it was something like this," He stated to Abercrombie, who looked confused.

Abercrombie said, "What do you mean?"

"It's a band trophy. Looks a bit older, but still a sweepstakes Band competition trophy."

"What is that?"

"When a band goes to a music festival, if they are bold, they can enter all of the categories in the contest. Usually, a concert performance, a music sight-reading contest, and sometimes a marching contest. If they get all first divisions in those contests, they win a sweepstakes trophy. It's hard to do, but Faraone's bands used to win them every year. He has a long streak of doing that. The band boosters called it a tradition of excellence- because a first division is an excellent rating. We have to get it out of that jagged crevice.

Abercrombie said, "I'll handle that if you watch my back."

"You got it, bro."

Abercrombie used another rock and started chipping away at the crevice and rock wall where the trophy was embedded. He hammered furiously.

The cavern shook and rumbled more, and the black ooze below them started to swirl and bubble. A giant opening appeared, and the oil started seeping into it. A booming voice filled the cavern. "I hunger!"

Mikey said, "Bro, please hurry. I think Sinistar is about to go all ham on us."

Abercrombie was successful, and they called up to Glitch to bring them up quickly as the crater cavern began to shake more, which made giant stones fall down towards them.

"Just great," said Mikey. "We survive everything else only to be crushed by some ordinary boulders. That figures." As the giant rocks cascaded, bounced, and careened off the walls down at them, Mikey closed his eyes tightly. "This is it, bro. It's been nice! Tell my pop I am sorry."

#

Eno reappeared in front of Bob but in a hologram state, "Bob Gross, you must find immediate shelter for the children. Do not dally. I have more pressing matters here with your son and friends. I fear there are some problems and some hard choices that will be made before the day's end is nigh. We will win the day, but I am not sure at what cost." He was in battle, and the hologram glitched a few times with him shooting his wand while musical chord explosions could be heard in the background.

Bob said, "Eno, what are you saying? Is Mikey in some sort of danger?"

"Aye, we all are, it seems. I will do my best to protect the young ones. You have my word." He continued to battle as he spoke.

Bob was worried now, "What can I do to help? Please make sure Mikey stays safe!"

Eno's hologram glitched and wavered. Bob could now hear "I hunger!" in the background, with Eno frantically shooting his wand. The hologram fizzled out in front of him abruptly.

Bob was horrified. What could he do from where he was? If he left the children, he would be leaving many kids his son's age. What kind of parent would do that? He felt selfish thinking about his own child instead of the others, but as a parent, he wanted his own kid's safety. "Dang, what do I do?" He halted the herd of Firemares and turned his horse in a new direction.

"Everyone, listen up. We have to go back to the castle. But don't worry, the snow king won't do anything to you now- he is powerless. I think we're all still in danger, and before we can go home, we have to fix one other issue." Bob got really serious. "We are the only hope of saving your friends and families back home. My own family is in danger right now, and I wouldn't ask you to do anything I wouldn't do. Please believe me. I know you all want this over, so I will promise you that this is the last thing we have to do. Then we can all go home safely."

The children agreed, even though some were obviously reluctant. They turned and followed Bob back towards the snow king's castle.

Kristin rode alongside Bob and said quietly, "What's going on, sir? Is Mikey in trouble? I saw some of Eno's holograms, but from an angle, I couldn't hear them really."

When Bob turned his gaze to look at her, she saw a tear roll down his face. He choked back his words. "I don't know Kristin. I don't know." He then wiped his face of tears and said, "All I know is that we have to do something to help them before something bad happens. I want to see if Layla can help us with what she knows about the castle. There's got to be a way to help, so we have to try."

"Fair enough. And I am sorry, Mikey is a good guy. He makes me laugh. You are a very lucky father to have a kid like him."

Bob smiled, "Thank you, Kristin. You are a good kid, too. Thank you for helping- in case I never get to tell you."

"Don't say that, sir. There's time to fix this." Then she imitated Eno, "The day's end is not nigh yet." They both smiled. "I did hear that part."

After riding for a while, the castle came into view, and they rode right to the front door. Bob told the children to stay together and that he would be back shortly. Try to gather some wood and build a fire- use the Firemare's feet to start a good bonfire to keep warm. Then he said, "Now, how about some hot cocoa?"

Kristin, Bob, and Presley went inside, placing the Polybius horn on the hand plate that Kristin still carried. They went straight to the throne room, and Layla was still there. She had drawn code all over the ground and was lying on her back in the middle of it, all counting and calculating things in the air. She was so enmeshed in thought that she didn't even notice them.

"Layla," said Bob. "What are you doing?"

Layla woke up from thought and looked at them with a questioning face. "What are you all doing back here? I thought you'd be long gone by now. By the way, how did you break the code to get out?" She looked directly at Kristin, "Are you an expert hacker, too? I have been trying for an hour, and I would really like to get out of here. It's the variables, right? I'm not passing them through the function calls properly I bet. What did you do?"

Kristin pulled out the horn and held it up towards Layla, "I just used this."

"Whoa, a cheat code! I like it. How did you get it?" Presley barked upon seeing it.

Kristin said, "He got it. Bit it right off of that mean ole snow king, didn't you, boy?" She was speaking in a baby voice to Presley. He wagged his tail happily.

Layla said, "May I?" Then Kristin handed it to her to inspect.

Bob then interrupted. "As cool as that was, we need your help, Layla. The others are in grave danger, so I want to know if there is anything here at the castle that can help us beat Sinistar again?"

Layla said, "Well, there's my disrupter, but it's small and might only reach 20 feet or so."

Bob said, "We need something bigger. Something that wouldn't just stop him but something that would end him. We have to put an end to this."

Layla thought and then said, "Well, there are those containers of essence. Do you think they could help? There's a lot of them under the castle floor- in the tunnels. It seems he never used the yellow ones, but I don't know why. The green ones cause nightmares."

Bob now had some hope and got eager, "Can you show us? Maybe the colors mean something?"

Layla took them down to the tunnels where she had been before. The trip there was difficult because of the previous war they had, but they got there without too much trouble. She showed them the green, red, and yellow stockpiles of canisters and explained what the red and green were, again being careful not to touch any, but she didn't know what the yellow was for. She also showed them the nightmare grenades she had made from the green essence.

"Interesting," Bob said, placing his hand on his chin in a thinking pose. To help him, he pulled out his pipe, which was unlit, and placed it in his mouth, which he claimed helped him "think even better."

CHAPTER TWENTY-TWO: The El Paso Star

The giant boulder headed toward Mikey, but Abercrombie swung heroically on his line and pushed Mikey out of the way just in time. The rock flew past and was drawn into the giant opening, which was Sinistar's mouth. "Dude. That was gas." Mikey said to Abercrombie.

"I am not sure what that means, but I think it means good?" Abercrombie said. "Youse youths nowadays, you're so hard to understand."

Mikey said smiling, "That's rather ironic, Bruh."

Eno called down, "Hurry with that artifact, young ones. I must cast this binding spell before this behemoth surfaces!"

As the crater shook, Mikey and Abercrombie made it up the ropes with Glitch's help, who pulled them up mechanically. They just had to hop and hop as they were lifted up and out of the crater. Mikey handed Eno the trophy, and he began the incantations to produce the spell. He spoke strange words, reminding Mikey of the 'Spell of Making' in the movie *Excalibur*, which he said to Abercrombie quietly, "A Nal Nathrack. Ufthas Bethsood, Dothe eeair Yenvay."

Abercrombie said. "Whatever you say, guy."

The trophy transformed into a ball of brilliant yellow light which Eno cast above the crater's center. Sinistar's engines came on one at a time, and he began to rise slowly up the crater out of the black ooze. "I live!"

The bright light then dove into the crater and slipped past Sinistar, going directly behind the massive robot nightmare. The glow from the light grew bigger, and giant glowing yellow fingers enveloped Sinistar and grabbed him on all sides like a hand would grab a doorknob.

His movement was temporarily halted, and he roared in anger loudly. It didn't look like the spell would last long. "What else can we do, Eno?" Said Mikey.

"We can only hope that my spell can bind him here long enough for the other world to assist on their end."

The sky was tearing apart once again. This tear was the target for Sinistar and his journey to the real-world dimension.

#

"Ok, let's get a move on. Yo, Ninja…You ride with me," said Faraone as an entire fleet of black hummers lined up with soldiers wearing uniforms with the initials "IDT" on their chests, getting into the vehicles quickly and in an orderly fashion. A Claxon was blaring, and lights were spinning on the top of all of the vehicles which had racks with very high-tech-looking turrets and boxes protruding from them, front and back. It made some of the fleets look like tanks. The side of the mountain disappeared as the commander screamed some orders in his headset, "Cloaking device off." The fleet hurriedly followed each other outside, creating tons of sand dust.

Before Faraone got in his truck with the ninja, he was looking inside some pelican cases and grabbed a weapon from one. It was a very large pistol made of mostly silver and as large as his forearm when held up. The metallic casing shined and sparkled in the lights, and Faraone said, "This one will do nicely." He then placed it on his gun rack in his truck and peeled out to follow the rest of the military convoy out of the secret base on the mountainside. As

244

he rumbled down the road, he loudly played AC DC's "*Back in Black*."

Bob, Kristin, and Layla rode furiously on Firemares through the desert landscape. Their hair was flowing, and they were travelling at top speeds across the surface of the varied terrains they passed over like lightning. Smoke trailed behind them, but they were also trailed by dozens of the floating cannisters that Polybius used to transport the children to the throne room. Layla had programmed them to follow her wrist computer, so where she went, they did, too.

Eno, Mikey, Abercrombie, and Glitch stood a bit away from the shaking crater that was holding Sinistar back from leaving, and then Mikey saw the riders approaching in the distance.

"I think it's my pop! Go pop, go!" exclaimed Mikey. "I need some music for this moment, backpack. Can you play some James Horner from the soundtrack, *Krull*? Maybe *Ride of the Firemares*?"

The song played made the moment even more exciting and magical for all who saw the riders and heard the music.

They arrived, and Bob immediately dismounted and ran to Mikey. They embraced. Bob said, "I thought I lost you, kiddo. Don't ever scare me like that again."

"I won't dad. I promise." Said Mikey.

Eno interrupted, "I see that you have brought forth some tubes. What will they do to assist our challenge?"

Bob smiled quirkily, "I think we have the right stuff to stop this thing. But we have to be sure. Mikey, can you dream walk once more into your aunt's room? You'll need to find something that tells us if we have the right color to stop Sinistar."

"Dad, I am not really sleepy right now. I am too scared to sleep." Said Mikey.

Eno said, "I can help you, Mike. I can cast a sleeping spell on you, but you won't be able to wake here until it is all over. Two outcomes are possible. If we fail, you will have escaped, and the rest of your friends will be trapped here forever. Sinistar will get out and destroy your world. We will all be safe here, but without you, Sinistar will surely destroy you all there. If we prevail, your friends and dad will join you in the real world, and we will have stopped Sinistar, forever trapping him in the dream world forever. Make your choice wisely."

Mikey patted his backpack. "Agreed. But if I do go, I know that I've got the best team to handle anything here. You are all my friends, and I won't fail you. We need a color to stop him, and it's in her room somewhere. I'm on it. Put me to sleep, kind sir."

Eno said, "Very well. Tell your backpack what color will stop him, and I will get the message here. We will take it from there." He then had Mikey lay down away from the crater and cast his sleep spell. Mikey was out. All could hear Sinistar roaring, "I hunger! Run coward! I am Sinistar!"

#

Mikey woke up in the hospital again. He took out the leads on his chest and pulled out the IV from his arm. "Ouch, that smarts!" He then turned off the machine alarms going off so the nurses wouldn't come rushing in. He quickly got dressed and had to sneak out of the hospital once again. He was on the second floor, so he told himself it wasn't too bad. He saw a cart full of hospital linens by a laundry chute.

"That's my ticket out of here!"

He crouched and ran to the cart and hid behind it. When nobody was around, he told himself, "Get in there, flyboy!" A quote from the movie *Star Wars*. Then he dove in and slid down to the first floor and into a pile of dirty laundry.

He eventually made it out of the hospital and ran to the Bunker Hill Memory Care facility where his aunt Irma lived. He signed in and asked, "Do you know where my aunt is right now?"

They told him it was dinner time, so she was probably in the main dining room.

"Thanks!" He ran around the corner and went towards her room instead. He noticed a familiar poster in the hall. It said, "One night only! Shen Yun performers direct from China. December 22nd performance El Paso Civic Center." He kept running past and went to her apartment. He had a key, so he unlocked it and went in. "Aunt Irma, are you here? It's housekeeping." No answer, and the lights were off.

Mikey quickly ran to her art desk and started thumbing through things looking for any notes or papers on colors. He didn't find any, but then as he was frustrated and about to give up, he saw the drawings on the wallboard. The entire adventure was drawn out in a sequence.

"My gosh, she knew what was happening all of the time. These drawings are telling the story!" He then noticed that there was one that had the new crater and his friends all around it, but it had been scribbled on with a black crayon like she was trying to cover something up. The sky had a tear in it, but no Sinistar was flying through it yet. The drawing was pinned over another, so he lifted it to reveal a drawing of the Franklin mountains and the El Paso star colored in yellow.

There was a poem scribbled at the bottom: "Blue, Green, and Red will make others dead. Yellow will prevent the fellow."

"BINGO was his name-o," said Mikey happily. Then he took his backpack off and talked into it. "Eno, come in. Breaker one nine to Eno. The phrase blue, green, and red will make others dead. Yellow will prevent the fellow. Over and out. Ten-four good, buddy. I hope you got that." He took down the scribbled drawing off the top of the other.

A voice behind him said coldly, "I did get that."

Mikey was startled and turned to see Mrs. White standing there menacingly.

"Oh, hey, Aunt White. Ha-how, are you today? Feeling good? I hope?"

Mrs. White said as coldly as before, "I'm actually feeling really bad right now. Really bad."

Mikey tried to run around her, but she raised her arm, and he lifted it off the ground. He had the drawing in his hand, and his feet were dangling.

"Do you think you could win? Do you take me for a fool?" She said, then flung him across the room where he hit the drawing desk, knocking off the drawing light and spilling all of the crayons everywhere on the floor by him.

Mikey tried to shake off the cobwebs in his head from the impact but was lying on the floor with the drawing. The drawing light had also landed there and was rolling back and forth on the tear in the sky that was in the drawing. He looked around as she started walking towards him.

"You cannot win. Your friends will perish, and Sinistar will come through valiantly into this world, and nothing will stop him!"

Mikey saw a yellow crayon and had an idea. He put his Walkman headphones on and pressed 'play' on his cassette tape player. It began to play *Magic Carpet Ride* by Steppenwolf. He grabbed the crayon and started making marks on the drawing towards the tear in the sky. Frantically, he drew the lines as his aunt approached.

"What do you think you are doing? You can't do that. Stop! I said stop drawing. Only I can do that!" She tried to snatch the drawing from the floor to look at it, but Mikey pulled away just in time. She said, "What have you done!?"

#

In the heart of the desolate dream world, the black crater began to tremble. From its depths, the sinister form of Sinistar, the evil robot with glowing red eyes and a metallic, menacing grin, emerged slowly. The ground quaked as Sinistar's powerful frame started to ascend, its mechanical engines coming on one at a time with a deafening roar. Above, the tear in the sky shimmered, the portal to the real world where Sinistar planned to wreak havoc.

Nearby, our heroes watched in horror. Glitch, the robotic snowman with a heart of circuits, stood firm, his icy exterior glinting in the dim light. Beside him, Abercrombie, the talking penguin with the Bostonian accent, paced in a circle nervously.

Kristin, the band girl with a makeshift backpack slung over her shoulder, exchanged worried glances with Layla, the hacker girl whose fingers frantically danced over a holographic keyboard. Bob held Presley, the small but brave puppy, close to his chest.

Bob said out loud, "Didn't we already live through this? Not again!"

#

Mikey's brow furrowed in concentration as he drew more yellow lines, each stroke representing a pod carrying a yellow essence vial. These vials were the key to stopping Sinistar, and they needed to pass through the tear in the sky before the evil robot could.

As Sinistar's engines started to carry him out of the crater and up into the air, the tear in the sky began to widen. Glitch's circuits buzzed with determination, and Abercrombie's wings flapped in nervous anticipation. Layla's fingers flew faster over her keyboard, trying to hack into Sinistar's systems.

Layla said, "I am not sure I can hack in fast enough to slow him this time!"

Mikey turned away from Irma, and his hand moved swiftly with the crayon. The yellow lines on the paper were now glowing with a magical light. He could feel the connection between the real world and the dream world strengthening. The pods, which were filled with the yellow essence, began to move instead of children this time. They were affected by the real world's drawing and raced quickly towards the tear in the sky.

"Come on, Mikey," Bob whispered, his eyes fixed on the tear. "You can do this."

With a final, decisive stroke, Mikey completed the last yellow line. The pods surged further forward, their glowing contents illuminating the dark landscape. Sinistar roared in fury as the first pod passed through the tear, followed by another and another.

"I am Sinistar!"

Glitch, Abercrombie, Kristin, Layla, Bob, and Presley watched in awe as the yellow essence vials streamed through the tear, their light pushing back the darkness.

All of the pods made it through, and on the other side of the tear was the IDT, ready to intercept them all. Several missiles shot up in the air from the hummers, and each exploded open a giant net that caught the pods. Parachutes deployed, and the hummers sped off to intercept each one.

Faraone pulled out a band bullhorn from his truck and yelled orders on it. "Take that one over there, and line that one up on the left of that one." The soldier went the wrong way. "Your other left, please."

They were building a giant star shape from the yellow vials around the mountain's portal tear. Other soldiers were hooking the vials up to cables that led to a generator and a computer setup. They just needed a little more time to get it activated.

In the dream realm, they knew the other team needed more time, but Layla was not having much luck. Presley growled at the evil robot, and something nobody expected occurred.

Glitch, the robotic snowman, was watching all of this chaos ensue, and he was worried that Mikey and his world would fall prey to Sinistar, and he wasn't going to let that happen. Not to his new friend, who had freed him from the evil snow king. These were all his new friends now, and he saw how worried they were along with how evil Sinistar was. He had to do something to help-something drastic to help his friends. He revved backwards and took a speeding roll at the giant crater and launched on the top of Sinistar, who had his giant mouth open, drawing in the black ooze and vegetation that was sucked into it.

"NO!!!" yelled Layla, and Glitch launched through the air and into Sinistar's mouth opening. As he went in, he turned, his lights all came on brightly, then he clicked madly at them and threw his arms up in celebration.

Abercrombie couldn't stop him either, and he fell at the crater's edge, trying to stop him as well.

Glitch's bright lights glowed inside the evil robot's mouth, bringing some light and colors to a frightening scene.

The evil robot's last engines came on, and he roared out of the crater and into the sky. But before it got up too high, he began to shake and slow. Ice crystals began to form on the outside of his surface. Glitch had done it. He had slowed the monster down by freezing Sinistar from the inside. The giant robot was not excelling very fast at all.

The heroes below cheered loudly and threw their arms up, mimicking Glitch's last movement. They all started yelling in unison, "Glitch! Glitch! Glitch!" He was a true hero, and his sacrifice helped the IDT soldiers get the yellow star built and turned on.

When the soldier activated the star, it lit up beautifully, illuminating the side of the mountains where the entire city of El Paso could see it shine. The essence in the vials glowed, swam wildly when activated, and the sound of laughter and children's dreams of fun and happiness could be heard from afar. The yellow essence was thrown out by Polybius because it did the opposite of what he wanted. It was grabbed from pleasant dreams, the kind of dreams where we are at our best, have scored the winning point, won the race, or had the best time with our friends and family members. Dreams where we could fly or run as fast as the wind or be anyone and come out the hero. The good dreams where memories of our past loved ones and past pets are with us, and we can once again love them. These magical dreams made yellow essence when captured, and this joyous ooze would not power anything evil in the dream realm, so Polybius took it away and stored it deep under the castle.

Sinistar's engines faltered, and with a final, enraged scream, the frozen, evil robot fell back into the black crater, the tear in the sky sealing shut.

In the real world, Mikey let out a breath he didn't realize he'd been holding. The magic paper lay before him. Its surface was now blank, and the battle was won. For now, the world was safe, thanks to the bravery of a dreamwalker and his friends in the dream world.

CHAPTER TWENTY-THREE: The Dance

Irma was sitting in the corner hugging her arms across her legs, and slightly rocking. "What do I do now? How will I avenge my love? I have failed." She cried and sobbed.

Mikey felt really bad about this and went to comfort her, but went cautiously. "Aunt Irma?" he said softly. "Are you Ok?"

Irma looked up weepily and said, "It is with a heavy heart and a slightly bruised ego that I must convey my profound regret for not achieving the desired outcome in my recent endeavor. Despite my earnest efforts and unwavering dedication, I find myself at the precipice of disappointment, much like a cat who misjudged the distance to the next windowsill. The task at hand proved to be an insurmountable challenge, and I must humbly acknowledge my shortcomings. It seems I have learned the hard way that even the best-laid plans of mice and English teachers can go awry.

I assure you that this experience has been a poignant lesson, one that I shall carry with me as a reminder of the importance of perseverance and resilience. After all, even Shakespeare had his off days."

Mikey said, "Um, Ok. I guess you'll be ok?"

Irma said, "I actually feel a bit relieved. I had so much hate built up inside that it transformed me into a different person entirely."

Mikey said I think I can help you in that department. He yelled at the door, "Come on in. We're ready for you!"

Just then several IDT soldiers came into the door in military fashion and stood in a semi-circle around Irma and Mikey.

Mikey said "Let er rip!"

The soldiers, grinning beneath their gas masks, moved in perfect synchrony. With a swift, practiced motion, they pulled the pins on their grenades. A burst of yellow dust exploded into the room, swirling like confetti caught in a playful breeze. The soft strains of Beethoven's Ode to Joy filled the air, its triumphant melody carried by a full, soaring choir. The voices harmonized with the unexpected sounds of children laughing and playing, their giggles bouncing off the walls like music itself. The entire scene felt surreal, almost whimsical, as the golden dust danced through the beams of light, and for a moment, it was as if the room had been transformed into a celebration of joy and innocence.

Irma could see forms of children playing and little dogs jumping and chasing their tails. Then she made out a form of a man coming towards her. He reached out his hand to her. She looked up and it was Bill! He said "Can I have this dance dear?"

In the soft glow of twilight, Irma found herself standing in the heart of a grand ballroom, its opulence overwhelming. The chandeliers above shimmered like a thousand stars, casting a golden light that danced across the polished marble floor. She wore a flowing, elegant gown of deep emerald, the silky fabric swishing softly with every step she took, brushing the floor like a delicate breeze. The air was filled with the gentle strains of Ode to Joy, gradually transitioning into a waltz that echoed off the gilded walls, each note carrying a weight of nostalgia that tugged at her heartstrings. As she took in the scene, the familiarity of the music swirled around her like a tender embrace, pulling her deeper into the moment.

As she looked around, her breath caught in her throat. His eyes, the same deep blue she had fallen in love with, were fixed on her with a tenderness that made her heart ache. He looked just as she remembered, his smile warm and inviting, his presence a beacon of comfort and love.

"Bill," she whispered, her voice trembling with emotion. "Is it really you?"

He nodded, stepping forward with a grace that seemed almost ethereal. "It's me, Irma," he said softly, his voice like a soothing balm to her soul. "I've missed you so much."

Tears welled up in her eyes as she reached out to him, her fingers brushing against his. The touch was electric, sending a shiver down her spine. "I've missed you too," she replied, her voice breaking. "Every single day."

Bill took her hand in his, pulling her gently into his arms. "Dance with me," he murmured, his breath warm against her ear. "Just one more time."

The music swelled around them as they began to move, their bodies swaying in perfect harmony. Irma closed her eyes, letting the memories wash over her. She could feel the strength of his embrace, the steady rhythm of his heartbeat against her cheek. It was as if time had stood still, and they were once again the young couple who had danced the night away under the stars.

As the final notes of the waltz faded into silence, Bill leaned down and pressed a tender kiss to her forehead. "I will always be with you, Irma," he whispered, his voice filled with love and reassurance. "In your heart, in your dreams, I will never truly be gone."

Irma opened her eyes, the ballroom dissolving into the soft light of dawn. She was back in her bedroom, the familiar surroundings a stark contrast to the dream. But as she lay there, a sense of peace washed over her. She knew that Bill's love would always be a part of her, a guiding light in the darkest of times. She was finally at peace and no longer full of anger. With a smile, she closed her eyes once more, holding onto the memory of their dance, and the promise that love never truly fades.

#

Mikey was able to dream walk back to his friends now and they threw a lavish party to celebrate at the snow king's castle. People from Shen Yun came from all over to see the new castle and even the monorail was fixed and picked up people from faraway lands to come to the castle when needed.

Abercrombie was made the new king and Layla was able to find her mom and bring her relatives to the castle to live. Glitch received a beautiful funeral which was attended by many in the land, complete with a celebration of his heroic deeds in the form of firework displays and drones that depicted some of the things he did. The sounds of funeral bells knelled throughout the city of Shen Yun for him. But, the most popular homage the people did, was mimicking him throwing up his new arms in triumph- which all imitated during the ceremony.

The heroes then fixed up the castle so that it could generate power with yellow essence only, which would not hurt anyone, nor drain them of life. Layla came up with that hack of course, which got her lifted up by all of her village and carried around in celebration for her cunning. The local villagers were in a state of xenophobia that led to the snow king's rule, but once the yellow essence was released countrywide, their fear was put at ease.

The Parasitic draw bats would now fill up on yellow essence and deliver it to charging stations at each village of Shen Yun, lighting up the village with new hope and love. They began to trust strangers again.

Imagine the countryside shrouded in darkness and ice, where the once vibrant fields lay barren and the rivers ran dry or were frozen. The air was thick with despair, and the trees stood as twisted shadows of their former selves. But then, a gentle breeze began to stir, carrying with it the whispers of hope and magic using the charging stations and the yellow essence.

As the first rays of light pierced through the gloom, the transformation began. The dark clouds dissipated, revealing a sky painted in hues of gold and lavender. The barren fields burst into life, with flowers of every color imaginable blooming in a symphony of beauty. The rivers, once dry or frozen, now flowed with crystal-clear water that sparkled like diamonds under the sun.

The trees, no longer twisted and gnarled, stretched their branches towards the sky, adorned with leaves that shimmered like emeralds. The air was filled with the sweet scent of blossoms and the melodious songs of birds that had returned to their homes.

In this magical transformation, the landscape became a tapestry of wonder. Rolling hills were covered in a carpet of soft, luminescent moss that glowed gently in the moonlight. Majestic waterfalls cascaded down cliffs, their waters creating rainbows that danced in the air. Enchanted forests emerged, where trees bore fruits that glowed with an inner light, and creatures of legend roamed freely once again.

The countryside, once a place of darkness, had become a realm of light and happiness, where every corner held a new and fantastical sight. It was a place where dreams came to life, and the impossible became possible.

The only thing left was to get the children back home. As much as they liked this new world, they missed their other friends, their pets, and their families.

Eno rigged up a Stargate portal with Layla's computer help and using the yellow, good essence as fuel, it was powered on. He said "I cannot get you back exactly where you came from because we are deep in the dream realm, but I can place you in your dimension. You may have many days travel to get home but you will make it back, I promise. I know you come from a place where desert is dominant; therefore, I will send you to a desert and hope that it is close."

Mikey and Bob got the children ready to go and had them all mount the Firemares for one last homebound ride. As they all went through the portal, Mikey played *Free-ride* by Edgar Mevers using the magical backpack. It was exciting for all of Shen Yun to see and wave them off in a large celebration. They had all been responsible to bringing life back to their world and the entire countryside celebrated them with more fireworks and even more glorious music.

Eno hadn't been totally correct with his coordinates and the children came out in the desert city of Karnali, southwest of Tibet. After quite the ride, the children all stayed the night at Hotel Tibet near the Simikot airport. They departed the next day and all flew home to be with their parents in El Paso.

Mikey and Bob with Presley, went back to their home in the Eastridge part of El Paso. Bob had new fervor to prepare the band this next season for the Bands of America competition and started listening to music he might choose and license.

Mikey and Presley had a lot of fun together, and the kids he saw around the dog park were actually really nice to him now. Things were looking up and he didn't have to only speak to his oboe anymore. He did practice on his oboe a lot more which helped his playing immensely. Kristin still won first chair in tryouts though, but he was cool with it and he hugged her when she won. She was surprised by the hug and actually gave him a kiss back on his cheek. He blushed.

#

Mikey said to his oboe, "That's the story old friend – or at least what was all told to me when I didn't remember some things. I told you it was an interesting story. I hope you liked it." Mikey put his oboe away and placed it back in his backpack. The city bus stopped and Mikey jumped out jovially and headed home. He put his headphones on and played his cassette tape for the short walk he had to make. The neighbors could hear the music because it was pretty loud in his headphones. *Find your way back* by Jefferson Starship. He felt it seemed appropriate. He snapped his fingers and gave old man Pettibon a shooter finger sign and winked. He still walked funny like something was in his pants. Old man Pettibon kept watering his plants and shook his head in disgust at the youth today.

The Interdimensional Dream Team returned to secretly saving the world from otherworldly and dimensional beings, and Mikey was recruited to assist. After all, he was one of the only dream walkers they actually knew about.

260

Faraone sped up to Bob and Mikey's driveway in his truck, then slammed on the brakes. "Mikey, c'mon we have a new mission. We found another dream walker and need your help boy. His name is Doctor Cello, and he is cloning people. We have to stop him. Get in and bring your backpack."

Mikey said, "I heard your truck coming a mile away Mr. Faraone. I'm ready." He reached into his backpack and pulled out a baseball cap embroidered with the letters IDT on it, and placed it on his head. "See ya, Pop." He hugged Bob tightly.

"Be careful son. Call if you need my help."

Mikey said "Slay." And made a peace symbol as he jumped up onto the passenger seat.

Faraone peeled out to the tune of *Back in Black* by AC DC once again, playing it loudly on his truck speakers. His license plate could be seen as they drove off…XCELNC.

THE END

INDEX - Definitions:

A

Abruptly (adverb): suddenly and unexpectedly.

Acronym (noun): an abbreviation formed from the initial letters of other words and pronounced as a word (e.g. ASCII, NASA).

Agape (adjective): (of the mouth) wide open, especially with surprise or wonder.

Anthropomorphism (noun): the attribution of human characteristics or human traits, emotions, or intentions to non-human entities like a god, animal, or object.

Apparition (noun): a ghost or ghostlike image of a person, the appearance of something remarkable or unexpected, typically an image of this type.

Arduous (adjective): involving or requiring strenuous effort; difficult and tiring.

B

Banal (adjective): it is so lacking in originality as to be obvious and boring.

Behemoth (noun): a huge or monstrous creature.

Bewilderment (noun): a feeling of being perplexed and confused.

Bifurcating (verb): divide into two branches or forks.

Bioluminescent (noun): the biochemical emission of light by living organisms; the light emitted by organisms such as fireflies and deep-sea fishes.

C

Careen (verb): move swiftly and in an uncontrolled way in a specified direction.

Catatonic (adjective): of or in an immobile or unresponsive stupor.

Circumspect (adjective): wary and unwilling to take risks.

Clattered (verb): make or cause to make a continuous rattling sound, fall or move with a continuous rattling sound.

Claxon (Noun): a kind of loud horn.

Consequential (adjective): following as a result or effect. Important; significant.

Contorted (adjective): twisted or bent out of the normal shape.

D

Darwinism (noun): the theory of the evolution of species by natural selection advanced by Charles Darwin.

Debris (noun): scattered pieces of waste or remains.

Demise (noun): a person's death.

Dialect (noun): a particular form of a language which is peculiar to a specific region or social group.

Diminish, diminished (verb): make or become less. Make (someone or something) seem less impressive or valuable.

Disillusioned (adjective): disappointed in someone or something that one discovers to be less good than one had believed.

Dismantle (verb): to take something apart, to dissect.

Dismantling (present participle): take (a machine or structure) to pieces.

Dispel (verb): *dispelling (present participle)* make (a doubt, feeling, or belief) disappear.

Dominant (adjective): most important, powerful, or influential.

Genetics: relating to or denoting heritable characteristics which are controlled by genes that are expressed in offspring even when inherited from only one parent. Often contrasted with recessive.

Ecology: denoting the predominant species in a plant (or animal) community. In decision theory, (of a choice) at least as good as the alternatives in all circumstances, and better in some.

Dubious (adjective): hesitating or doubting; not to be relied upon; suspect.

E

Emanated (verb): originate from; be produced by.

Emblazon, emblazoned (verb): conspicuously inscribe or display a design on.

Erratic, erratically (adjective): not even or regular in pattern or movement; unpredictable.

Eschew (verb): deliberately avoid using; abstain from.

Essence (noun): the intrinsic nature or indispensable quality of something, especially something abstract, that determines its character.

Extrapolate (verb): extend the application of (a method or conclusion, especially one based on statistics) to an unknown situation by assuming that existing trends will continue or similar methods will be applicable.

F

Feign (verb): pretend to be affected by (a feeling, state, or injury).

Fermion (noun): a subatomic particle, such as a nucleon, which has half-integral spin and follows the statistical description given by Fermi and Dirac.

Fermata (noun): a pause of unspecified length on a note or rest; a mark over a note or rest that is to be lengthened by an unspecified amount.

Fetter (noun): a chain or manacle used to restrain a prisoner, typically placed around the ankles.

Flabbergasted (adjective): greatly surprised or astonished.

Flourish (verb): (of a person, animal, or other living organism) grow or develop in a healthy or vigorous way, especially as the result of a particularly favorable environment.

Foible (noun): a minor weakness or eccentricity in someone's character.

G

Goa (noun): (Procapra picticaudata), also known as the Tibetan gazelle, is a species of antelope that inhabits the Tibetan plateau.

Grimace (verb): to distort one's face in an expression usually of pain, disgust, or disapproval.

H

Heathen (noun): an unenlightened person; a person regarded as lacking culture or moral principles.

I

Imbecilic (adjective): very stupid or foolish; idiotic.

Immensely (adverb): to a great extent; extremely.

Immemorial (adjective): originating in the distant past; very old.

Inert (adjective): lacking the ability or strength to move.

Interdimensional (adjective): between dimensions.

Interloper (noun): a person who becomes involved in a place or situation where they are not wanted or are considered not to belong.

Inquisitive (adjective): curious or inquiring, unduly curious about the affairs of others; prying.

J

Jovial (adjective): cheerful and friendly.

K

Knell (noun): the sound of a bell rung slowly to announce a death.

L

Loquacious (adjective): tending to talk a great deal; talkative.

Luminescent (adjective): emitting light not caused by heat.

M

Maladjusted (adjective): failing or unable to cope with the demands of a normal social environment.

Malevolent (adjective): having or showing a wish to do evil to others.

Masticate (verb): chew (food).

Melee (noun): a confused fight, skirmish, or scuffle.

Methodical (adjective): done according to a systematic or established form of procedure.

Mezzo forte (noun): a moderately high volume of sound.

Mischievous (adjective): (of a person, animal, or their behavior) causing or showing a fondness for causing trouble in a playful way. (of an action or thing) causing or intended to cause harm or trouble.

Moniker (noun): a name.

Murmuration (noun): flock.

Myriad (noun): a countless or extremely great number. (adjective): countless or extremely great in number.

N

Nebulous (adjective): in the form of a cloud or haze; hazy.

Nefarious (adjective): (typically of an action or activity) wicked or criminal.

Nonchalantly (adverb): in a casually calm and relaxed manner.

O

Ominous (adjective): giving the impression that something bad or unpleasant is going to happen; threatening; inauspicious.

Ostinato (noun): a continually repeated musical phrase or rhythm.

P

Parasitic (adjective): (of an organism) living as a parasite.

Perplexed (adjective): completely baffled; very puzzled.

Personification (noun): the attribution of a personal nature or human characteristics to something nonhuman, or the representation of an abstract quality in human form.

Pianissimo (noun): a passage marked to be performed very softly.

Polybius: (c. 200–c. 118 bc), Greek historian. His forty books of Histories (only partially extant) chronicled the rise of the Roman Empire from 220 to 146 bc.

Polybius (Urban legend): is a fictitious 1981 arcade game that features an urban legend. The legend describes the game as part of a government-run crowdsourced psychology experiment based in Portland, Oregon. Gameplay supposedly produced intense psychoactive and addictive effects in the player. These few publicly staged arcade machines were said to have been visited periodically by men in black for the purpose of data-mining the machines and analyzing these effects. Supposedly, all of these *Polybius* arcade machines then disappeared from the arcade market.

This urban legend has persisted in video game journalism and through continued interest, and it has inspired video games with the same name.

Preferential (adjective): of or involving preference or partiality; constituting a favor or privilege.

Profusely (adverb): to a great degree; in large amounts.

Pulverize (verb): to reduce (as by crushing, beating, or grinding) to very small particles: atomize.

Purgatory (noun): (in Roman Catholic doctrine) a place or state of suffering inhabited by the souls of sinners who are expiating their sins before going to heaven.

Q

Query (noun): used in writing or speaking to question the accuracy of a following statement or to introduce a question.

R

Recessive (adjective): *genetics-* relating to or denoting heritable characteristics controlled by genes that are expressed in offspring only when inherited from both parents, i.e., when not masked by a dominant characteristic inherited from one parent.

Rectify (verb): put right; correct.

Reverberate (verb): (of a loud noise) be repeated several times as an echo; (of a place) appear to vibrate or be disturbed because of a loud noise.

Rhododendron (noun): a shrub or small tree of the heath family, with large clusters of bell-shaped flowers and typically with large evergreen leaves, widely grown as an ornamental.

S

Salient (adjective): most noticeable or important. Prominent; conspicuous. (of an angle) pointing outward.

Semblance (noun): the outward appearance or apparent form of something, especially when the reality is different.

Sibling (noun): each of two or more children or offspring having one or both parents in common; a brother or sister.

Smitten (verb): from **Smite**. Strike with a firm blow; *(be smitten)* be strongly attracted to someone or something.

Syntax (noun): the arrangement of words and phrases to create well-formed sentences in a language; the arrangement of words and phrases in a specific order.

T

Temerity (noun): excessive confidence or boldness; audacity.

Temporal (adjective): relating to time.

Tenure (noun): the holding of an office.

Transcendent (adjective): beyond or above the range of normal or merely physical human experience.

U

Unfurl, Unfurling (verb): make or become spread out from a rolled or folded state, especially in order to be open to the wind.

Utilitarian (adjective): designed to be useful or practical rather than attractive.

V

Vacuous (adjective): devoid of intelligence.

W

Writhe (verb): make continual twisting, squirming movements or contortions of the body.

X

Xenophobia (noun): s fear of foreigners or strangers.

Y

Yoke (verb): become joined or linked together.

Z

Zeal (noun): prompt willingness.